THE
SECRET
CIRCLE

Also by L.J. Smith

Secret Circle

Part I: The Initiation, The Captive Part I

Night World

Volume 1: Secret Vampire, Daughters of Darkness, Enchantress
Volume 2: Dark Angel, The Chosen, Soulmate
Volume 3: Huntress, Black Dawn, Witchlight

Vampire Diaries

Volume 1 (Books 1 & 2): The Awakening, The Struggle
Volume 2 (Books 3 & 4): The Fury, The Reunion
Book 5: The Return: Nightfall
Coming soon
Book 6: The Return: Shadow Souls
Book 7: The Return: Midnight

THE
SECRET
CIRCLE

THE CAPTIVE PART II
AND
THE POWER

L. J. SMITH

Hodder
Children's
Books

A division of Hachette Children's Books

Secret Circle © 1992 by Lisa Smith and Daniel Weiss Associates

Secret Circle bind-up 2: The Captive Part II and The Power first published
in the USA in 2008 by HarperTeen, an imprint of Harper Collins Publishers.

This Secret Circle edition published 2009 by Hodder Children's Books

4

ISBN-13: 978 0 340 99954 7

Typeset in Meridien Roman by Avon DataSet Ltd,
Bidford-on-Avon, Warwickshire

Printed and bound in Great Britain by
CPI Bookmarque Ltd, Croydon, Surrey

The paper and board used in this paperback by Hodder Children's Books
are natural reyclable products made from wood grown in
sustainable forests. The manufacturing processes conform to the
environmental regulations of the country of origin.

Hodder Children's Books
a division of Hachette Children's Books
338 Euston Road,
London NW1 3BH
An Hachette UK company
www.hachette.co.uk

For Lauren and Brian, who know love is the Power

PROLOGUE

The figure floated there motionless except for eddies within itself.

Then it drifted towards Cassie.

She was the one who seemed to be facing it straight on. A sudden thought came into her mind. When Adam had first taken the crystal skull out of his backpack on the beach, it had seemed to be looking directly at her. And again – at the skull ceremony, she remembered. When Diana had pulled the cloth off the skull then, those hollow eyesockets had seemed to be staring right into Cassie's eyes.

Now this thing was staring at her in the same way.

THE
CAPTIVE
PART II

CHAPTER

1

The voices from above were getting nearer. Cassie couldn't move; a grey blanket seemed to have enfolded her senses. Chris was pulling at her arm.

'C'mon, Cassie! They're comin'!'

Faintly, Cassie heard from above: 'If you'll line up in single file, we'll be going down a narrow stairway...'

Chris was pulling Cassie off the narrow stairway. 'Hey, Doug, give me a hand here!'

Cassie made a supreme effort. 'We have to go home,' she said urgently to Chris. She drew herself up and tried to speak with authority. 'I have to go back and tell Diana – something – right now.'

The brothers looked at each other, perplexed but dimly impressed.

'Okay,' Chris said, and Cassie sagged, the greyness washing over her again.

With Doug pulling in front and Chris trying to prop her up from behind, they led her rapidly through the dark, winding corridors of the dungeon. They seemed as comfortable in the darkness as rats, and they guided her unerringly through the passageways until a neon sign announced EXIT.

On the drive north, the pumpkins thumped and rolled in the back seat like a load of severed heads. Cassie kept her eyes shut and tried to breathe normally. The one thing she knew was that she couldn't tell the Henderson brothers what she was thinking. If they found out what she suspected about Kori, anything might happen.

Just drop me off at Diana's,' she said when they finally returned to Crowhaven Road. 'No – you don't have to go in with me. Thanks.'

'Okay,' Chris said, and they let her off. Then he stuck his head back out the window. 'Uh, hey – thanks for getting that mutt off me,' he said.

'Sure,' Cassie said light-headedly. 'Any time.' As they rolled away she realised they had never even asked her why she needed to talk to Diana. Maybe they were so used to doing inexplicable things themselves that they didn't wonder when other people did.

Mr Meade answered the door, and Cassie realised that it must be late if he was home from the office. He called up to Diana as Cassie climbed the stairs.

'Cassie!' Diana said, jumping up as she saw Cassie's face. 'What's the matter?'

Adam was sitting on the bed; he rose too, looking alarmed.

'I know it's late – I'm sorry – but we have to talk. I was in the Witch Dungeon—'

'You were where? Here, take this; your hands are like ice. Now start over again, slowly,' Diana said, sitting her down and wrapping her in a sweater.

Slowly, stumbling sometimes, Cassie told them the story: how Chris and Doug had picked her up and taken her to Salem. She left out the part about the pumpkin patch, but told how they'd gone to the Witch Dungeon, and how, listening to the lecture, she had suddenly seen the connection. Pressing to death – rockslides; hanging – broken necks.

'But what does it mean?' Diana said when she'd finished.

'I don't know, exactly,' Cassie admitted. 'But it looks like there's some connection between the three deaths and the way Puritans used to punish people.'

'The dark energy is the connection,' Adam said quietly. 'That skull was used by the original coven, which lived in the time of the witch trials.'

'But that wouldn't account for Kori,' Diana protested. 'We didn't activate the skull until after Kori was dead.'

Adam was pale. 'No. But I found the skull the day before Kori died. I took it out of the sand...' His eyes met Cassie's, and she had a terrible feeling of dismay.

'Sand. "To Hold Evil Harmless",' she whispered. She looked at Diana. 'That's in your Book of Shadows. Burying an object in sand or earth to hold the evil in it harmless. Just like—' She stopped abruptly and bit her tongue. God, she'd almost said, 'Just like you buried the skull on the beach to keep it safe.'

'Just like I found it,' Adam finished for her. 'Yes. And you think that when I took it out, that alone activated it. But that would mean the skull would have to be so strong, so powerful...' His voice trailed off. Cassie could see he was trying to fight the idea; he didn't want to believe it. 'I did feel *something* when I pulled it out of that hole,' he added quietly. 'I felt dizzy, strange. That could have been from dark energy escaping.' He looked at Cassie. 'So you think that energy came to New Salem and killed Kori.'

'I – don't know what to think,' Cassie said wretchedly. 'I

3

don't know why it *would*. But it can't be coincidence that every single time we interact with the skull, somebody dies afterwards, in a way that the Puritans used to kill witches.'

'But don't you see,' Diana said excitedly, 'it *isn't* every time. Nobody used the skull right before Jeffrey died. It was absolutely safe—' She hesitated and then went on quickly. 'Well, of course I can tell *you* two – it was safe out on the beach. It's still buried there now. I've been checking it every few days. So there isn't a one-to-one correspondence.'

Cassie was speechless. Her first impulse was to blurt out, 'Somebody did too use the skull!' But that would be insane. She could never tell Diana that – and now she was utterly at a loss. A shaking was starting deep inside her. Oh, God, there *was* a one-to-one correspondence.

It was like that slogan, *Use a gun; go to jail*. Use the skull; kill somebody. And she, Cassie, was responsible for the last time the skull had been used. She was responsible for killing Jeffrey.

Then she got another terrible jolt. She found Adam's keen blue-grey eyes fixed on her. 'I know what you're thinking,' he said.

Cassie swallowed, frozen.

'You're trying to think of a way to protect me,' he said. 'Neither of you likes the idea that my pulling the skull out of the sand had something to do with Kori's death. So you're trying to discredit the theory. But it won't work. There's obviously *some* connection between the skull and all three deaths – even Kori's.'

Cassie still couldn't move. Diana touched his hand.

'If it is true,' she said, her green eyes blazing with intensity, 'then it isn't your fault. You couldn't know that removing the skull would do any harm. You couldn't *know*.'

But I did know, Cassie thought. Or at least I should have known. I knew the skull was evil; I sensed it was capable of killing. And I still let Faye take it. I should have fought her harder; I should have done anything to stop her.

'If anyone's to blame,' Diana was going on, 'it's me. I'm the coven leader; it was my decision to use the skull in the ceremony. If the dark energy that knocked Faye over went out and killed Mr Fogle and Jeffrey afterwards, it's my fault.'

'No, it isn't,' Cassie said. She couldn't stand any more. 'It's mine – or at least it's everybody's...'

Adam looked from one girl to the other, then burst into strained laughter and dropped his head into his hand.

'Look at us,' he said. 'Trying to clear each other and each take the blame ourselves. What a joke.'

'Pretty pathetic,' Diana agreed, trying to smile.

Cassie was fighting tears.

'I think we'd better stop thinking about whose fault it is, and start thinking about what to do,' Adam went on. 'If the dark energy that escaped at the ceremony killed both Mr Fogle and Jeffrey, it may still be out there. It may do something else. We need to think about ways to stop it.'

They talked for several hours after that. Adam thought they should search for the dark energy, maybe do some scrying around the graveyard. Diana thought they should continue combing all the Books of Shadows, even the most indecipherable ones, to see if there was any advice about dealing with evil like this, and to learn more about the skull.

'And about Black John, too,' Cassie suggested mechanically, and Diana and Adam agreed. Black John had used the skull in the beginning, had 'programmed' it.

Perhaps his intentions were still affecting it.

But all the time they were talking, Cassie was feeling – outside. Alienated. Adam and Diana really *were* good, she thought, watching them talk fervently, fired with the discussion. They really had acted with the best of intentions. She, Cassie, was different. She was – evil.

Cassie knew things that they didn't know. Things she could never tell them.

Diana was nice when the time came for Cassie to go. 'Adam had better drive you home,' she said.

Adam did. They didn't speak until they reached Cassie's house.

'How're you hanging on?' he said quietly then.

Cassie couldn't look at him. She had never wanted comfort more, never wanted to throw herself into his arms as much as she did now. She wanted to tell him the whole story about Faye and the skull, and listen to him say that it was all right, that she didn't have to face it alone. She wanted him to hold her.

She could feel him wanting that too, just inches away in the driver's seat.

'I'd better go inside,' she said shakily.

Adam was gripping the steering wheel so hard it looked as if he were trying to break it.

'Good night,' she said softly, still without looking at him.

There was a long, long pause while she felt Adam fight with himself. Then he said, 'Good night, Cassie,' in a voice drained of all energy.

Cassie went inside. She couldn't talk to her mother or her grandmother about this either, of course. She could just imagine it: 'Hi, Mom; you remember Jeffrey Lovejoy? Well, I helped kill him.' No, thank you.

It was a strange thought, knowing you were evil. It floated around in Cassie's mind as she lay in bed that night, and just before she fell asleep it got weirdly mixed up with visions of Faye's honey-coloured eyes.

Wicked, she could almost hear Faye chuckling throatily. You're not evil, you're just *wicked*... like me.

The dream started out beautifully. She was in her grandmother's garden, in the summer, when everything was blossoming. Lemon balm spilled a golden pool on the ground. Lavender, lily of the valley, and jasmine were throwing such sweet scents into the air that Cassie felt giddy.

Cassie bent to snap off a stem of honeysuckle, with its tiny, creamy flowerheads. The sun shone down, warming her shoulders. The sky was clear and spacious. Strangely, although this was her grandmother's garden, there was no house nearby. She was all alone in the bright sunshine.

Then she saw the roses.

They were huge, velvety, red as rubies. No roses like that grew wild. Cassie took a step towards them, then another. Dew stood in the curl of one of the rose petals, quivering slightly. Cassie wanted to smell one of them, but she was afraid.

She heard a throaty chuckle beside her.

'Faye!'

Faye smiled slowly. 'Go ahead, smell them,' she said. 'They won't bite you.' But Cassie shook her head. Her heart was beating quickly.

'Oh, come on, Cassie.' Faye's voice was coaxing now. 'Look over there. Doesn't that look interesting?'

Cassie looked. Behind the roses something impossible had happened. Night had fallen, even though it was still daylight where Cassie was standing. It was a cool black-and-purple night, broken by stars but not a trace of moon.

'Come with me, Cassie,' Faye coaxed again. 'It's just a few little steps. I'll show you how easy it is.' She walked behind the rosebush and Cassie stared at her. Faye was standing in darkness now, her face shadowed, her glorious hair merging with the gloom.

'You might as well,' Faye told her softly, inexorably. 'After all, you're already like me – or had you forgotten? You've already made your choice.'

Cassie's hand let the honeysuckle spray fall. Slowly, slowly, she reached out and picked one of the roses. It was such a deep red, and so soft. Cassie stared down into it.

'Beautiful, isn't it?' Faye murmured. 'Now bring it here.'

Mesmerised, Cassie took a step. There was a line of wavering shadow on the ground, between the darkness and the day. Cassie took another step and a sudden sharp pain in her finger made her gasp.

The rose had pricked her. Blood was streaming down her wrist. All the thorns on the roses were crimson, as if they'd been dipped in blood.

Appalled, she looked up at Faye, but she saw only darkness and heard only that mocking chuckle. 'Maybe next time,' Faye's voice floated out of the shadows.

Cassie woke up with her heart pounding, eyes staring into the blackness of her room. When she turned the light on, she almost expected to see blood on her arm. But there was no blood, and no mark of any thorn on her finger.

Thank God, she thought. It was a dream, just a dream. Still, it was a long time before she could fall asleep again.

She woke again to the ringing of the phone. By the colour of the light against the eastern window she knew she'd slept late.

'Hello?'

'Hello, Cassie,' a familiar voice said in her ear.

Cassie's heart jumped. Instantly the entire dream flashed before her. In a panic, she expected Faye to start talking throatily about roses and darkness.

But Faye's voice was ordinary. 'It's Saturday, Cassie. Do you have any plans for tonight?'

'Uh... no. But—'

'Because Deborah and Suzan and I are having a little get-together. We thought you might like to come.'

'Faye... I thought you were mad at me.'

Faye laughed. 'I was a little – miffed, yes. But that's over now. I'm *proud* of your success with the guys. It just shows you what a little witchery will do, hmm?'

Cassie ignored this; she'd had a sudden thought. 'Faye, if you're planning to use the skull again, forget it. Do you want to know how dangerous it is?' She started to tell Faye what she'd discovered in the Witch Dungeon, but Faye interrupted.

'Oh, who cares about the skull any more?' she said. 'This is a *party*. So we'll see you at around eight, then, all right? You *will* show up, won't you, Cassie? Because there might be – unfortunate consequences if you didn't. Bye!'

Deborah and Suzan will be there, Cassie told herself as she walked up to Faye's house that night. They won't let Faye actually kill me. The thought gave her some comfort.

And Faye, when she opened the door, seemed less sinister than usual. Her golden eyes were glimmering with something like mischief and her smile was almost playful.

'Come in, Cassie. Everybody's in the den,' she said.

9

Cassie could hear music as they approached a room off the entrance hall. It was furnished in the same opulent and luxurious style as the rest of the house. Noise from a huge TV was competing with some song by Madonna being blasted out of a magnificent stereo unit. With all this technology, the dozens of candles stuck in various kinds of holders around the room seemed incongruous.

'Turn that stuff down,' Faye ordered. Suzan, pouting, pointed a remote control at the stereo, while Deborah muted the TV. Apparently Faye had forgiven them as well.

'Now,' Faye said, with a feline smile at Cassie, 'I'll explain. The housekeeper has the day off, and my mother is sick in bed—'

'As usual,' Deborah interrupted, to Cassie. 'Her mom spends ninety-five per cent of her life in bed. Nerves.'

Faye's eyebrows arched and she said, 'Yes, well, it's certainly *convenient*, isn't it? At times like this.' She turned back to Cassie and went on, 'So we're going to have a little pizza party. You'll help out getting things ready, won't you?'

Cassie was tingling with relief. A pizza party. She'd been imagining – oh, all sorts of strange things. 'I'll help,' she said.

'Then let's get started. Suzan will show you what to do.'

Cassie followed Suzan's directions. They lit the red and pink candles and started a low, crackling fire in the fireplace. They lit incense, too, which Suzan said was composed of ginger root, cardamom, and neroli oil. It was pungent, but delicious smelling.

Faye, meanwhile, was placing crystals about the room. Cassie recognised them – garnets and carnelians, fire opals and pink tourmelines. And Suzan, Cassie noticed, was wearing a carnelian necklace which harmonised with her strawberry-blonde hair, while Faye was wearing more than her usual number of star rubies.

Deborah switched off the lamps and went to fiddle with the stereo. The music that began to rise was like nothing Cassie had ever heard. It was low and throbbing, some primal beat that seemed to get into her blood. It started out softly, but seemed to be getting almost imperceptibly louder.

'All right,' Faye said, standing back to survey their work. 'It's looking good. I'll get the drinks.'

Cassie looked over the room herself. Warm; it looked warm and inviting, especially when compared with the chilly October weather outside. The candles and the fire made a rosy glow, and the soft, insistent music filled the air. The incense was spicy, intoxicating, and somehow sensuous, and the smoke threw a slight haze over the room.

It looks like an opium den or something, Cassie thought, simultaneously fascinated and horrified, just as Faye came back with a silver tray.

Cassie stared. She'd expected, maybe, a six-pack of soda – or maybe a six-pack of something else, knowing Deborah. She should have known Faye would never stoop to anything so inelegant. On the tray was a crystal decanter and eight small crystal glasses. The decanter was half full of some clear ruby-coloured liquid.

'Sit down,' Faye said, pouring into four of the glasses. And then, at Cassie's doubtful look, she smiled. 'It's not alcoholic. Try it and see. Oh, go *on*.'

Warily, Cassie took a sip. It had a subtle, faintly sweet taste and it made her feel flushed with warmth right down to her fingertips.

'What's in it?' she asked, peering into her glass.

'Oh, this and that. It's – stimulating, isn't it?'

'Mmm.' Cassie took another sip.

'And now,' Faye smiled, 'we can play Pizza Man.'

There was a pause, then Cassie said, 'Pizza Man?'

'Pizza Man He Delivers,' Suzan said, and giggled.

'Otherwise known as watching guys make fools of themselves,' Deborah said, grinning savagely. She might have gone on, but Faye interrupted.

'Let's not *tell* Cassie; let's just show her,' she said. 'Where's the phone?' Deborah handed her a cordless phone.

Suzan produced the yellow pages, and after a few moments of thumbing and scanning, read out a number.

Faye dialled. 'Hello?' she said pleasantly. 'I'd like to order a large pizza, with pepperoni, olives, and mushrooms.' She gave her address and phone number. 'That's right, New Salem,' she said. 'Can you tell me how long it will be? All right; thanks. 'Bye.'

She hung up, looked at Suzan, and said, 'Next.'

And then, to Cassie's growing astonishment, she did it all over again.

Six times.

By the end of it, Faye had ordered seven large pizzas, all with the same toppings. Cassie, who was feeling somewhat dizzy from the smell of incense, wondered just how many people Faye was planning to feed.

'Who's coming to this party – the entire Mormon Tabernacle Choir?' she whispered to Suzan. Suzan dimpled.

'I hope not. It's not choirboys we're interested in.'

'That's enough,' said Faye. 'Just wait, Cassie, and you'll see.'

When the doorbell rang the first time, Faye, Suzan, and Deborah went into the parlour and looked through the window. Cassie followed and looked too. The porch light revealed a young man holding a greasy cardboard box.

'Hmm,' said Faye. 'Not bad. Not terrific, but not bad.'

'I think he's fine,' Suzan said. 'Look at those shoulders. Let's take him.'

With Cassie trailing behind, they all went into the hall.

'Well, hello,' Faye said, opening the door. 'Do you mind coming inside and putting it over here? I left my purse in the other room.' As Cassie watched with widening eyes, they escorted the guy into the warmth of the luxurious, richly scented den. Cassie saw him blink, then saw a stupefied expression cross his face.

Deborah took the pizza from him. 'You know,' Faye said, biting the pen she had poised over a cheque book, 'you look a little tired. Why don't you sit down? Are you thirsty?'

Suzan was pouring a glassful of the clear ruby liquid. She held it out to him with a smile. The delivery boy wet his lips, looking dazed. Cassie could understand why. She thought there was probably no guy in the world who could resist Suzan, with her cloud of strawberry-gold hair and her low-cut blouse, holding out a crystal glass. Suzan leaned over a little farther as she offered it to him, and the guy took the drink.

Deborah and Faye exchanged knowing glances. 'I'll go move his car around the side,' Deborah murmured, and left.

'My name's Suzan,' Suzan said to the guy, as she sank into the cushiony couch beside him. 'What's yours?'

Deborah had barely returned when the doorbell rang again.

CHAPTER

2

'**Y**uck,' Deborah said, as they peered out the parlour window again. This delivery guy was skinny, with lank hair and acne.

Faye was already moving to the front door. 'Pizza? We didn't order any pizza. I don't care who you called to confirm it, we don't want it.' She shut the door in his face, and after a few minutes of hanging around the porch he went away.

As his delivery van was pulling out, another one pulled in. The tall, blond guy with the cardboard box kept looking behind him at the receding rival van as he walked to the door.

'Now *this* is more like it,' Faye said.

When they brought the blond delivery guy into the den, Suzan and the muscular one were entangled on the couch. The pair disengaged themselves, the boy still looking foggy, and Faye poured the new guest a drink.

Within the next hour, the doorbell rang four more times and they collected two more delivery boys. Suzan divided her attention between the muscular one and a new one with high cheekbones who said he was part Native American. The other new one, who looked younger than the others and had soft-brown eyes, sat nervously next to Cassie.

'This is weird,' he said, looking around the room, and taking another gulp from his glass. 'This is so weird... I don't know what I'm doing. I've got deliveries to make...' Then he said, 'Gee, you're pretty.'

Gee? thought Cassie. Gosh. Golly. Oh, my *God*. 'Thanks,' she said weakly, and glanced around the room for help.

None was forthcoming. Faye, looking sultry and exuding sensuality, was running one long crimson fingernail up and down the blond guy's sleeve. Suzan was sunk deep in the couch with an admirer on either side. Deborah was sitting on the arm of an overstuffed chair, eyes slitted and rather scornful.

'Can I put my arm around you?' the brown-eyed boy was asking hesitantly.

Boys aren't toys, Cassie thought. Even if this one did look like a teddy bear. Faye had brought these guys here to play with, and that was wrong... wasn't it? They didn't know what they were doing; they didn't have any *choice*.

'I just moved up here last summer from South Carolina,' the boy was going on. 'I had a girl back there... but now I'm so lonely...'

Cassie knew the feeling. This was a *nice* guy, her age, and his brown eyes, though a little glassy, were appealing. She didn't scream when he put his arm around her, where it rested warmly and a little awkwardly around her shoulders.

She felt light-headed. Something about the incense... or the crystals, she thought. The music seemed to be pulsing inside her. She should be embarrassed by what was going on in this room – she *was* embarrassed – but there was something exciting about it too.

Some of the candles had gone out, making it darker.

The warmth around Cassie's shoulders was nice. She thought of yesterday night, when she'd wanted so much for someone to comfort her, to hold her. To make her feel not alone.

'I don't know why, but I really like you,' the brown-eyed boy was saying. 'I never felt like this before.'

Why not do it? She was already – bad. And she wanted to be close to *somebody* . . .

The brown-eyed boy leaned in to kiss her.

That was when Cassie knew it was wrong. Not the way kissing Adam was wrong, but wrong for *her*. She didn't want to kiss him. Every individual cell in her body was protesting, panicking. She wiggled out from under him like an eel and jumped up.

Faye and the blond guy were also on their feet, heading out of the room. So were Suzan and her unmatched pair.

'We're just going upstairs,' Faye said in her husky voice. 'There's more room up there. Lots of rooms, in fact.'

'No,' Cassie said.

A hint of a frown creased Faye's forehead, then she smiled and went over to Cassie, speaking in low tones. 'Cassie, I'm disappointed in you,' she said. 'After your performance at the dance, I really thought you were one of us. And it's not *nearly* as wicked as some other things you've done. You can do anything you want with these guys, and they'll like it.'

'No,' Cassie said again. 'You told me to come over and I did. But I don't want to stay.' Her eyes were smarting and she had trouble keeping her voice steady.

Faye looked exasperated. 'Oh, all right. If you don't

want to have fun, I can't make you. Go.'

Relief washed over Cassie. With one glance back at the brown-eyed boy, she hurried to the door. After last night's dream, she'd been so frightened... she hadn't been sure what Faye would do to her. But she was getting away.

Faye's voice caught her at the door, and she waited until she had Cassie's full attention before speaking.

'Maybe next time,' she said.

Cassie's entire skin was tingling as she hurried away from Faye's house. She just wanted to get home, to be safe...

'Hey, wait a minute,' Deborah called after her.

Reluctantly, Cassie turned and waited. She was braced as if for a blow.

Deborah came up quickly, her step light and controlled as always. Her dark hair was tumbling in waves around her small face and falling into her eyes. Her chin was slightly out-thrust as usual, but her expression wasn't hostile.

'I'm leaving too. You want a ride?' she said.

Instantly memories of the last 'ride' she'd accepted flashed through Cassie's mind. But she didn't exactly like to refuse Deborah. After Faye's parting words, Cassie was feeling small and soft and vulnerable – like something that could be easily squashed. And besides... well, it wasn't often Deborah made a gesture like this.

'Okay, thanks,' Cassie said after only a moment's hesitation. She didn't ask if they should be wearing helmets. She didn't think Deborah would appreciate the question.

Cassie had never been on a motorcycle before. It seemed bigger when she was trying to get on it than it had looked just standing there. Once she was on, though, it felt surprisingly stable. She wasn't afraid of falling off.

'Hang on to me,' Deborah said. And then, with an incredibly loud noise, they were moving.

It was the most exhilarating feeling – flying through the air. Like witches on broomsticks, Cassie thought. Wind roared in Cassie's face, whipped her hair back. It whipped Deborah's hair into Cassie's eyes so she couldn't see.

As Deborah accelerated, it became terrifying. Cassie was sure she'd never gone this fast before. The wind felt icy cold. They were racing forward into darkness, far too fast for safety on a rural road. The houses on Crowhaven were far behind. Cassie couldn't breathe, couldn't speak. Everything was the wind and the road and the feeling of speed.

I'm going to die, Cassie thought. She almost didn't care. Something this electrifying was worth dying for. She was sure Deborah couldn't take this next corner.

'Relax!' Deborah shouted, her voice snatched away by the wind. 'Relax! Don't fight the way I'm leaning.'

How can you relax when you're plunging at practically a hundred miles an hour into darkness? Cassie thought. But then she found out how: you give yourself up to it. Cassie resigned herself to her fate, and let the speed and the wind take her. And, magically, everything was all right.

She was aware, eventually, that they were heading back up Crowhaven Road, past Diana's house, past the others. They overshot Cassie's house and stormed around the vacant lot at the point of the headland.

Dust sprayed up on either side. Cassie saw the cliff whip by and buried her head in Deborah's shoulder. Then they were leaning, they were slowing, they were spiralling to a stop.

'So,' said Deborah, when the world was still again,

'what'd you think?'

Cassie lifted her head and made her fingers stop clutching. Every inch of her was as icy as if she'd been standing in a freezer. Her hair was matted and her lips and ears and nose were numb.

'It was wonderful,' she gasped. 'Like flying.'

Deborah burst into laughter, jumped off, and slapped Cassie on the back. Then she helped Cassie off. Cassie couldn't stop shivering.

'Look over here,' Deborah said, stepping over to the edge of the cliff.

Cassie looked. Far below, the dark water crashed and foamed around the rocks. It was a long way down.

But there was something beautiful, too. Over the vast grey curve of ocean, an almost half-full moon hung. It cast a long wavering trail of light along the water, pure silver on the darkness.

'It looks like a road,' Cassie said softly, through chattering teeth. 'Like you could ride on it.'

She looked at Deborah quickly, not sure how the biker girl would take to such a fancy. But Deborah gave a short nod, her narrowed eyes still on the silver path.

'That would be the ultimate. Just ride till you fly straight off the edge. I guess that was what the old-time witches wanted,' she said.

Cassie felt a warmth even through her shivering. Deborah felt what she herself had felt. And now Cassie understood why Deborah rode a motorcycle.

'We better go,' Deborah said abruptly.

On the way back to the motorcycle Cassie stumbled, falling to one knee. She looked back and saw that she had tripped on a piece of brick or stone.

'I forgot to tell you; there used to be a house here,' Deborah said. 'It got torn down a long time ago, but there're some pieces of foundation left.'

'I think I just found one,' Cassie said. Rubbing her knee, she was starting to get up when she noticed something beside the brick. It was darker than the soil it was resting on and yet it shone faintly in the moonlight.

She picked it up and found that it was smooth and surprisingly heavy. And it *did* shine; it reflected the moonlight like a black mirror.

'It's hematite,' said Deborah, who'd come back to look. 'It's a powerful stone – for iron-strength, Melanie says.' She knelt down suddenly beside Cassie, tossing tangled hair out of her eyes. 'Cassie! It's your working crystal.'

A thrill which seemed to come from the stone rippled through Cassie. Holding the smooth piece of hematite was like holding an ice cube, but all the things that Melanie had said would happen when she found her own personal crystal were happening now. It fitted her hand, it felt natural there. She liked the weight of it. It was *hers*.

Elated, she lifted her head to smile up at Deborah, and in the chilly moonlight Deborah smiled fiercely back.

It was when she was dropping Cassie off at Number Twelve that she said, 'I heard you came to see Nick yesterday.'

'Oh – um,' Cassie said. That meeting with Nick in the garage seemed like centuries ago, not yesterday. 'Uh, I didn't come to *see* him,' she stammered. 'I was just walking by...'

Deborah shrugged. 'Anyway, I thought I'd tell you – he gets in bad moods sometimes. But that doesn't mean you should give up. Other times he's okay.'

Cassie floundered, completely amazed. 'Uh – well – I didn't mean – I mean, thanks, but I wasn't really...'

She couldn't find a way to finish, and Deborah wasn't waiting anyway. 'Whatever. See you later. And don't lose that stone!' Dark hair flying, the biker girl zoomed off.

Up in her room, Cassie's legs felt weak from tension, and she was tired. But she lay in bed for a while and held the hematite on her palm, tilting it back and forth to watch the light slide over it. For iron-strength, she thought.

It wasn't like the chalcedony rose; it gave her no feeling of warmth and comfort. But then the chalcedony rose was all mixed up in her mind with Adam and his blue-grey eyes. Diana had the rose now, and Diana had Adam.

And Cassie had a stone which brought a strange coolness to her thoughts, a coolness that seemed to extend to her heart. For iron-strength, she thought again. She liked that.

'And so that's what Cassie believes, that each of the deaths – even Kori's – is connected to the skull, and to Puritan ways of killing people,' Diana said. She looked around the circle of faces. 'Now it's up to us to *do* something about it.'

Cassie was watching Faye. She wanted to see the reaction in those hooded golden eyes when Diana explained about the dark energy that had escaped during the skull ceremony, killing Jeffrey. Sure enough, when Diana got to that part, Faye shot a glance at Cassie, but there was nothing apologetic or guilty about it. It was a look of conspiracy. *Only you and I know*, it said. *And I won't tell if you won't.*

I'm not that stupid, Cassie telegraphed back angrily, and Faye smiled.

It was Sunday night and they were all sitting on the beach. Diana hadn't been able to find out much from her own Book of Shadows about dealing with evil objects like the skull, and she was calling for everyone's help.

It was the first full meeting of the Circle in three weeks, since the day after Mr Fogle had been found dead. Cassie scanned the faces above thick jackets and sweaters – even New Englanders had to bundle up in this weather – and wondered what was going on in each individual witch's head.

Melanie was grave and thoughtful as usual, as if she neither believed nor disbelieved Cassie's theory, but was willing to test it out scientifically. Laurel just looked appalled. Suzan was examining the stitching on her gloves. Deborah was scowling, unwilling to give up the idea that outsiders had killed Kori. Nick – well, who could tell what Nick thought? Sean was chewing his fingernails.

The Henderson brothers were agitated. For a terrible instant Cassie thought they were going to turn their energy on Adam, blame him for Kori's being killed. But then Doug spoke up.

'So how come we're still sittin' around talking? Let *me* have the skull – *I'll* take care of it,' he said, teeth bared.

'Yeah – let Doug have it,' Sean chimed in.

'It can't be destroyed, Doug,' Melanie said patiently.

'Oh, yeah?' Chris said. 'Put it in with a pipe bomb—'

'And nothing would happen. Crystal skulls can't be destroyed, Doug,' Melanie repeated. 'That's in all the old lore. You wouldn't even scratch it.'

'And there's no really safe place to store it,' Diana said. 'I might as well tell you all, I've got it buried somewhere, and yesterday I set up a spell to tell me if the place is disturbed. It's vital that the skull *stays buried*.'

Cassie had a sick feeling in her stomach. Diana was looking around the group, focussing on Deborah, Faye, and the Hendersons. It would never occur to her to look at me, Cassie thought, and somehow this made her feel sicker than ever.

'Why can't we take it back to the island?' Suzan said, surprisingly, showing she was listening after all.

Adam, who had been sitting quietly, his fine, humorous face unusually moody, answered. 'Because the island won't protect it any more,' he said. 'Not since I took the skull.'

'Sort of like one of those Egyptian tombs with a curse on it,' said Laurel. 'Once you break in, you can't undo what you've done.'

Adam's lip quirked. 'Right. And we're not strong enough to cast a new spell of protection that would hold it. This skull is *evil*,' he said to all of them. 'It's so evil that burying it in sand won't do anything but keep it from being activated at the moment. There's no way to purify it' – he looked at Laurel – 'and no way to destroy it' – he looked at Doug and Chris – 'and no place to keep it safe.' He looked at Suzan.

'Then what do we do?' Deborah demanded, and Sean squeaked, 'What do we *do*?'

'Forget about it?' Faye suggested with a lazy smile. Adam shot her a dark look. Diana intervened.

'Adam had the idea of searching for the dark energy again with a pendulum, seeing if there are any new trails,' she said. She turned to Cassie. 'What do you think?'

Cassie dug her fingernails into her palms. If they traced the dark energy and it led them straight back to Faye's house, the place where it had most recently escaped... Faye was looking at her sharply, wanting her to veto the suggestion. But Cassie had an idea.

'I think we should do it,' she told Diana evenly.

Faye's stare turned menacing, furious. But there was nothing she could say.

Diana nodded. 'All right. We may as well start now. It's a long walk to the graveyard, so I thought we might try picking up the trail around here. We'll go out on Crowhaven Road and see if there's anything to follow.'

Cassie could actually feel her chest quivering with the beating of her heart as they walked off the beach. She thrust one hand into her pocket to feel the cold, smooth piece of hematite. Iron-strength, that was what she needed right now.

'Are you crazy?' Faye hissed as they climbed the bluff and headed for the road. She caught Cassie's arm in a punishing grip, holding her back from the others. 'Do you know where that trail *goes*?'

Cassie shook the arm off. 'Trust me,' she said shortly.

'*What?*'

Cassie whirled on the taller girl. 'I said, trust me! I know what I'm doing – and you don't.' And with that she began to climb again. Iron-strength, she thought dizzily, impressed with herself.

But she still found it hard to breathe when Diana stood out in the middle of Crowhaven Road – near Number Two, Deborah's house – and held up the peridot crystal.

Cassie watched it, feeling the concentration of all the minds around her. She waited for it to spin in circles.

It did – in the beginning. The chain twisted first one way and then the other, like a wound-up swing on a playground. But then, to Cassie's horror, it began to seesaw, pointing up and down Crowhaven Road. Down, the way they'd travelled the first time, the way that had eventually led to the cemetery, and up towards the headland.

Towards Faye's.

Cassie's legs felt as if they were sinking into cotton as she followed the group. Faye had no trouble holding her back now. 'I told you,' she said vehemently out of the side of her mouth. '*Now* what, Cassie?

If that trail leads to my house, I'm not going down alone.'

Cassie clenched her teeth and choked out, 'I thought we couldn't trace it at ground level. That energy came out through your bedroom ceiling on the second floor, and it was going straight up. I thought it would be too high to track.'

'You obviously thought wrong,' Faye hissed.

They were passing the vacant house at Number Three. They were passing Melanie's house. Laurel's house was in front of them; they were passing it. Faye's house was just ahead.

Cassie thought she actually might faint. She was almost unaware that she was clutching Faye's arm as hard as Faye was clutching hers. She waited for the peridot to turn aside and lead them all to Faye's doorstep.

But Diana was walking on.

Cassie felt a violent surge of relief – and of bewilderment. Where were they *going*? They were passing Number Seven, another vacant house. Passing the Hendersons', passing Adam's, passing Suzan's. They were passing Sean's – oh, my God, Cassie thought, we're not going to *my* house?

But they were passing Number Twelve as well. Diana was following the pendulum's swing, leading them out on to the point of the headland.

And there the crystal began to spin in circles again.

'What's going on?' Laurel said, looking around in astonishment. 'What are we doing here?'

Adam and Diana were looking at each other. Then they both looked at Cassie, who came slowly forward from the rear of the group. Cassie shrugged at them.

'This is the place where Number Thirteen used to be,' Diana said. 'Right, Adam? The house that was torn down.'

'I heard it burned down,' Adam said. 'Before we were born.'

'No, it wasn't that long ago,' said Melanie. 'It was only about sixteen or seventeen years ago – that's what I heard. But before that it was vacant for centuries. Literally.'

'How many centuries?' Cassie said, too loudly. For some reason she found her fingers clenched around the piece of hematite in her pocket.

The members of the coven turned to her, looking at her with eyes that seemed to shine slightly in the moonlight.

'About three,' Melanie said. 'This was Black John's house. Nobody ever lived in it after he died in 1696.'

The hematite burned against Cassie's palm with icy fire.

CHAPTER 3

'This is all too weird for me,' Laurel said, shivering.

'But what does it *tell* us?' Deborah challenged.

'It's another link to Black John,' Adam said. 'Other than that, nothing.'

'So it's a dead end, like the cemetery,' Faye said, looking pleased.

Cassie had the feeling they were wrong, but she couldn't explain why, so she kept her mouth shut. Something else was worrying her, worrying her terribly. The piece of hematite that right now felt as heavy as a bit of neutron star in her pocket... it had come from the ruins of Black John's house. It might even have belonged to him. Which meant that she had to tell Diana about it.

People were wandering around, breaking up into small groups. The meeting, for all intents and purposes, was over. Cassie took a deep breath and went to Diana.

'I didn't get a chance to talk to you earlier,' she said. 'But I wanted to tell you about something that happened yesterday.'

'Cassie, you don't have to tell me. I know it wasn't like Faye said.'

Cassie blinked, thrown off balance. 'What did Faye say?'

'We don't even have to talk about it. I know it's not true.'

'But what did she *say*?'

Diana looked uncomfortable. 'She said – you were over at her house last night, playing – well, some kind of game.'

'Pizza Man,' Cassie said distinctly. When Diana stared at her, she explained, 'Pizza Man He Delivers.'

'I know what it's called,' Diana said. She was scanning Cassie's face. 'But I'm sure you would never...'

'*You're* sure? You can't be sure,' Cassie cried. It was too much – Diana's blind insistence on her innocence. Didn't Diana realise that Cassie was bad, evil?

'Cassie, I *know* you. I know you wouldn't do anything like that.'

Cassie was feeling more and more agitated. Something inside her was getting ready to snap. 'Well, I was there. And I did do it. And' – she was getting close to the source of the anguish inside her – 'you don't know what kind of things I would or wouldn't do. I've already done some things—'

'Cassie, calm down—'

Cassie reeled a step backwards, stung. 'I *am* calm. Don't tell me to calm down!'

'Cassie, what's wrong with you?'

'Nothing's wrong with me. I just want to be left alone!'

Diana's eyes sparked green. She was tired, Cassie knew, and anxious. And maybe she'd reached a snapping point, too. 'All right,' she said, with unaccustomed sharpness in her normally gentle voice. 'I'll leave you alone, then.'

'Fine,' Cassie said, her throat swollen and her eyes stinging. She didn't want to fight with Diana – but all this anger and pain inside her had to go *somewhere*. She'd never known how awful it was to have people insist you were good, when you *weren't*.

Her fingers unclenched from the piece of hematite, and she left it in her pocket as she turned around and walked away. She stared down over the edge of the cliff at the swirling waves below.

Faye moved in beside her, bringing a scent of sweet, musky perfume. 'Show it to me.'

'Huh?'

'I want to see what's in your pocket that you've been holding on to like it might run away.'

Cassie hesitated, then slowly drew the smooth, heavy stone out.

Still facing the ocean, Faye examined it. 'A hematite crystal. That's rare.' She held it up to the moonlight and chuckled. 'Did Melanie ever tell you about some of hematite's more – unusual properties? No? Well, even though it looks black, if you cut it into thin slices, they're transparent and red. And the dust that comes off the stone turns the liquid that cools the cutting wheel as red as blood.'

She gave the stone back to Cassie, who held it loosely, looking down at it. No matter where it came from, it was *her* crystal now. She'd known that from the moment she'd seen it. How could she give it up?

'I found it here, by the foundation of the house,' she said dully.

Faye's eyebrows lifted. Then she collected herself. 'Hm. Well – of course, anybody could have dropped it here in the past three hundred years.'

A strange sense of excited relief filtered through Cassie.

'Yes,' she said. 'Of course. Anybody could have.' She put the crystal back in her pocket. Faye's hooded golden eyes were gleaming at her, and Cassie felt herself nod. She didn't have to give up the crystal after all.

Adam was calling people back into a group. 'Just one thing before everybody leaves,' he was saying. He seemed oblivious to the little drama that had been enacted between Cassie and Diana a few minutes earlier.

'I have an idea,' he said, when the Club had gathered around again. 'You know, I just realised that everything connected with the dark energy has led to death, to the dead. The cemetery; that ghost-shape Cassie and Deborah and Nick and I saw on the road; even this place – a ruined house built by a dead man. And – well, the weekend after next is Samhain.'

There was a murmur from the group. Adam looked at Cassie and said, 'You know, Halloween. All Saints' Eve, November Eve, whatever. But no matter what you call it, it's the night when the dead walk. And I know it might be dangerous, but I think we should do a ceremony, either here or at the cemetery, on Halloween. We'll see what we can call up.' He turned to Diana. 'What do you think?'

This time the response was silence. Diana looked concerned, Melanie doubtful, Sean openly scared. Doug and Chris were grinning their wild grins, and Deborah was nodding fiercely. Faye had her head cocked to one side, considering; Nick stood with his arms across his chest, stone-faced. But it was Laurel and Suzan who spoke up.

'But what about the *dance*?' Laurel said, and Suzan said, 'Saturday night is the Halloween dance and I've already got my shoes.'

'We always have a party on Halloween,' Melanie explained to Cassie. 'It's a big witch holiday. But this year Halloween falls on Saturday, and the school dance is the same night. Still,' she said slowly, 'I don't see why we couldn't do both. We could leave the dance around eleven thirty and still have plenty of time for a ceremony here.'

'And I think it *should* be here,' Diana said, 'and not the graveyard. That's just *too* dangerous, and we might call up more than we bargained for.'

Cassie thought of the shadowy form she and Adam had seen at the graveyard. A bit too belligerently, she asked. 'What are we planning to do with whatever we *can* call up?'

'Talk to it,' Adam said promptly. 'In the old days people called up the spirits of the dead on Halloween and asked them questions. The spirits had to answer.'

'It's the day when the veil between the worlds is the thinnest,' Laurel clarified. 'Dead people come back and visit their living relatives.' She looked around the group. 'I think we should do the ceremony.'

There was agreement from the Circle, some of it hesitant, some enthusiastic. But everyone nodded.

'Right,' Adam said. 'Halloween night, then.' Cassie thought it was unusual that he was taking over the job of coven leader this way, but then she looked at Diana. Diana looked as if she were holding some turmoil inside her tightly under control. For a moment Cassie felt sorry for her, but then her own misery and conflict welled up. She left the meeting quickly, without speaking to Diana.

In the weeks before Halloween, the real cold set in, although the leaves were still bronze and crimson. Cassie's bedroom smelled of camphor because her grandmother had brought old quilts out of storage to pile on her bed.

The last of the herbs had been gathered, and the house was decorated with autumn flowers, marigolds and purple asters. Every day after school Cassie found her grandmother in the kitchen, cooking oceans of apple sauce to jar, until the whole house smelled of hot apple pulp and cinnamon and spices.

Pumpkins mysteriously appeared on everybody's back porch – but only Cassie and the Hendersons knew where they came from.

Things didn't get better with Diana.

A guilty part inside Cassie knew why. She didn't *want* to fight with Diana – but it was so much easier not having to worry about her all the time. If she wasn't always talking to Diana, wasn't over at Diana's house every day, she didn't have to think about how hurt Diana would be if Diana ever found out the truth. The shameful secrets inside Cassie didn't rub her so much when Diana was at a distance.

So when Diana tried to make up, Cassie was polite but a little cool. A little – detached. And when Diana asked why Cassie was still mad, Cassie said she *wasn't* still mad, and why couldn't Diana just leave things alone? After that, Diana did.

Cassie felt as if a thin, hard shell were growing all over her.

She thought about what Deborah had said about Nick. *He gets in bad moods sometimes, but that doesn't mean you should give up.* Of course, there was no way Cassie could go back and ask Nick again. At least, there was no way the old Cassie could have. There seemed to be a new Cassie now, a stronger, harder one – at least on the outside. And she had to do *something*, because every night she thought about Adam and ached, and she was afraid of what might happen if she went to that dance unattached.

The day before Halloween she walked up to Nick's garage again.

The skeleton-car looked just the same. Its entire engine was out, resting on a sort of bottomless table made of pipes. Nick was underneath the table.

Cassie knew better than to ask him what he was doing this time. She saw him see her feet, saw his gaze travel up. Then he scooted out from under the table and stood up.

His dark hair was spiky with sweat, and he wiped his forehead with the back of a greasy hand. He didn't say anything, just stood there looking at her.

Cassie didn't give herself time to think. Focussing all her attention on an oil stain on his T-shirt, she said rapidly, 'Are you going to the Halloween dance tomorrow?'

There was a long, long silence. Cassie stared at the oil stain while Nick stared at her face. She could smell rubber and warm metal as well as grease and a faint hint of gasoline. She felt as if she were hanging suspended in air.

Then Nick said, 'No.'

Everything came crashing down. Cassie felt it, and for some reason she was suddenly able to look Nick in the face.

'Oh,' she said flatly. Oh, stupid, *stupid*, she was thinking. The new Cassie was as dumb as the old one. She should never have come here.

'I don't see why you want to know in the first place,' Nick said. Then he added, 'It's got something to do with Conant, doesn't it?'

Cassie tensed. 'Adam? What are you talking about? What could my asking you to a dance have to do with Adam?' she said, but she could feel the blood rise to her face.

Nick was nodding. 'I thought so. You've really got

it bad. And you don't want him to know, so you're looking for a substitute, right? Or are you trying to make him jealous?'

Cassie's face was burning now, but hotter was the flame of rage and humiliation inside her. She wouldn't cry in front of Nick, she *wouldn't*.

'Sorry for bothering you,' she said, and, feeling stiff and sore, she turned around to walk away.

'Wait a minute,' Nick said. Cassie went on walking and reached the golden October sunlight. Her eyes were fixed on the fading scarlet leaves of a red maple across the street.

'Wait,' Nick said again, closer. He'd followed her out. 'What time do you want me to pick you up?' he said.

Cassie turned around and stared at him.

God, he *was* handsome, but so cold... even now he looked completely dispassionate, indifferent. The sun caught blue glints off his dark hair, and his face was like a perfectly carved ice sculpture.

'I don't want to go with you any more,' Cassie told him bleakly, and started away again.

He moved in front of her, blocking her without touching her. 'I'm sorry I said the thing about trying to make Conant jealous. That was just...' He stopped and shrugged. 'I didn't mean it. I don't know what's going on, and it's none of my business, anyway. But I'd like to go to the dance with you.'

I'm hallucinating, Cassie thought. I've got to be. I thought I just heard Nick apologise... and then say he'd *like* to go with me. I must have a fever.

'So what time do you want me to pick you up?' Nick said again.

Cassie was having trouble breathing, so her voice was faint. 'Um, about eight would be fine. We're all changing into our costumes at Suzan's house.'

'Okay. I'll see you there.'

On Halloween night, in Suzan's Greek Revival house, the girls of Crowhaven Road prepared themselves. This night was different than the evening of the Homecoming dance. For one thing, Cassie knew what she was doing now. Suzan had taught her how to do her own make-up, in exchange for Cassie helping Suzan with her costume.

They'd all taken baths with fresh sage leaves; Laurel's orders, for enhancing their psychic powers. Cassie had also washed in milk of roses – rosewater and oil of sweet almonds – for softening her skin and to smell nice. Cassie's grandmother had helped her plan and make her costume, which consisted mainly of panels of thin gauze.

When she was finished that night, Cassie looked in Suzan's mirror and saw a girl slender as a candle flame, dressed in something like mist, with an elusive, glancing beauty. The girl had hair like smoky topaz curling around a delicate face, and as Cassie watched, rosy shadows bloomed on her pale skin.

She looked soft and touchable and sensuous, but that was all right, because she would be with Nick. Cassie dabbed perfume behind her ears – not magnet oil but simply attar of roses – and tossed her scented hair back. Well, there was a certain wistfulness in the girl's wildflower-blue eyes, but that couldn't be helped. Nothing was going to cure that, ever.

She wasn't wearing any crystal to allure, only the hematite for iron-strength in a pouch under her costume.

'What are you?' Deborah said, looking into the mirror over her shoulder.

'I'm a muse. It's an old-time Greek thing; my grandmother

showed it to me in a book. They weren't goddesses, just sort of divine guides. They inspired people with creativity,' Cassie said. She looked at herself uncertainly. 'I guess I'm Calliope; she was muse of poetry. The others were muses of history and stuff.'

Melanie spoke up. 'Witches believe that there was only one muse before they got split up into nine. She was the spirit of the arts, all of them. So maybe tonight you're her.'

Cassie turned to look at their costumes. Deborah was a rocker, all silver bangles, studs, and black leather. Melanie was Sophia, the biblical spirit of wisdom, with a sheer veil over her face and a wreath of silver stars in her hair.

Suzan had taken Cassie's suggestion and dressed up as Aphrodite, goddess of love. Cassie had gotten the idea from Diana's prints and her grandmother's book of Greek myths. 'Aphrodite was supposed to be born from the sea,' she said now. 'That's the reason for all the shells.'

Suzan's hair was loose around her shoulders, and her robe was the colour of sea foam. Iridescent sequins, seed pearls, and tiny shells decorated the mask she held in her hand.

Laurel was a fairy. 'A *nature* spirit,' she said, pivoting to show long, curving dragonfly wings. She was wearing a garland of leaves and silk flowers on her head.

'Everyone looks great,' a soft voice said, and Cassie turned and caught her breath. Diana wasn't even dressed up, or at least she was only wearing her ceremonial costume, the one she wore at Circles. But she appeared to be wreathed in her own light and she was beautiful beyond description.

Laurel spoke quietly in Cassie's ear. 'She's not

making fun of it or anything, you know. Halloween's our most magical holiday of the year. She's honouring it.'

'Oh,' Cassie murmured. Her eyes slid to Faye.

Faye, she guessed, was a witch. The kind that guys were afraid of. She was wearing a sleeveless black dress, like a parody of the white shift Diana wore at meetings of the Circle. It was slit up both sides to the hip, and cut to show every curve. The material shimmered like silk when she walked.

There are going to be some hearts broken at the dance tonight, Cassie thought.

Downstairs, the doorbell rang, and the girls all went down in their fluttering draperies and rippling gowns to meet the guys. The Club was going to this dance in a group, as they planned to leave in a group at eleven thirty.

Nick was Cassie's date, but in that first moment all she could see was Adam. He was amazing. The branched ends of stag antlers sprouted from a crown of oak leaves on his head, and he was wearing a mask of oak leaves and acorns.

'He's Herne, the horned god,' Melanie said. 'Sort of like Pan, you know, a nature god. He's god of animals, too – that's why he gets to take Raj with him.'

Raj *was* there, trying to thrust his nose forward to give Cassie one of his embarrassingly warm greetings. Adam – or Herne; it unnerved Cassie how natural he looked with the horns and the oak leaves – held the dog back.

The other girls were laughing at the guys' costumes. 'Sean,' Laurel said, 'you're skinny enough without showing all your bones.' He was dressed as a skeleton.

Chris and Doug had strange symbols painted on

their faces: black and red triangles, yellow lightning bolts. Their long hair was even more dishevelled than usual. 'We're Zax,' they said, and everyone said, *'Who?'*

Chris answered: 'Zax the magician. He pulls cigarettes out of the air.'

'It's from some science-fiction show they saw once,' Suzan explained finally.

Faye's slow, lazy voice broke in. 'And just what are you supposed to be, Nick? The Man in Black?'

Cassie looked at Nick for the first time. He wasn't wearing a costume, just black jeans and a black pullover sweater. He looked very handsome, very cool.

'I'm supposed to be *her* date,' he said calmly, and without another look at Faye he held out his hand to Cassie.

Faye can't mind, Cassie told herself as they walked to the line of cars outside. Faye doesn't want him any more; she shouldn't care who he goes with. But there was a thin coil of uneasiness in her stomach as she let Nick guide her to the Armstrong car. Deborah and Laurel got in the back.

On the porches around them, jack-o'-lanterns had fiery grins and dancing flames for eyes. It was a crystal moonlit night.

'A haunted night,' Laurel said from the back seat. 'Tonight spirits gather at all the windows and doors, looking in. We always put a white candle in the window to guide them.'

'Or a plate of food to feed them, so they don't try to come inside,' Deborah said in a hollow voice.

Cassie laughed, but there was a slightly false note in the laughter. She didn't want spirits looking in her windows. And as for what Laurel had said two weeks ago, about dead relatives coming back to visit the living

– well, Cassie didn't want that, either. She didn't know any of her dead relatives, except her father, and he probably wasn't really dead. No, on the whole, she'd rather just leave all dead people alone.

But the Circle was planning to do just the opposite tonight.

The gym was decorated with owls, bats, and witches flying across giant yellow moons. Black and orange crepe paper was wound around the girders and streamed from the basketball hoops. There were dancing skeletons, spitting cats with arched backs, and surprised-looking ghosts on the walls.

It was all so fun and harmless. The ordinary students who'd come to dance and masquerade and drink purple poison punch had no idea of the real darkness that lurked outside. Even the ones who hated the Club didn't know the full truth.

Diana and Adam arrived together, making what must have been the most impressive entrance New Salem High School had ever seen. Diana, in her simple white shift, with her bare throat and arms looking as fresh as baby's skin, and her aureole of shining hair falling down her back, looked like a shaft of moonlight that had somehow wandered accidentally into the gym.

And Adam – Adam always had a presence, a way of innately commanding respect from anyone smart enough really to look at him. Tonight, as Herne, he was more arresting than ever. He seemed to *be* the forest god, perilous and mischievous, awe-inspiring but not unkind. Above all, he looked wild. There was nothing domesticated about him; he belonged in the open spaces, running underneath the stars. Raj stayed beside him, looking more like a wolf than a dog, and none of the chaperons said a word of objection.

'You know what happens tonight,' a voice murmured, breath warm on Cassie's neck.

Cassie said, 'What, Faye?' without turning around.

'Well, the coven leaders who represent the goddess Diana and the horned god have to make an alliance. They have to...' Faye paused delicately. '... merge, shall we say? To represent the union of male and female principals.'

'You mean they...?'

'It can be done symbolically,' Faye said blandly. 'But somehow I don't think Adam and Diana will be satisfied with symbolism, do you?'

CHAPTER
4

Cassie stood petrified. Her heart was going like a trip-hammer, but that was the only part of her capable of motion.

Adam and Diana... they *couldn't*. Only, of course, they could. Diana was laughing up at Adam now, tossing her straight, shining hair back. And although Cassie couldn't see Adam's eyes behind the mask, his lips were smiling.

Cassie turned, almost blundering into Nick, who was bringing her some punch, and rushed off into the dimness.

She found a dark corner under a Chinese lantern that had gone out. Shielded by a curtain of black and orange streamers, she stood there, trying to get hold of herself, trying not to see the pictures her mind was showing her.

The next thing she knew, she could smell wood smoke and ocean breeze, along with a faint, indefinable scent of animal and oak leaves. Adam.

'Cassie,' he said. Just that, as if Herne were calling her in her dreams, inviting her to throw off the covers in the middle of the night and come dancing in the autumn leaves.

And then, in a more ordinary voice, he said quietly, 'Cassie, are you okay? Diana says—'

'What?' Cassie demanded, in a way that would have been fierce if her voice hadn't been trembling.

'She's just worried that you're not all right.'

'I'm all right!' Cassie was struggling not to let the tears escape. 'And anyway – I'm tired of people talking about me behind my back. Faye says, Diana says – I'm *tired* of it.'

He took both her cold hands in his. 'I think,' he said in a subdued voice, 'that you're just tired, period.'

I am, Cassie thought. I'm tired of having secrets. And I'm tired of fighting. If I'm already evil, what's the point of fighting?

Just at the moment, to think was to act. Before she knew what she was doing, her hands had turned inside Adam's, so that her fingers were clasping his. *Not by word or look or deed*, what a laugh, she thought. We've already broken it a thousand times. Why not really break it? That way at least she would have something concrete to feel bad about. That way Diana wouldn't have him first.

That was the crux of it. Diana might have everything else, but she wouldn't have Adam first.

I could do it, Cassie thought. Suddenly, her mind was working coolly and rationally, far removed from all the twisted pain in her chest. Adam was vulnerable to her because he was honourable, because he would never dream of her scheming to get him.

If she started to cry right now... If she got him close enough to hold her, then relaxed against him, making herself soft in his arms... If she laid her head on his shoulder so that he could smell her hair... If she sighed and let her head fall back... would he be able to resist kissing her?

Cassie didn't think so.

There were places darker than this corner. Safe places in the school. The home-ec room with the lock anyone could pick, the storage compartment where the gymnastics mats were kept. If Adam kissed her and she kissed him back, could anything stop them from going there?

Cassie didn't think so.

And Diana, sweet *stupid* innocent Diana, would never know the difference. If Adam said he'd had to take Cassie for a walk to calm her down, Diana would believe him.

No, there was nothing to stop Cassie and Adam... except the oath. How did it go again? *Fire burn me, air smother me, earth swallow me, water cover my grave.* Cassie wasn't afraid of that. Fire was burning her body already, and air was smothering her – she couldn't breathe. There was nothing to stop her. She leaned in closer to Adam, head drooping like a flower on a slender stem, feeling the first easy tears come. She heard the catch in her breath, and felt his fingers tighten on hers in concern, and awareness.

'Cassie – God...' he whispered.

A fierce rush of triumph swept through Cassie. He couldn't help himself. It was going to happen. *Oak and holly, leaf and briar/ Touch him with the secret fire...*

What was she *doing*?

Using magic on *Adam*? Snaring him with words that had come from some deep well of knowledge within herself? It was wrong, dishonourable, and not just because members of the Club didn't work spells on each other unasked.

It was wrong because of Diana.

Diana, who'd been Cassie's friend when no one else

would speak to her. Who'd championed her against Faye and the whole school. Even if Cassie couldn't deal with being close to Diana right now, the memory of Diana was like a star shining in her mind. If she betrayed that, she betrayed everything that meant anything.

Evil or not, Cassie couldn't do it.

She extracted her hands from Adam's strong fingers.

'I'm all right,' she said, her voice soft and weak, all its bones crushed.

He was trying to get hold of her hands again. That was the problem with magic, you couldn't always stop what you'd started. 'Adam, really,' she said. Then, desperately, she added, 'Diana's waiting.'

Saying Diana's name helped. He stood for a moment, then escorted her back, Herne bringing a wayward nymph home to the Circle. Cassie went over to Laurel for safety; Nick was nowhere in sight. Well, she didn't blame him.

Diana was talking to Sally Waltman, who was there and looking hard as nails, despite the loss of Jeffrey. That left Adam and Cassie with Laurel and Melanie and their dates, and Sean and Deborah. A merry group of witches. Next to them was a group of outsiders.

A slow dance was starting. The group of outsiders broke up, moving onto the dance floor. All except one.

That one remained standing there, isolated, on the fringe of the Club. She was a junior Cassie vaguely recognised from French class, a shy girl, not beautiful, but not ugly, either. Right now she was trying to pretend that she didn't mind being abandoned, that she didn't care.

Cassie's heart went out to her. Poor girl. Once, Cassie had been just like her.

'Want to dance?' It was Adam's voice, warm and

friendly – but he wasn't talking to Cassie, he was talking to the outsider girl. Her face lit up, and she went happily with him out onto the floor, the scales of her mermaid costume flashing and twinkling. Cassie watched them go with a pang.

But not of jealousy. Of love – and respect.

'The parfit gentil knight,' Melanie said.

'What?' said Cassie.

'It's from Chaucer. We learned it in British lit class. That's what Adam is, the perfect gentle knight,' Melanie explained.

Cassie thought about this for a while. Then she turned to Sean. 'Hey, skinny, want to shake your bones?' she said.

Sean's face lit up.

Well, Cassie thought as she and Sean began swaying to the music, one thing was for sure: this dance *wasn't* anything like the last one. With Adam, the gym had seemed a place of beauty and enchantment. Now all she saw were paper cutouts and naked pipes overhead. At least Sean-the-Day-Glo-skeleton didn't try to pull her in too close.

Afterwards, other guys approached her, but Cassie made a beeline for Nick, who'd rematerialised, and hid behind him. At least this part of her plan worked – the other guys retreated. It was strange to be something everybody wanted and couldn't have. Nick didn't ask her why she'd rushed off, and she didn't ask him where he'd disappeared to.

They danced a few times. Nick didn't try to kiss her.

And then it was time to leave. After saying good-bye to their bewildered, slightly indignant dates, the members of the Club gathered at the exit, and not even the strawberry-blonde goddess Aphrodite was late.

Even the two identical Zaxes, their slanted blue-green eyes sparkling, were waiting outside the door. Then they all started off into the darkness. The moon had set, but the stars seemed to be on fire.

It was cold on the point of the headland. They sat on bits of the foundation of the razed house, while Deborah and Faye built a bonfire in the centre. Other people were bringing provisions out of the cars. Cassie had expected everyone to be solemn, but the Circle was in a party mood, excited by the night, laughing and joking, defying the danger of what they were going to do in an hour or so. Cassie found herself enjoying the celebration, not thinking about the future.

There was lots of food. Dried pumpkin seeds ('Without *salt*,' Laurel said), pumpkin bread and gingerbread baked by Diana, boxes of chocolate- and orange-frosted doughnuts from Adam, a bowl of mixed Halloween candy provided by Suzan, soft drinks and spiced cider, and a large paper bag of Chris's that rattled.

'Nuts! Yeah! For virility!' Doug yelled to the other guys, with an uncouth gesture.

'Hazelnuts symbolise wisdom,' Melanie said patiently, but the Henderson brothers just sneered.

And there were apples: winesaps, greenings, macintoshes. 'Apples for love and death,' Diana said. 'Especially at Halloween. Did you know they were sacred to the goddess Hera?'

'Did you know the seeds contain cyanide?' Faye added, smiling oddly. She'd been smiling oddly at Cassie ever since Cassie had emerged from behind the streamer curtain with Adam at the dance. Now, leaning over to take a piece of gingerbread, she murmured in Cassie's ear, 'What happened back there when he followed you? Did you blow your chance?'

'It isn't nice to fool around with guys who're taken,' Cassie whispered tiredly, as if explaining to a five-year-old.

Faye chuckled. 'Nice? Is that what you want for your epitaph? "Here lies Cassie. She was... nice"?'

Cassie turned her head away.

'I know an apple spell,' Laurel was saying to the group. 'You peel an apple in one long spiral, then throw the peel over your shoulder, and if it doesn't break, it forms the initial of your true love.'

They tried this, without much success. The peelings kept breaking, Suzan cut herself on Deborah's knife, and when Diana did manage to throw a peeling over her shoulder, it only formed a spiral.

'Well, that's sacred to the goddess at least,' Laurel said, frowning. 'Or to the Horned One,' she added mischievously, looking at Adam.

Cassie had been deliberately breaking her apple peels; the whole fortune-telling thing made her uneasy. And not just because Melanie mentioned cheerfully, 'They used to execute witches for this kind of divination on Halloween.'

'I've got another one,' Laurel said. 'You throw a nut in the fire, say a pair of names, and see what happens. Like Suzan and David Downey,' she added impishly. 'If the nut pops, they're meant for each other. If it doesn't, they're doomed.'

'If he loves me, pop and fly; if he hates me, burn and die!' Suzan quoted dramatically as Laurel tossed a hazelnut in. The round little nut just sizzled.

'Laurel and Doug,' Chris snickered, throwing in another.

'Chris and Sally Waltman!' Doug countered.

'Cassie and Nick!'

Deborah tossed that one in, grinning, but Faye was noticeably unsmiling.

'Adam...' she said, holding a nut up high between long red nails and waiting until she had everyone's attention. Cassie stared at her, poised on the edge of her brick. '... and Diana,' Faye said finally, and flicked the hazelnut into the flames.

Cassie, mesmerised, watched the nut where it lay on glowing embers. She didn't want to look at it; she had to.

'There are lots of other Halloween traditions,' Laurel was going on. 'It's time to remember old people, people who're coming to the winter of their lives – or that's what my Granny Quincey says.'

Cassie was still staring at that one hazelnut. It seemed to be jiggling – but was it going to pop?

'It's getting late,' Adam said. 'Don't you think we should get started?'

Diana brushed pumpkin-bread crumbs off her hands and stood. 'Yes.'

Cassie only took her eyes off the fire for an instant, but in that instant, there was a sound like gunfire. Two or three nuts had exploded at once, and when Cassie looked back she couldn't see the one Faye had thrown. It had popped – or she'd lost track of it. She couldn't tell which.

A heartbeat later it flashed through her mind to wonder about Deborah's nut – for Cassie and Nick. But she couldn't tell what had become of that one, either.

'All right, now,' Diana said. 'This is going to be a different kind of Circle. It's going to be more powerful than anything we've ever used before, because we need more protection than we've ever needed before. And it's going to take everybody's help.' She followed this with an earnest glance at Faye, who replied with a look of utmost innocence.

Cassie watched Diana draw a circle inside the ruined foundation with her black-handled knife. The bonfire was at the centre. Everyone was serious now, their eyes following the path of the knife as it cut through the soil, making an almost perfect ring with a single gap at the north-east corner.

'Everyone get inside, and then I'll close it,' Diana said. They all filed inside and sat along the inner perimeter of the ring. Only Raj was left on the outside, watching anxiously and whining a little in his throat.

'After this,' Diana said, closing the gap with a sweep of the knife, 'no one leaves the protection of the circle. What we're summoning up inside will be dangerous, but what'll be hanging around outside will be even worse.'

'How dangerous?' Sean said nervously. 'What's inside, I mean.'

'We'll be safe as long as we don't go near the fire or touch it,' Diana said. 'No matter how strong a spirit it is, it won't be able to part from the fire we use to summon it. All right,' she added briskly, 'now I'm going to call on the Watchtower of the East. Powers of Air, protect us!'

Standing facing the dark eastern sky and ocean, Diana held a burning stick of incense and blew it eastwards across the circle. 'Think of air!' she told the coven members, and at once Cassie not only thought of it, but felt it, heard it. It started as a gentle breeze blowing from the east, but then it began to gust. It became a blast, a roaring wind beating in their faces, blowing Diana's long hair backwards like a banner. And then it diverted, flowing around the circumference of the circle, enclosing them.

Diana took a burning stick out of the fire and moved to stand in front of Cassie, who was seated at the southernmost edge of the circle. Waving the stick over Cassie's head, she said, 'Now I'm calling on the Watchtower of the South. Powers of Fire, protect us!'

She didn't need to say, *think of fire*. Cassie could already feel the heat radiating on her back, could picture the pillar of flame bursting up behind her. It raced around like sparks across gunpowder, to form a circle of wildfire just outside the circle of wind.

It's not real, Cassie reminded herself. They're just symbols we're visualising. But they were awfully concrete-looking symbols.

Diana moved again. Dipping her fingers in a paper cup, she sprinkled water across the western perimeter, between Sean and Deborah. 'I'm calling on the Watchtower of the West. Powers of Water, protect us!'

It surged up, a phantom glass-green wave, cresting higher and higher. The swell flowed around to encompass the circle with a wall of water.

Lastly, Diana moved north, facing Adam and scattering salt across the northern line. 'Watchtower of the North,' she said, in a voice that wavered slightly and showed how much this was taking out of her. 'Powers of Earth, protect us!'

The ground rumbled beneath them.

It caught Cassie off guard, and the rest of the group was even more startled than she was. They weren't used to earthquakes here in New England, but Cassie was a native Californian. She saw that Sean was about to jump up.

'Deborah, get Sean!' she cried.

In an instant, the biker girl had grabbed Sean and was forcibly holding him from running. The tremors became more and more violent – and then with a sound like a thunderclap, the ground split. A chasm opened all around the circle, spewing up a strong, sulphurous smell.

It isn't real. It isn't real, Cassie reminded herself. But surrounding her she saw the phantoms of the four elements Diana had invoked, layered one after another. A circle of raging wind, then a ring of fire, then a wall of seawater, and finally a chasm in the earth. Nothing from the outside could pass those boundaries – and Cassie wouldn't like to bet on anything from the inside getting out safely, either.

Shakily, Diana walked over to sit down in her place between Nick and Faye. 'Okay,' she said, almost in a whisper. 'Now we all concentrate on the fire. Look into it and let the night do the rest. Let's see if anything comes to talk to us.'

Cassie's eyes shifted to Melanie, beside her. 'But if we're protected from everything outside, who's going to be able to come talk to us?' she murmured.

'Something from *here*,' Melanie whispered back, looking down at the barren earth inside the circle. Inside the foundations of the house.

'Oh.'

Cassie gazed into the flames, trying to clear her mind, to be open to whatever might be trying to cross the veil between the invisible world and this one. Tonight was the night, and now was the time.

The fire began smoking.

Just a little at first, as if the wood were damp. But then the smoke got darker – still transparent, but blacker. It streamed upwards and hung in a cloudy mass above the bonfire.

Then it began to change.

It was twisting, swelling, like thunderheads rolling together. As Cassie stared, her breath clogging in her throat, it began to mould itself, to form a shape.

A man-shape.

It seemed to develop from the top down, and it was wearing old-fashioned clothes, like something out of a history book. A hat with a high crown and a stiff brim. A cloak or cape which hung down from broad shoulders, and a wide, severe linen collar. Breeches tied below the knees. Cassie thought she could make out square-toed shoes, but at times the lower legs just dwindled into the smoke of the fire. One thing she noticed, the smoke never actually detached from the fire, it always remained connected by a thin trail.

The figure floated there motionless except for eddies within itself.

Then it drifted towards Cassie.

She was the one who seemed to be facing it straight on. A sudden thought came into her mind. When Adam had first taken the crystal skull out of his backpack on the beach, it had seemed to be looking directly at her. And again – at the skull ceremony, she remembered. When Diana had pulled the cloth off the skull then, those hollow eyesockets had seemed to be staring right into Cassie's eyes.

Now this thing was staring at her in the same way.

'We should ask it a question,' Melanie said, but even her usually calm voice was unsteady. There was a feeling of menace about the cloudy shape, of evil. Like the dark energy inside the skull, only stronger. More immediate.

Who are you? thought Cassie, but her tongue was frozen, and anyway, she didn't need to ask. There was no doubt at all in her mind who the shape in front of her was.

Black John.

Then came Diana's voice, clear and carefully calm. 'We've invited you here because we've found something of yours,' she said. 'We need to know how to control it. Will you talk to us?'

There was no answer. Cassie thought the thing was moving closer to her – but maybe it was just an illusion.

'There are terrible things going on,' Adam said. 'They have to be stopped.'

No illusion. It was coming closer.

'Are *you* controlling the dark energy?' Melanie asked abruptly, and Laurel's voice blended with hers: 'You're dead! You've got no right to be interfering with the living.'

'What's your problem, anyway?' Deborah demanded.

Too fast, Cassie thought. Too many people asking questions. The shape was drifting steadily closer. Cassie felt paralysed, as if she were in danger that no one else saw.

'Who killed Kori?' Doug Henderson was snarling.

'Why did the dark energy lead us to the cemetery?' Deborah jumped in.

'And what happened to Jeffrey?' Suzan added.

The trail of smoke connecting the shape to the fire was stretched out thin, and the shape was right in front of Cassie. She was afraid to look into that cloudy, indistinct face, but she had to. In its contours she thought she could recognise the face she'd glimpsed inside the crystal skull.

Get up, Cassie.

The words weren't real words, they were in her mind. And they had some power over her. Cassie felt herself shift position, begin to rise.

Come with me, Cassie.

The others were still asking questions, and dimly Cassie could hear barking far away. But much louder was the voice in her mind.

Cassie, come.

She got to her feet. The swirling darkness seemed to be less transparent now. More solid. It was reaching out a formless hand.

Cassie reached out with her own hand to take it.

CHAPTER

5

'Cassie, no!'

Later Cassie would realise it was Diana who had shouted. At the time the words came to her only through a fog, and they sounded slow and dragging. Meaningless, like the continued mad barking that was going on somewhere far away. Cassie's fingertips brushed the transparent black fingertips before her.

Instantly, she felt a jolt like the thrill that the hematite had given her. She looked up, shocked, from her own hand to the smoky, swirling face, and she *recognised* it—

Then everything shattered.

There was a great splash and icy-cold drops of water splattered Cassie from head to foot. At the same instant there was the hissing sound of red-hot embers being suddenly drenched. The smoky man-thing changed, dwindling, dissolving, as if it were being sucked back into the fire. A fire that now was nothing more than a sodden black mess of charred sticks.

Adam was standing on the other side of the circle, holding the cooler, whose contents had doused the fire.

Raj was behind him, hair bristling, lips skinned back from his teeth.

Cassie stared from her own outstretched hand to Adam's wide eyes. She swayed. Then everything seemed to go soft and grey around her, and she fainted.

'You're safe now. Just lie still.' The voice seemed to come from a great distance, but it had a note of gentle authority. Diana, Cassie thought vaguely, and a great longing swept over her. She wanted to hold Diana's hand, but it was too much trouble to move or try to open her eyes.

'Here's the lavender water,' came another voice, lighter and more hasty. Laurel. 'You dab it on, like this...'

Cassie felt a coolness on her forehead and wrists. A sweet, clean smell cleared her head a little.

She could hear other voices now. '... maybe, but I still don't know how the hell Adam did it. I couldn't move – felt like I was frozen.' That was Deborah.

'Me, too! Like I was stuck to the ground.' That was Sean.

'Adam, will you please sit down now so Laurel can look at you? *Please?* You're hurt.' That was Melanie, and suddenly Cassie could open her eyes. She sat up and a cool damp cloth fell off her forehead into her lap.

'No, no – Cassie, lie still,' Diana said, trying to push her back down. Cassie was staring at Adam.

His wonderful unruly hair was blown every which way. His skin was reddened, like a skier with a bad case of windburn, and his clothes looked askew and damp. 'I'm all right,' he was saying to Melanie, who was trying to sit him in a chair.

'What happened? Where are we?' Cassie said. She was lying on a couch in a shabby living room she knew she should recognise, but she felt very confused.

'We brought you to Laurel's house,' said Diana. 'We didn't want to scare your mom and grandma. You fainted. But Adam saved your life.'

'He went *through* the four circles of protection,' Suzan said, with a distinct note of awe in her voice.

'Stupid,' Deborah commented. 'But impressive.'

And then came Faye's lazy drawl: 'I think it was a tremendously devoted thing to do.'

There was a startled pause. Then Laurel said, 'Oh, well, you know Adam and duty. I guess he *is* devoted to it.'

'*I* would've done it – so would Doug – if we could've got up,' Chris insisted.

'And if you could've thought of it – which you couldn't,' Nick said dryly and a little grimly. His expression was dark.

Cassie was watching as Laurel dabbed with a damp towel at Adam's face and hands. 'This is aloe and willow bark,' Laurel explained. 'It should keep the burns from getting worse.'

'Cassie,' Diana said gently, 'do you remember what happened before you fainted?'

'Uh... you guys were asking questions – too many questions. And then – I don't know, this voice started talking in my head. That thing was staring at me...' Cassie had a sudden thought. 'Diana – at the skull ceremony in your garage, you know how you had the skull under a cloth?' Diana nodded. 'Did you have it facing any particular way under the cloth?'

Diana looked startled. 'Actually, there was something about that that worried me. I put the skull facing the place where I'd sit in the circle – but when I took the cloth off, it was facing the other way.'

'It was facing *me*,' Cassie said. 'Which means either somebody moved it or... it moved itself.' They were looking at each other, both puzzled and uneasy, but *communicating*. Cassie felt closer to Diana than she had in weeks. Now was the time to make up, she thought.

'Diana,' she began, but just then she noticed something. Adam's mask of horns and oak leaves was sitting on a chair beside Diana, and one of Diana's slender hands was resting on it, caressing it as if for comfort. It was an unconscious gesture – and a completely revealing one. A bolt of resentment shot through Cassie's heart. Herne and the goddess Diana – they *belonged* together, right? And Diana knew it. Later tonight they'd probably perform that little ceremony Faye had been talking about.

Cassie looked up and found Faye looking at her, golden eyes hooded and ironic. Faye smiled faintly.

'What is it?' Diana was saying. 'Cassie?'

'Nothing.' Cassie stared down at the threadbare violet rug on the hardwood floor. 'Nothing. I feel all right now,' she added. It was true, the disorientation was almost gone. But the memory of that smoky face stayed with her.

'What an ending to our Halloween,' Laurel said.

'We should have stayed at the dance,' said Suzan, sitting back and crossing her legs. 'We didn't learn anything – *and* Cassie got hurt,' she added, after a moment's thought.

'But we did learn something. We learned that Black John's ghost is still around – and it's malevolent,' Adam said. 'It certainly wouldn't answer any of our questions.'

'And it's strong,' Diana said. 'Strong enough to influence all of us, to keep us from moving.' She looked at Cassie. 'Except Cassie. I wonder why.'

Cassie felt a flash of discomfort, and she shrugged.

'It doesn't matter how strong it is,' Melanie said. 'Halloween's over in a few hours, and after that it won't have any power.'

'But we still don't know any more about the skull. Or about Kori,' Doug said, unusually serious.

'And *I* don't think we even know that Black John is – how did you put it, Adam? Malevolent,' came Faye's husky slow voice. 'Maybe he just didn't feel like talking.'

'Oh, don't be ridiculous,' began Laurel.

Before an argument could break out, Diana said, 'Look, it's late, and we're all tired. We're not going to get anything solved tonight. If Cassie really is okay, I think we should all go home and get some rest.'

There was a pause, and then nods of agreement.

'We can talk about it at school – or at Nick's birthday,' Laurel said.

'I'll take Cassie home,' Nick said at the door.

Cassie glanced at him quickly. He hadn't said much while she'd been lying on the couch – but he'd *been* there. He'd come along with the rest of them to make sure she was all right.

'Then Deborah can come with me,' Melanie said. 'She rode in with you, right?'

'Can you drive me, too? I really am tired,' Diana said, and Melanie nodded easily.

Cassie scarcely noticed the rest of the good-byes. What she was noticing was that Adam was leaving in his Jeep Cherokee, heading north, and Diana was going with Melanie and Deborah, going south.

No Herne-and-Diana ceremony *tonight*, Cassie thought, and a wash of relief went through her. Relief – and a ripple of mean gladness. It was wrong, it was bad – but she felt it.

Just as she got into Nick's car, she saw Faye smiling at her with raised eyebrows, and before she knew it, Cassie had smiled back.

* * *

The next day when Cassie stepped out of her house she stopped in shock. The sugar-maple trees across the street had changed. The blazing autumn colours that had reminded her of fire were gone. So were the leaves. Every branch was bare.

It looked like a Halloween skeleton.

'Nick won't let us do much for his birthday tomorrow,' Laurel said. 'I wish we could give him a *real* surprise party.'

Deborah snorted. 'He'd walk right out.'

'I know. Well, we'll try to think of something he won't think is too infantile. And' – Laurel brightened – 'we can make up for it on the other birthdays.'

'What other birthdays?' Cassie said.

All the girls of the Club looked at her. They were sitting in the back room of the cafeteria, having a special conference while the guys kept Nick away.

'You mean you don't *know* about the birthday season?' Suzan asked in disbelief. 'Diana didn't tell you?'

Diana opened her mouth and then shut it again. Cassie guessed she didn't know how to say that she and Cassie didn't talk that much any more, at least not in private.

'Let's see if I can keep it straight,' Faye said with a low chuckle, eyes on the ceiling. She began to count on fingers tipped with long, gleaming scarlet nails. 'Nick's is November third. Adam's is November fifth. Melanie's is November seventh. Mine – and oh, yes, Diana's, too – is November tenth...'

'Are you *kidding*?' Cassie broke in.

Laurel shook her head as Faye went relentlessly on. 'Chris and Doug's is November seventeenth, Suzan's is the twenty-fourth, and Deborah's is the twenty-eighth. Laurel's is, um...'

'December first,' Laurel said. 'And Sean's is December third, and that's it.'

'But that's . . .' Cassie's voice trailed off. She couldn't believe it. Nick was only a month older than Sean? And *all* the witch kids were eight or nine months older than she was? 'But you and Sean are juniors, like me,' she said to Laurel. 'And my birthday's July twenty-third.'

'We just missed the cut-off date,' Laurel said. 'Everybody born after November thirtieth has to wait another year for school. So we had to watch everybody else go off to kindergarten while we stayed home.' She wiped away imaginary tears.

'But that's still . . .' Cassie couldn't express herself. 'Don't you think that's pretty incredible? All of you guys being born within a month of each other?'

Suzan dimpled wickedly. 'It was a very wet April that year. Our parents all stayed inside.'

'It *seems* odd, I admit,' Melanie said. 'But the fact is that most of our parents got married the spring before. So it really isn't that surprising.'

'But . . .' Cassie still thought it *was* surprising, although clearly all the members of the Club were so used to it they didn't wonder about it any more. And why don't I fit in the pattern? she thought. I guess it's because I'm half outsider. She shrugged. Melanie was probably right; anyway, there was no point in worrying. She let the subject drop and they went back to planning Nick's party.

They finally decided to combine all the birthdays for that first week – Nick's, Adam's, and Melanie's – and hold the party on Saturday, November seventh.

'*And*,' Laurel said, when they explained their plan to the boys, 'this one is going to be *really* different. Don't ask now – it's going to be *unique*.'

'Uh, it's not some health-food kind of thing, is it?' Doug said, looking suspicious.

The girls looked at each other and stifled laughter. 'Well – it *is* healthy – or at least some people think so,' Melanie said. 'You'll just have to come and see.'

'But we'll freeze to death,' Sean said, horrified.

'Not with this,' Laurel laughed. She held up a thermos.

'Laurel.' Adam was having a hard time not laughing himself. 'I don't care how hot whatever you've got in there is – it's not going to keep us warm in *that*.'

A silver moon, slightly more than half full, was shining down on an obsidian sea. It was the sea Adam was pointing to.

'It's not Ovaltine,' Deborah told him impatiently. 'It's something *we* mixed up.'

The five boys were facing the girls, who were lined up behind Laurel. There was a bonfire going on the beach, but at this distance it did nothing to cut the icy wind.

'They're obviously not going to believe us,' Faye said, and Diana added, 'I guess we'll just have to show them.'

Laurel passed the thermos around. Cassie took a deep breath and then a gulp. The liquid was hot and medicinal-tasting – like one of Laurel's nastier herbal teas – but the instant she swallowed it, a tingling warmth swept over her. Suddenly she didn't need her bulky sweater. It was positively hot out here on the beach.

'To the sea, ye mystics,' Melanie said. Cassie wasn't sure what it meant, but like the other girls, she was shedding suddenly unnecessary clothing. The boys were goggling.

'*I* want a birthday party like this,' Sean said urgently, as Faye unzipped her red jacket. 'Okay? Okay? I want—'

The guys were mildly disappointed when it turned out the girls had bathing suits on underneath.

'But what are *we* supposed to do?' Adam said, sniffing at the thermos and grinning at the bikini-clad girls.

'Well...' Faye smiled. 'You can always improvise.'

'Or,' Diana put in, 'you can look behind the big rock. There just *might* be a pile of swimming trunks there.'

'Now this really is different,' Laurel said happily to Cassie some time later, while they were both floating in water up to their chins. 'A midnight swimming party in November. This is *witchy*.'

'Be more witchy if we were all sky-clad,' Chris commented, shaking his shaggy blond head like a wet dog.

Cassie and Laurel looked at each other, then at Deborah, who was bobbing nearby.

'Good idea,' Deborah said, nodding at the other girls. 'How about you first, Chris?'

'Wait a minute – I didn't mean – hey, Doug – *help*!'

'Come on, girls,' Laurel shouted. 'Chris wants to go skinny-dipping, only he's a little shy.'

'Help! Guys, help!'

It turned into a sort of combination of tag and aquatic wrestling. Everyone joined in. Cassie found herself being chased by Nick and she fled, kicking up great splashes while he cut cleanly through the surf behind her. He got close enough to grab her.

'Help!' Cassie shrieked, half laughing, so that she accidentally drank some salt water. But there was no help in sight. Laurel and Deborah were heading an assault on the Henderson brothers, and Adam and Diana were far away, their sleek heads bobbing side by side.

Nick tossed wet hair – blacker than onyx in the

moonlight – out of his eyes and grinned at her. Cassie had never seen him smile before. 'Surrender,' he suggested.

'Never,' Cassie said, with as much dignity as she could muster while wavelets slapped her. Nick *was* handsome – but she didn't want him to get hold of her out here. He made another grab at her and Cassie shrieked for help again, and suddenly there was a heaving wave between them.

'Go on! Get out of here!' Faye said. Her eyes gleamed wickedly under long, wet lashes. 'Or do we have to *make* you? Cassie, grab him around the neck while I get his trunks!'

Cassie had no idea how to grab a guy as strong as Nick around the neck, especially when she was laughing so hard, but she surged forward. Faye dived like a dolphin, and Nick twisted and made a hasty retreat, swimming away as fast as he could.

Cassie looked at Faye and found Faye smiling sideways at her. Cassie grinned.

'Thanks,' she said.

'Any time,' Faye said. 'You know I'm glad to do anything for my friends. And we are friends, aren't we, Cassie?'

Cassie thought about that, treading water in the silver-glinting ocean. 'I guess,' she said, finally, slowly.

'That's good. Because, Cassie, there's a time coming up when I'm going to need all my friends. This Tuesday, when the moon is full, the Circle is going to have a meeting.'

Cassie nodded, not getting it for a moment. Of course they were going to have a meeting. And another party; it was Faye's and Diana's birthday. They were both seventeen—

'The leadership vote!' Cassie said, taking an involuntary

gulp of salt water again. She stared at Faye with a sudden terrible apprehension. 'Faye...'

'That's right,' Faye said. In the moonlight she looked like a mermaid, staying afloat effortlessly. Her glorious mane of hair hung soaking wet down her back like twining seaweed. Her eyes held Cassie's. 'I want to be leader of this coven, Cassie. I *will* be leader. And you're going to help me.'

'No.'

'Yes. Because this time I'm serious. I've been going easy on you, letting you have your way, not making you play by the rules. But that's over now, Cassie. This is the one thing I want more than anything else in the world, and you *are* going to help me. Otherwise...' Faye looked over her shoulder to where Adam and Diana were still bobbing, far away. Then she turned back.

'Otherwise, I'll do it,' she said. 'I'll tell Diana – and not just about that little cuddling session on the bluff. I'll tell her about the way you and Adam were kissing at the Homecoming dance – did you think nobody would see that? And the *real* reason Adam went through four circles of protection to save you at Halloween. And' – she floated closer to Cassie, her hooded golden eyes as unblinking as the eyes of a falcon – 'I'll tell her about the skull. How you stole it from her and gave it to me, so we could kill Jeffrey.'

'That's not what happened! I'd never have let you have it if I'd known—'

'Are you sure, Cassie?' Faye smiled, a slow, conspiratorial smile. 'I think, deep down, that you and I are just the same. We're... sisters under the skin. And if you don't vote for me on Tuesday, I'll let everyone know the truth about you. I'll tell them what you really are inside.'

Evil, Cassie thought, staring out at the ocean. It reflected the moonlight back like a mirror, like a piece of hematite, and it surrounded her. She couldn't say a word.

'Think about it, Cassie,' Faye said pleasantly. 'You have until Tuesday night to decide.' And then she swam away.

It was Tuesday night.

The full moon was directly overhead, the circle had been cast. The members of the Club sat around it. Diana, who was wearing all the symbols of the Queen of the Witches, had called on the four elements to protect them, but now she was silent. It was Melanie who was calling for the vote, from oldest to youngest.

'Nicholas,' she said.

'I told you before,' Nick said. 'I won't vote. I'm *here*, because you two insisted' – he glanced from Faye to Diana – 'but I abstain.'

With a strange feeling of unreality, Cassie watched his handsome, cold face. Nick had abstained, why couldn't she? But she knew that would never satisfy Faye, unless Faye had already won. And Cassie was no closer to knowing which way to vote tonight than she had been three days ago. If only she had a little more time—

But there was no time. Melanie was speaking again.

'Adam.'

Adam's voice was firm and clear. 'Diana.'

From a pile of red and white stones in front of her, Melanie put forward one white. 'And as for me, I vote for Diana too,' she said, and put out another white stone. 'Faye?'

Faye smiled. 'I vote for myself.'

Melanie put out a red stone. 'Diana.'

'I vote for myself too,' Diana said quietly.

A third white stone. Then Melanie said, 'Douglas.'

Doug grinned one of his wildest grins. 'I'm voting for Faye, naturally.'

'Christopher.'

'Uh…:' Chris looked confused. Despite Faye's frown and Doug's frantic coaching, he was squinting into nothingness as if searching for a lost decision. Finally, he seemed to find it and he looked at Melanie. 'Okay; Diana.'

Everyone in the circle stared at him. He glared back defiantly. Cassie's fingers clenched on the piece of hematite in her pocket.

'Chris, you feeb—' Doug began, but Melanie shut him up.

'No talking,' she said, and put out a fourth white stone next to the two red. 'Suzan.'

'Faye.'

Three red, four white. 'Deborah.'

'Who do you think?' Deborah snapped. 'Faye.'

Four red, four white. 'Laurel,' said Melanie.

'Diana's always been our leader, and she always will be,' Laurel said. 'I vote for her.'

Melanie put a fifth white stone out, a trace of a smile hovering on her lips. 'Sean.'

Sean's black eyes shifted nervously. 'I…' Faye was staring at him relentlessly. 'I… I… *Faye*,' he said, and hunched up his shoulders.

Melanie shrugged and put out another red stone. Five red, five white. But although her grey eyes remained serious, her lips were definitely curved in a smile. All of Diana's adherents had relaxed, and they were flashing smiles at each other across the circle.

Melanie turned confidently to the last member of the coven and said, 'Cassandra.'

CHAPTER
6

There was silence under the silver disk of moon.

'Cassie,' Melanie said again.

Now everyone was looking at her. Cassie could feel the heat of Faye's golden eyes on her, and she knew why Sean had squirmed. They were hotter than the pillar of fire Diana had summoned up to protect them at Halloween.

As if compelled, Cassie glanced the other way. Diana was looking at her too. Diana's eyes were like a pool adrift with green leaves. Cassie couldn't seem to look away from them.

'Cassie?' Melanie said for the third time. Her voice was tinged with the slightest note of doubt.

Still unable to look away from Diana's eyes, Cassie whispered, 'Faye.'

'*What?*' cried Laurel.

'Faye,' Cassie said, too loudly. She was clutching the piece of hematite in her pocket. Coldness from it seemed to seep through her body. 'I said Faye, all right?' she said to Melanie, but she was still looking at Diana.

Those clear green eyes were bewildered. Then, all at once, understanding came into them, as if a stone had been tossed into the tranquil pool. And when Cassie saw that, saw Diana really *understand* what had just happened, something inside her died forever.

Cassie didn't know any longer why she was voting for Faye. She couldn't remember now how all this had started, how she'd gotten on this path in the first place. All she knew was that the coldness from her hand and arm was trickling through her entire body, and that from here on, there was no turning back.

Melanie was sitting motionless, stunned, not touching the pile of red and white stones. She seemed to have forgotten about them. It was Deborah who leaned forward and picked up the sixth red stone, adding it to Faye's pile.

And somehow that act, and the sight of the six red stones beside the five white ones, made it real. Electricity crackled in the air as everyone sat forward.

Slowly, Melanie said, 'Faye is the new leader of the coven.'

Faye stood up.

She had never seemed so tall before, or so beautiful.

Silently, she held out a hand to Diana.

But it wasn't a gesture of friendship. Faye's open hand with the long crimson nails was *demanding*. And in response to it, very slowly, Diana got to her feet as well. She unclasped the silver bracelet from her upper arm.

Adam had been staring, thunderstruck. Now he jumped to his feet. '*Wait* a minute—'

'It's no use, Adam,' Melanie said, in a deadened voice. 'The vote was fair. Nothing can change it now.'

Faye took the silver bracelet with the mysterious, runic inscriptions, and clasped it about her own bare, rounded arm. It shone there against the honey-pale skin.

Diana's fingers trembled as she undid the garter. Laurel,

muttering something and brushing tears out of her eyes with an angry gesture, moved forward to help her, kneeling before Diana and tugging at the circle of green leather and blue silk. It came free and Laurel stood up, looking as if she wanted to throw it at Faye.

But Diana took it and placed it in Faye's hand.

Faye was wearing the shimmering black shift that she'd worn to the Halloween dance, the one slit up both sides to the hip. She buckled the garter around her left thigh.

Then Diana put both hands to her hair and lifted off the diadem. Fine strands of hair the colour of sunlight and moonlight woven together clung to the silver crown as she removed it.

Faye reached out and almost snatched it from her.

Faye held the circlet up high, as if showing it to the coven, to the four elements, to the world. Then she settled it on her own head. The crescent moon in its centre gleamed against her wild black mane of hair.

There was a collective release of breath from the Circle.

Cassie didn't know how she'd gotten to her feet, but suddenly she was running. She bolted out of the circle and ran beside the ocean, her feet sinking into wet sand. She ran until something caught her from behind and stopped her.

'Cassie!' Adam said. His eyes looked straight into hers, as if he was searching for her soul.

Cassie hit out at him.

'Cassie, I know you didn't want to do it! She made you, somehow, didn't she? Cassie, tell me!'

Cassie tried to shake him off again. Why was he bothering her? She was furious, suddenly, with Adam and Diana and their everlasting *faith* in her.

'I know she made you,' Adam said forcefully.

'Nobody made me!' Cassie almost shouted. Then she stopped fighting him and they stood and stared at each other, both breathing hard.

'You'd better get back there,' Cassie said. 'We're not supposed to be alone – remember? Remember our oath? Not that I guess you *need* to think about it much any more. It's pretty easy to keep these days, isn't it?'

'Cassie, what's going *on*?'

'Nothing is going on! Just go, Adam. Just—' Before Cassie could stop herself she had grabbed Adam's arms and pulled him forward. And then she kissed him. It was a hard, angry kiss, and the next moment when she released him she was as stunned as he was.

They stared at each other speechlessly.

'Go back,' Cassie said, hardly able to hear her own voice through the pounding in her ears. It was over, it was all over. She was so cold... not just her skin, but inside her, deep in her core, she was freezing. Freezing over like black ice. Everything was black around her.

She pushed Adam away and made for the distant glow of the bonfire.

'Cassie!'

'*I'm* going back. To congratulate our new leader.'

It was chaos back at the circle. Laurel was crying, Deborah was shouting, Chris and Doug were glaring like a couple of tomcats about to fight and calling each other names. Sean was hovering behind Faye to keep his distance from a disdainful Melanie. Suzan was telling Chris and Doug to grow up, while Faye laughed. Of all of them, only Nick and Diana were utterly still. Nick was smoking silently, away from the rest of the group, watching them with narrowed eyes.

Diana was just standing there, exactly where she'd been

when Cassie left. She didn't seem to see or hear any of the disturbance around her.

'Will you all just shut up?' Deborah was yelling when Cassie reached them. 'Faye's the one in charge now.'

'That's right,' Suzan said. Chris and Doug were shoving each other now. Suzan saw Cassie and said appealingly, '*Isn't* that right, Cassie?'

It was strange, how quickly the silence descended. Everyone was looking at Cassie again.

'That's right,' Cassie said, in a voice hard as stone.

Chris and Doug stopped shoving. Laurel stopped crying. No one moved as Cassie walked over behind Faye. From that position she might have been supporting Faye – or she might have been about to stab her in the back.

If Faye was afraid, she didn't show it. 'Okay,' she said to the others. 'You heard it. I'm leader. And now I'm going to give my first order.' She turned her head slightly to address Cassie. 'I want *you* to get the skull. As for the rest of you – we're going to the cemetery.'

'*What?*' Laurel screamed.

'I'm leader and I'm going to *do* something with my power instead of just sitting on it. There's energy trapped in that skull, energy that we can use. Cassie, go get it.'

Everyone was talking now, arguing, bellowing at each other. Things had never been like this when Diana was leader. Adam was yelling at Faye, demanding to know if she had gone crazy. Only Nick and Diana remained still, Nick watching, Diana staring at something only she could see.

Melanie was trying to restore calm, but it was doing no good. Some distant, clinical part of Cassie's mind noted that if Diana were to interfere now, if Diana would come forward and take over, the coven would listen to her. But Diana did nothing. And the shouting just got louder.

'*Get* it, Cassie,' Faye was snarling between clenched teeth. 'Or I'll get it myself.'

Cassie could feel Power building around her. The sky overhead was stretched tight as a drum, tight as a harp string waiting to be plucked. The ocean behind her throbbed with pent-up force. She could feel it in the sand under her feet, and see it in the leaping flames of the bonfire.

She remembered what she'd done to the Doberman in the pumpkin patch. Some power had burst out from her, focussed like a laser beam. Cassie felt as if something like that was concentrating in her now. She was connected to everything and it was all waiting for her to unleash it.

'Black John will let us have his power – he'll *give* it to us if we just ask the right way,' Faye was shouting. 'I *know*; I've communicated with him. But we have to go and ask him.'

Communicated with him – when? Cassie thought. When she, Cassie, had let Faye take the skull the first time? Or at some point later?

'But why the *cemetery*?' Melanie was crying. 'Why there?'

'Because that's what he *says*,' Faye snapped back impatiently. 'Cassie, for the last time! Get the skull!'

The elements were ranged behind her... Cassie stared at the back of Faye's neck. But then she remembered something. The look in Diana's eyes when Cassie had voted against her... oh, what good would it do to kill Faye now? Everything was over.

Cassie spun around and headed for the place where the skull was buried.

'How does she even know—?' Melanie was beginning, and Faye's laughter cut her off. So that was over, too, the secret about Cassie stealing the skull was out. Diana hadn't told anyone *exactly* where the skull was buried, not even Adam. Cassie ran so she wouldn't have to hear more.

She dug in the centre of the blackened stones until her fingernails scraped the cloth that wrapped the skull. Then she dug around it and pulled it out of the sand, surprised, as always, by how heavy it was. Cassie staggered as she picked the skull up and started back to Faye.

Deborah ran to meet her. 'This way,' she said, diverting Cassie before she could reach the group. 'Come on!' They climbed the bluff and Cassie saw Deborah's motorcycle.

'Faye planned this,' Cassie said. She looked at Deborah, her voice rising slightly. 'Faye had this planned!'

'Yeah. So what?' Deborah looked perplexed; a good lieutenant used to taking orders from her superior. What did Cassie care if Faye had it planned? 'She figured she would have a hard time getting all the others to come, but she wanted to make sure we got there,' Deborah explained.

'I don't see how she's going to get *any* of the others to come,' Cassie said, looking down at the group below. But a strange madness seemed to have taken hold of some of them; whatever Faye was saying was whipping them into a frenzy. Suzan was heading for the bluff, and Doug was half dragging Chris. Faye was pushing Sean.

'That's seven; Faye said that's all we need,' Deborah said, turning from the bluff. 'Come on!'

This motorcycle ride was like the last, in that the speed was as great, the moon even brighter. But this time Cassie wasn't afraid, even though she could only hold on to Deborah with one arm. The other was hugging the skull to her lap. They reached the cemetery and a minute later heard engines. The Samurai was arriving with Chris and Doug and Suzan. Behind it was Faye's Corvette. Faye got out of the driver's side and Sean tumbled out of the passenger door.

'Follow me,' Faye said. Long hair switching behind her, she made for the north-east corner. With every step she took, her bare, shapely legs flashed pale, showing the garter on her thigh and a black-handled dagger tucked in the garter. When the ground began to rise, she stopped.

Cassie stopped, too, clutching the skull to her chest with both arms, frighteningly aware of where they were standing. In a row here, broken only by a mound in the earth, were the graves of Faye's father, Sean's mother, and all the other dead parents from Crowhaven Road. Sean was snivelling now, and only Deborah's grip on him was keeping him from running away.

Faye turned to face them. Even in the worst of times, the tall, dramatically beautiful girl had a natural authority, an ability to intimidate people. Now that seemed enhanced by the symbols of the Queen of the Witches: the diadem, the bracelet, the garter. An aura of power and glamour surrounded her.

'It's time,' Faye said, 'to take back the energy that belonged to the original coven, and that Black John stored in the skull. Black John wants us to have that power, to use against our enemies. And we can get it back – *now*.'

Taking the black-handled dagger out of her garter, Faye unsheathed it and drew a quick, imperfect circle in the dried-up grass. 'Get in,' she said, and the others took their places.

She's got them moving so fast they're not thinking about what they're doing, Cassie thought. No one questioned Faye; everyone seemed caught up in the driving urgency Faye was creating. Even Sean had stopped whining and was staring, rapt.

And Faye made a stunning sight as she held the knife up and rapidly called on the elements for protection. Too fast, Cassie was thinking – such slight protection when all their efforts on Halloween hadn't been enough. But she couldn't speak either; they were all caught on a roller-coaster ride and nobody could stop it. Least of all Cassie, who was so numb and cold...

'Put the skull in the centre, Cassie,' Faye said. Her voice was breathless and her chest was rising and falling quickly. She looked more excited than she had ever looked about Jeffrey, or Nick, or that guy from the pizza place she'd taken upstairs.

Cassie knelt and placed the cloth-wrapped thing in the middle of Faye's flawed circle.

'And now,' Faye said, in that queer, exultant voice, staring down at the sandy lump between her feet, 'we can reclaim the power that should have been ours all along. I call on all the elements to witness—'

'Faye, stop!' Adam shouted, appearing running between the gravestones.

The rest of the coven was behind him, including Diana, who still looked as if she were moving in her sleep. Even Nick, silent and watchful as always, was in the rear.

Faye snatched up the covered skull and held it cradled in her two hands. 'You had your chance,' she said. 'Now it's my turn.'

'Faye, just stop a minute and *think*,' Adam said. 'Black John isn't your friend. If he's really communicated with you, whatever he's told you is lies—'

'*You're* the liar!' Faye shot back.

'Chris, Doug – that skull killed Kori. If you let that dark energy loose again—'

'Don't listen to him!' Faye shouted. She looked like some barbarian queen as she stood there, long legs apart, silver glinting against the black of her shift and the darker black of her hair. Cassie realised that while Adam was talking to her, Laurel and Melanie were circling, one on either side.

Faye realised it, too. 'I won't let you stop me! This is the beginning of a new Circle!'

'*Please*, Faye—' Diana cried, desperately, seeming to wake up at last.

'By Earth, by Air, by Fire, by Water!' Faye shouted, and she jerked the cloth off the skull and held it in both hands over her head.

Silver. The full moon shone down on the crystal and seemed to blaze there, and it was as if another face were suspended above Faye's; a livid, unnatural, skeletal face. And then – darkness began to pour forth from it. Something blacker than the sky between the stars was streaming out of the skull's eye sockets, out of its gaping nose-hole and between its grinning teeth. Snakes, thought Cassie, staring hypnotised at what was happening. Snakes and worms and the old kind of dragons, the kind whose heavy scales scrape the ground and who spit poison when they breathe. Everything bad, everything black, everything loathsome and crawling and evil seemed to be flooding out of that skull, although none of it was real. It was only darkness, only black light.

There was a sound like the humming of bees, only higher, more deadly. It was growing. Faye was standing under that dreadful cascade of darkness, and the sound was like two ice picks driving into Cassie's ears, and somewhere a dog was barking...

Someone has to stop this, Cassie realised. No – *I* have to stop this. *Now.*

She was getting to her feet when the skull exploded.

* * *

Everything was quiet and dark.

Cassie wanted it to stay that way.

Somebody groaned beside her.

Cassie sat up slowly, looking around, trying to piece together what had happened. The cemetery looked like a killing field. Bodies were strewn all over. There was Adam, stretched out with one arm reaching towards the circle and Raj beside him. There was Diana with her shining hair in the leaves and dirt. There was Nick, getting to his hands and knees, shaking his head.

Faye was lying in a pool of black silk, her dark hair covering her face. Her hands with their long red nails were cupped, open – but empty. There was no sign of the skull.

Someone groaned again, and Cassie looked to see Deborah sitting up, rubbing her face with one hand.

'Are they dead?' Deborah said hoarsely, staring around.

'I don't know,' Cassie whispered. Her own throat hurt. All those bodies and the only movement was the fluttering of Diana's hair in the wind. And Nick, who was stumbling towards the circle.

But then there was a stirring – people were starting to sit up. Sean was whimpering. Suzan was, too. Deborah crawled over to Faye and pushed Faye's hair back.

'She's breathing.'

Cassie nodded; she didn't know what to say. Adam was bending over Diana – she looked quickly away from that. Melanie and Laurel were up, and so were Chris and Doug, looking like punch-drunk fighters. Everyone seemed to be alive.

Then Cassie saw Laurel gasp and point. 'Oh, my *God*. The mound. Look at the mound.'

Cassie turned – and froze. Her eyes went back and forth over the scene without believing it.

The mound her grandmother had told her was for storing artillery was broken open. The rusty padlock was gone, and the iron door was jammed against the piece of concrete. But that wasn't all. The top of the mound, where the sparse cemetery grass had grown, was cracked like an overripe plum. Like the cocoon of an insect that had burst free.

And all up and down the line of graves by the fence, tombstones were tilting crazily. The ones nearest the mound, the ones with the names of the parents of Crowhaven Road, were split and shattered. *Riven*, Cassie thought, the old-fashioned word coming from nowhere, singularly appropriate.

Something from inside the mound smelled bad.

'I've got to see,' Deborah muttered. Cassie had never admired anyone so much as she did Deborah just then, making her staggering way towards the open mound. Deborah had more physical courage than anyone Cassie had ever known. Dizzily, Cassie got up and lurched beside her, and they both fell to their knees at the edge of the evil-smelling fissure.

The moon shining inside showed that it was empty. But there was a coating like slime on the raw earth down there.

Then light and motion caught Cassie's eye.

It was in the sky, the sky to the north-east. It was something like the aurora borealis, except that it flickered intermittently, and it was entirely red.

'That's above Crowhaven Road,' Nick said.

'Oh, God what's happening?' Laurel cried.

'Looks like fire,' Deborah muttered, still hoarse.

'Whatever it is, we'd better get there,' Nick said.

Adam was holding Diana, trying to revive her. Suzan and Sean were huddled, and Chris and Doug still looked punchy. But Melanie and Laurel were on their feet, if shaken.

'Nick's right,' Melanie said. 'Let Adam take care of things here. Something's happening.'

Cassie glanced at Faye, her fallen leader, lying on the ground. Then she turned and followed Melanie without a word.

It didn't matter that the five who started unsteadily towards the road had just recently been on opposite sides of a fight. There was no time to think about anything that petty now. Cassie got on the back of Deborah's motorcycle, and Melanie and Laurel jumped into Nick's car. The others would have to follow when they could – and if they wanted to.

Wind roared in Cassie's ears like the sound of the sea. But the feeling of power she'd had earlier, the connection with the elements, was broken. She couldn't *think* – her mind was fuzzy and cloudy as if she had a bad cold. All she knew was that she had to get to Crowhaven Road.

'It's not fire,' Deborah shouted as they approached. 'No smoke.'

Dark houses flew by – Diana's, Deborah's. The empty Georgian at Number Three. Melanie's, Laurel's, Faye's. The vacant Victorian. The Hendersons', Adam's, Suzan's, Sean's...

'It's at your house, Cassie,' Deborah shouted.

Yes. Cassie knew it would be. Something inside her had known even before they started out.

A maple tree showed up like a black skeleton against the red light that engulfed the house at Number Twelve. But the red wasn't fire. It was some witch-light, a crimson aura of evil.

Cassie remembered how much she had hated this house when she'd first seen it. She'd hated it for being huge and ugly, with its peeling grey clapboards and its sagging eaves and unwashed windows. But now she cared about it. It was her family's ancient home; it belonged to her. And more important than anything, her mother and grandmother were inside.

CHAPTER 7

Cassie jumped off the motorcycle and ran up the driveway. But as soon as she entered the red light, she slowed. Something about the light made it hard to move through it, hard even to breathe. It was as if the air here had thickened.

In slow motion, Cassie fought her way to the door. It was open. Inside, the ordinary lights, the lamps in the hallway, looked feeble and silly against the red glow that pervaded everything, like flashlights in the daytime.

Then Cassie saw something that made her breath catch.

Footprints.

Something had tracked mud across her grand-mother's pine-board floor. Only it wasn't mud. It was black as tar and it steamed slightly, like some primordial muck from hell. The prints went up the stairs and then back down again.

Cassie was afraid to go any farther.

'What is this?' Nick shouted, coming in behind her. His shout didn't go very far in the thickened air; it sounded muffled and dragging. Cassie turned towards him, and it was like turning in a dream, where every motion is reduced to a crawl.

'Come on,' Nick said, pulling at her. Cassie looked behind her and saw Deborah and Melanie and Laurel in the doorway, also moving in slow motion.

Cassie let Nick guide her and they fought their way up the stairs. The red glow was dimmer up here; it was hard to see any prints. But Cassie followed them more by intuition than by sight down the hall to the door of her mother's room, and she pointed to it. She was too frightened to go in.

Nick's hand grasped the doorknob, turned it. The door slowly flew open. Cassie stared at her mother's empty bed.

'*No!*' she screamed, and the red light seemed to catch the word and draw it out endlessly. She forgot to be frightened then and ran forward – slowly – into the middle of the room. The bed was rumpled, slept-in, but the covers had been thrown back and there was no sign of her mother.

Cassie looked around the deserted room in anguish. The window was closed. She had a terrible sense of loss, a terrible premonition. Those black and steaming footprints went to the side of her mother's bed. Some *thing* had come and stood here, beside her mother, and then…

'Come on! Downstairs,' Nick was shouting from the doorway. Cassie turned to him – and screamed.

The door was swinging slowly shut again. And in the shadows behind it was a pale and ghostly figure.

Cassie's second scream was cut off as the figure stepped forward, showing a drawn white face and dark hair falling loose over slender shoulders. It was wearing a long, white nightgown. It was her mother.

'*Mom,*' Cassie cried, and she launched herself forward,

throwing her arms around her mother's waist. Oh, thank God, thank God, she thought. Now everything would be all right. Her mother was safe, her mother would take care of things. 'Oh, Mom, I was so scared,' she gasped.

But something was wrong. Her mother wasn't hugging her back. There was no response at all from the upright but lifeless body in the nightgown. Cassie's mother just *stood* there, and when Cassie pulled back, she saw her mother was staring emptily.

'Mom? *Mom?*' she said. She shook the slender white figure. '*Mom!* What's the matter?'

Her mother's beautiful eyes were blank, like a doll's eyes. Unseeing. The black circles underneath seemed to swallow them up. Her mother's arms stayed limp at her sides.

'Mom,' Cassie said again, almost crying now.

Nick had pushed the door open again. 'We have to get her out of here,' he told Cassie.

Yes, Cassie thought. She tried to convince herself that it was the light, that maybe outside of the red glow her mother would be okay. They each took one of the limp arms and led the unresisting figure into the hallway. Melanie, Laurel, and Deborah converged from different directions.

'We looked in all the rooms on this floor,' Melanie said. 'There's no one else up here.'

'My grandmother—' Cassie began.

'Help us get Mrs Blake downstairs,' Nick said.

At the bottom of the stairs, the black prints turned left and then crossed and recrossed. A thought flashed into Cassie's mind.

'Melanie, Laurel, can you take my mom outside? Out of the light? Will you make sure she's safe?' Melanie nodded, and Cassie said, 'I'll be out as soon as I can.'

'Be *careful*,' Laurel said urgently.

Cassie saw them leading her mother to the door, then she made herself stop looking. 'Come on,' she said to Nick and Deborah. 'I think my grandma's in the kitchen.'

A line of footprints led that way, but it wasn't just that, it was a *feeling* Cassie had. A terrible feeling that her grandmother was in the kitchen, and that she wasn't alone.

Deborah walked like a stalking huntress, following the black marks down the twisting hallways to the old wing of the house, the one built by the original witches in 1693.

Nick was behind Cassie, and Cassie realised vaguely that they were protecting her, giving her the safest place in line. But there was no safe place in this house now. As they crossed the threshold into the old wing, the red light seemed to get stronger, and the air even thicker. Cassie felt her lungs labouring.

Oh, God, it *looked* like fire in here. The red light was everywhere and the air burned Cassie's skin. Deborah stopped and Cassie almost ran into her. She struggled to see over Deborah's shoulder, but her eyes were sore and streaming.

She felt Nick behind her, his hand gripping her shoulder hard. Cassie tried to make her eyes focus, squinting into the thick red light.

She could see her grandmother! The old woman was lying in front of the hearth, by the long wooden table she had worked at so often. The table was on its side, and herbs and drying racks were scattered on the floor. Cassie started towards her grandmother, but there was something else there, something her mind didn't want to take in. Nick was holding her back, and Cassie stared at the thing bending over the old woman.

It was burned, black, hideous. It looked as if its skin was

hard and cracked. It had the shape of a man, but Cassie couldn't see eyes or clothes or hair. When it looked up at them she got a brief, terrifying impression of a skull shining silver through the blackness of its face.

It had seen them now. Cassie felt as if she and Nick and Deborah were welded together; Nick was still holding her, and she was clutching Deborah. She wanted to run, but she *couldn't*, because there was her grandmother on the floor. She couldn't leave her grandmother alone with the burned thing.

But she couldn't fight, either. She didn't know how to fight something like this. And Cassie could no longer feel any connection to the elements; in this horrible oven of a room she felt as if she were cut off from everything outside.

What weapons did they have? The hematite in Cassie's pocket wasn't cool any more; when she thrust her hand in to touch it, it burned. No good. Air and Fire and Earth were all against them. They needed something this creature didn't control.

'Think of water,' she shouted to Nick and Deborah. Her voice was stifled in the oppressive blistering air. 'Think of the ocean – cold water – ice!'

As she said it, she thought herself, trying to remember what water was like. Cool... blue... endless. Suddenly she remembered looking over the bluff when she'd first come to her grandmother's house, seeing a blue so intense it took her breath away. The ocean, unimaginably vast, spread out before her. She could picture it now; blue and grey like Adam's eyes. Sunlight glinted off the waves, and Adam's eyes were sparkling, laughing...

Wind rattled the windows in their casements, and the faucet in the sink began to shake. It burst a leak somewhere at its base and a thin stream of white water sprayed up. Something burst in the dishwasher, too, and water gushed on the floor. Water was hissing out of the pipe under the sink.

'Now!' Deborah shouted. 'Come on, get him now!'

Cassie knew it was wrong even as Deborah said it. They weren't strong enough, not nearly strong enough to take this thing on directly. But Deborah, always heedless of danger, was lunging forwards, and there was no time to scream a warning or make her stop. Cassie's heart failed her and her legs went weak in the middle of the rush towards the black thing.

It would kill them – one touch of those burned, hardened hands could kill – but it was giving way before them. Cassie couldn't believe they were still alive, still moving, but they were. The thing was backing away, it was crouching, it was running. It turned and went through what had been the old front door, searing the handle black as it went. It went out into the darkness and then it was gone.

The door hung open, rattling in the wind. The red light died. Through the doorway Cassie could see the cool silver-blue of moonlight.

She dragged in a deep breath, grateful just to be able to breathe without hurting.

'We did it!' Deborah was laughing. She pounded Nick on the arm and back. 'We did it! All right! The bastard ran!'

It *left*, Cassie thought. It left, deliberately. We didn't win anything.

Then she turned sharply to Nick. 'My mother! And Laurel and Melanie – they're out there—'

'I'll go check them. I think it's gone for now, though,' he said.

For now. Nick knew the same thing she did. It wasn't

defeated; it had withdrawn.

On trembling legs, Cassie went and knelt by her grandmother on the floor.

'Grandma?' she said. She was afraid the old woman was dead. But no, her grandmother was breathing heavily. Then Cassie was afraid that if the wrinkled eyelids opened, the eyes underneath would stare blankly like a doll's – but they were opening now, and they saw her, they knew her. Her grandmother's eyes were dark with pain, but they were rational.

'Cassie,' she whispered. 'Little Cassie.'

'Grandma, you're going to be all right. Don't move.' Cassie tried to think of anything else she'd heard about injured people. What to do? Keep them warm? Keep their feet elevated? 'Just hang on,' she told her grandmother, and to Deborah she said, 'Call an ambulance, fast!'

'*No*,' her grandmother said. She tried to sit up and her face contracted with pain. One knobby-knuckled hand clutched at the thin robe over her nightgown. Over her heart.

'Grandma, don't move,' Cassie said frantically. 'It's going to be all right, everything's going to be all right...'

'No, Cassie,' her grandmother said. She was still breathing in that tortured way, but her voice was surprisingly strong. 'No ambulance. There's no time. You need to listen to me; I have something to tell you.'

'You can tell me later.' Cassie was crying now, but she tried to keep her voice steady.

'There won't *be* a later,' her grandmother gasped, and then she settled back, her breathing careful and slow. She spoke distinctly, kneading Cassie's hand in her own. Her eyes were so dark, so anguished – and so kind. 'Cassie, I don't have much time left, and you need to listen. This is important. Go to the fireplace and look on the right-hand side for a loose brick. It's just about the level of the mantel. Pull it out and bring me what's inside the hole.'

Cassie stumbled to the hearth. A loose brick – she couldn't *see*; she was crying too hard. She felt with her fingers, scraping them on the roughness of mortar, and something shifted under them.

This brick. She dug her fingernails into the crumbled mortar around it and worked it back and forth until it came out. She dropped it and reached into the cool dark hollow now exposed.

Her fingertips found something smooth. She eased it closer with her nails, then grasped it and pulled it out.

It was a Book of Shadows.

The one from her dream, the one with the red leather cover. Cassie took it back to her grandmother and knelt again.

'He couldn't make me tell where it was. He couldn't make me tell anything,' her grandmother said, and smiled. 'My own grandmother showed me that was a good place to hide it.' She stroked the book, then her age-spotted hand tightened on Cassie's. 'It's yours, Cassie. From my grandmother to me to you. You have the sight and the power, as I did, as your mother does. But you can't run away like she did. You have to stay here and face him.'

She stopped and coughed. Cassie looked at Deborah, who was listening intently, and then back at her grandmother. 'Grandma, *please*. Please let us call the ambulance. You can't just give up—'

'I'm not giving anything up! I'm giving it all to *you*. To you, Cassie, so you can carry on the fight. Let me do that before I die. Otherwise it's all been meaningless, everything.' She coughed again. 'It wasn't supposed to be like this. That girl – Faye – she fooled me. I didn't think she would move this fast. I thought we would have more time – but we don't. So, now listen.'

She drew a painful breath, fingers holding Cassie's so hard it hurt, and her dark old eyes stared into Cassie's. 'You come from a long line of witches, Cassie. You know that. But you don't know that our family has always had the clearest sight and the most power. We've been the strongest line and we can see the future – but the others don't always believe that. Not even our own kind.'

Her eyes lifted to look at Deborah. 'You young people, you think you come up with everything new, don't you?' Her seamed old face wrinkled in a laugh, although there was no sound. 'You don't have much respect for old folks, or even for your parents. You think we lived our lives standing still, don't you?'

She's wandering, Cassie thought. She doesn't know what she's saying. But her grandmother was going on.

'Your idea about getting out the old books and reviving the old traditions – you think you were the only ones to come up with that, don't you?'

Cassie just shook her head helplessly, but Deborah, brows drawn together in a scowl, said, 'Well, weren't we?'

'No. Oh, my dears, no. In my day, when I was a little girl, we played with it. We had meetings sometimes, and those of us with the sight would make notes of what we saw, and those with the healing touch would talk about herbs and things. But it was your parents' generation who got up a real coven.'

'Our *parents*?' Deborah said in disbelief. 'My parents are so scared of magic they practically puke if you mention it. *My* parents would *never*—'

'That's now,' Cassie's grandmother said calmly, as Cassie tried to hush Deborah. 'That's now. They've forgotten – they made themselves forget. They had to, you see, to survive. But things were different when they were young. They were just a little older than you, the children of Crowhaven Road. Your mother was maybe nineteen, Deborah, and Cassie's mother was just seventeen. That was when the Man in Black came to New Salem.'

'Grandma...' Cassie whispered. Icy prickles were going up and down her spine. This room, which had been so hot, was making her shiver. 'Oh, Grandma, please...'

'You don't want to know. I know. I understand. But you have to listen, both of you. You have to understand what you're up against.'

With another cough, Cassie's grandmother shifted position slightly, her eyes going opaque with memory. 'That was the fall of 1974. The coldest November we'd had in decades. I'll never forget him on the doorstep, kicking the snow off his boots. He was going to move into Number Thirteen, he said, and he needed a match to light the wood he was carrying. There was no other kind of heat in that old house; it had been empty since he'd left it the first time.'

'Since *what*?' Cassie said.

'Since 1696. Since he'd left the first time to go to sea, and drowned when his ship went down.' Her grandmother nodded without looking at Cassie. 'Oh, yes, it was Black John. But we didn't know that then. How much suffering could have been prevented if we *had*... but there's no use thinking about that.' She patted Cassie's hand. 'We lent him matches, and the girls and young men on the street helped him rebuild that old house. He was a few years older than they were, and they looked up to him. They admired him and his travels – he could tell the most marvellous stories. And he was handsome – handsome in a way that didn't show his black heart underneath. We were all fooled, all under his spell, even me.

'I don't know when he started talking to the young people about the old ways. Pretty soon, I guess; he worked fast. And they were ready to listen. They thought we parents were old and stodgy if we opposed them. And to tell the truth, not many of us objected very strongly. There's good in the old ways, and we didn't know what *he* was up to.'

The shivers were racing all over Cassie's body by now, but she couldn't move. She could only listen to her grandmother's voice, the only sound except for the thin hiss of water in that quiet kitchen.

'He got the likeliest of the young ones together and paired them off. Yes, that's about the size of it, although we parents didn't know then. He made matches, giving this girl to this boy, and this boy to that girl, and somehow he made it all seem reasonable to them. He even broke up pairs that had planned to marry – your mother, Deborah, was going to marry Nick's dad, but *he* changed that. Switched her from one brother to the other, and they let him. He had such a grip on them they would have let him do anything.

'They did the marriages in the old way, handfasting. Ten weddings in March. And we all celebrated, like the idiots we were. All those young people so happy, and never a quarrel between them, we thought; how lucky they were! They were just like one big group of brothers and sisters. Well, the group was *too* big for one coven, but we didn't think about that.

'It was good to see the respect they had for the old ways, too. They had the Beltane fire in May and at midsummer they gathered Saint-John's-wort and mistletoe. And in September I remember all of them laughing and shouting as they brought the John Barleycorn sheaf in to represent the harvest. They didn't know what the other John was planning.

'We knew by then the babies were coming soon, and that was another reason to celebrate. But it was in October that some of the older women started to worry. The girls were all so pale and the pregnancies seemed to take so much out of them. Poor Carmen Henderson was flesh and bones except for her belly. *That* looked like she was carrying twin elephants. There wasn't much celebrating at Samhain; the girls were all too sick.

'And then on November third, it started. Your uncle Nicholas, Deborah, the one you never knew, called me to come to his wife's bedside. I helped Sharon have little Nick, your cousin. He was a fighter from the first minute; I'll never forget how he squalled. But there was something else, something I'd never seen in a baby's eyes, and I went home thinking about it. There was a *power* there I'd never seen before.

'And two days later it happened again. Elizabeth Conant had a baby boy, with hair like Bacchus's wine and eyes like the sea. That baby *looked* at me, and I could feel his power.'

'Adam,' Cassie whispered.

'That's right. Three days later Sophie Burke went into labour – her that kept her own name even when she married. Her baby, Melanie, was like the others. She looked two weeks old when she was brand-new, and she saw me as clearly as I saw her.

'The strangest ones born were Diana and Faye. Their mothers were sisters and they had their babies at the same moment, in two separate houses. One baby was bright like sunlight and the other one was dark as midnight, but those two were connected somehow. You could tell even at that age.'

Cassie thought of Diana and a pang went through her, but she pushed it away and went on listening. Her grandmother's voice seemed to be getting weaker.

'Poor little things... it wasn't their fault. It isn't *your* fault,' the old woman said, focussing suddenly on Deborah and Cassie. 'Nobody can blame you. But by December third, *eleven* babies had been born, and they were all strange. Their mothers didn't want to admit it, but by January there was no way to deny it. Those tiny babies could call on the Powers, and they could scare you if they didn't get what they wanted.'

'I knew,' Cassie whispered. 'I knew it was too weird for all of those kids to be born within one month... I *knew*.'

'Their parents knew, too, but they didn't know what it meant. It was Adam's father, I think, who put it all together for them. Eleven babies, he said – he guessed that with one more that made a coven. And who was the one more? Why, the man who'd arranged for all those babies to be born, the man who was going to lead them. Black John had come back to make the strongest Circle this country had ever seen – not from this generation, but from the next, Adam's father said. From the infants.

'Nobody believed the story at first. Some parents were scared, and some were just plain stupid. And some didn't see how Black John could come back from the dead after all those years. That's one mystery that hasn't been solved yet.

'But gradually some of the group were convinced. Nick's father, who'd lost his own fiancée, seen her married off to his younger brother – he listened. And Mary Meade, Diana's mother; she was as smart as she was pretty. Even Faye's father, Grant Chamberlain... he was a cold man, but he knew his infant daughter could set the curtains on fire without touching them, and he knew that wasn't right. They got some of the others talked around, and one cold night, the first of February, the bunch of them set off to talk to *him* about it.'

CHAPTER

8

Cassie's grandmother shook her head. 'To talk! If they'd come to us, to the older women, we might have warned them. Me and Laurel's grandma, and Adam's grandma, and Melanie's great-aunt Constance – we could have told them a few things, maybe saved them. But they went alone, without telling anyone. On Imbolc, February first, more than half the group that *he* had put together went to challenge him. And out of that group, not one came back.'

Tears were running slowly down the seamed old cheeks. 'So you see, it was the brave ones, the strong ones that went and died. The ones that are left are the ones too scared or too stupid to see the danger – I'm sorry, Deborah, but it's true.' Cassie remembered that both Deborah's parents were alive. 'All the best of Crowhaven Road went to fight Black John that Imbolc Night,' her grandmother said.

'But *how*?' Cassie whispered. She was thinking of that row of gravestones in the cemetery. 'How did they die, Grandma?'

'I don't know. I doubt if anyone alive knows, unless

it's...' Her grandmother broke off and shook her head, muttering. 'There was fire in the sky, and then a storm. A hurricane from the sea. The older women got together the babies that had been left with them, and the young parents that hadn't gone with the group, and we managed to save them. But the next day the house at Number Thirteen was burned to the ground, and all the ones who'd gone to challenge Black John were dead.

'We never found most of the bodies. They were washed out to sea, I suppose. But one thing we did find was the burned corpse at Number Thirteen. We knew it was *him* by the ring he wore, a shiny black stone we used to call lodestone. I forget the modern name. We took *him* out to the old burying ground and put him in the bunker. Charles Meade, Diana's father, dropped that chunk of concrete in front of it. We figured that if he'd come back once, he might try again someday, and we meant to stop him if we could. And after that the parents that had survived hid their Books of Shadows and did their best to keep their children away from magic. And it's strange, but most of them forgot what they could. I guess because they couldn't remember and stay sane. Still, it's funny, now, how much they've forgotten.'

The cracked voice had been growing weaker and weaker, but now Cassie's grandmother grasped Cassie's wrist hard. 'Now, listen to me, child. This is important. Some of us didn't forget, because we couldn't. I'd named my daughter for a prophetess, and she did the same for her daughter, because we've always had the second sight. Your mother couldn't bear what her gift showed her, and so she ran away from New Salem; she ran all the way to the other coast. But I stayed, and I've watched all my premonitions come true, one by one. The babies that were born on Crowhaven Road in that single month grew up different, despite everything their parents could do. They were drawn to the Powers and the old ways from the beginning. They all grew up strong – and some of them grew up bad.

'I've watched it happen, and in my mind I've heard Black John laughing. They burned his body, but they couldn't burn his spirit, and it's always been here, waiting, hanging around the old burying ground and the vacant lot at Number Thirteen. He was waiting for his coven, the one he'd planned, the one he'd gotten born. He was waiting for them to come of age. He was waiting for them to bring him back.

'I knew it would happen – and I knew only one thing could stand against him when it did. And that's *you*, Cassie. You have the strength of our family, and the sight, and the Power. I begged your mother to come home, because I knew that without you the children of Crowhaven Road would be lost. They'd turn to *him*, the way their parents did, and he'd be their leader and their master. You are the only one who can stop him from taking them now.'

'So that's what you and Mom fought about,' Cassie said in wonder. 'About *me*.'

'We fought about courage. She wanted to protect you, and I knew that by protecting you we'd lose all the others. You had a destiny even before you were born. And the worst was that we couldn't tell you about it – that was what the prophecies said. You had to come here all unknowing and find your own way, like some innocent sacrifice. And you did. You've done everything we could have wanted. And the time was coming when we could have explained it all to you ... but she fooled us, that Faye. By the way, how'd she do it?'

'I ...' Cassie didn't know what to say. 'I helped her, Grandma,' she said finally. 'We found the crystal skull that belonged to Black John, and it was full of dark energy. Every time we used it, somebody died. And then—' Cassie took a deep, ragged breath. 'Then, tonight, Faye told us to bring the skull to the cemetery. And when she uncovered it there – I don't know – all this darkness came out…'

Cassie's grandmother was nodding. '*He* was master of dark things. Just like the real Man in Black, the lord of death. But, Cassie, do you really understand?' With a supreme effort, the old woman tried to sit up to look in Cassie's face. 'When you took the skull to his burying place and let that energy out, it was enough to bring him back. He's *here* now; he's come back again. Not a ghost or a spirit, but a man. A walking, breathing man. He'll look different the next time you see him; once he's had a chance to pretty himself up. And he'll try to fool you.' She sank back wearily.

'But, oh, Grandma – I helped let him loose. I'm sorry. I'm so sorry…' Tears swam in Cassie's eyes.

'You didn't know. *I* forgive you, child, and what's done is done. But you have to be ready for him…' Cassie's grandmother's eyes drifted shut, and her breath had a frightening sound.

'Grandma!' Cassie said, shaking her in panic.

The old eyes opened again, slowly. 'Poor Cassie. It's a lot to face. But you have strength, if you look for it. And now you have this.' Feebly, she pressed the Book of Shadows again into Cassie's hands. 'The wisdom of our family, and the prophecies. Read it. Learn it. It'll answer some of the questions I don't have time for. You'll find your way…'

'Grandma! Grandma, *please*…'

Her grandmother's eyes were still open, but they were changing, filming over, as if they didn't see her any more. 'I don't mind going now that I've told the

story... but there's something else. Something you need
to know...'

'Cassie!' The voice came from the doorway, and it
startled Cassie so much that she jerked and looked up.
Laurel was standing there, her elfin face white with
concern. 'Cassie, what's *happening* in here? Are you
okay? Do you want a doctor?' She was staring at Cassie's
grandmother on the floor.

'Laurel, not now!' Cassie gasped. She was crying,
but she held on harder to her grandmother's knotted
old hands. 'Grandma, please don't go. I'm frightened,
Grandmother. I *need* you!'

Her grandmother's lips were moving, but only the
faintest of sounds came out. '... never be afraid, Cassie.
There's nothing frightening in the dark if you just
face it...'

'Please, Grandma, please. Oh, *no*...' Cassie's head
dropped down to her grandmother's chest and she sobbed.
The knotted hands weren't holding hers any more. 'You
said you had something else to tell me,' she wept. 'You
can't go...'

An almost inaudible breath came from her grandmother's
chest. Cassie thought it was the word 'John.' And then,
'... nothing dies forever, Cassie...'

The chest against Cassie's forehead heaved once and
was still.

Outside, a yellowing moon hung low in the sky.

'The Mourning Moon,' Laurel said quietly. 'That's what
this one is called.'

It was appropriate, Cassie thought, although her eyes
were dry now. There were more tears inside her, building
up, but they would have to wait. There was something
that had to be done before she could rest and cry. Even

after her grandmother's story, she had so many questions, so much to figure out – but first, she had to do this one thing.

There were a bunch of cars parked near the street. The rest of the coven was there – no, not all of them. Cassie saw Suzan and Sean and the Hendersons, and Adam and Diana. But she didn't see the person she was looking for.

'Melanie and Nick took your mom to Melanie's aunt Constance,' Laurel said hesitantly. 'They thought it was the best place for her, tonight. She was still kind of spacey – but I know she'll be okay.'

Cassie swallowed and nodded. She *wasn't* sure; she wasn't sure of anything. She only knew what she had to do right now.

Never be afraid, Cassie. There's nothing frightening in the dark if you just face it.

Just face it. Face it and stand up to it.

Then Cassie saw who she was looking for.

Faye was in the shadows beyond the headlights of the cars. Her black shift and her hair blended in with the gloom, but the pallor of her face and the silver ornaments she wore stood out.

Cassie walked up to her without hesitation. At that moment, she could have hit Faye, strangled her, killed her. But all she said was, 'It's over.'

'What?' Faye's eyes gleamed a little, yellow as the moonlight. She looked sick and unsettled – and dangerous. Like a pile of dynamite ready to go off.

'It's over, Faye,' Cassie repeated. 'The blackmail, the threats... it's all over. I'm not your prisoner any more.'

Faye's nostrils flared. 'I'm warning you, Cassie, this isn't the time to push me. I'm still leader of the coven. The vote was fair. You can't do anything to change it...'

'I'm not trying to change it – *now*. Right now I'm just saying that you don't have a hold over me any more. It's finished.'

'It's finished when *I* say it's finished!' Faye snarled. Cassie realised then how close Faye was to snapping, how dangerous Faye's mood really was. But it didn't matter. Maybe it was even better this way, to get it all over with at once.

'I'm not joking, Cassie,' Faye was going on heatedly. 'If you can turn on me, I can do the same to you...'

Cassie took a deep breath and then said, 'Go ahead.'

There's nothing frightening in the dark if you just face it.

'Fine,' Faye said between her teeth. 'I will.'

She turned around and strode to the place where Diana and Adam were standing, arms around each other. Adam was practically supporting Diana, Cassie saw, and for a moment her heart failed her. But it had to be done. Despite the oath, despite Diana's pain, it had to be done.

Faye turned back once to look at Cassie. A look that said, clearly, *you'll be sorry*. Cassie wondered in sudden panic if it was true. Would she be sorry? Was she doing the wrong thing after all, defying Faye at the wrong time? Wouldn't it be better to wait, to think about this...

But Faye was turning back to Diana, malicious triumph written all over her face. The coven wasn't happy with Faye tonight, but Faye was still the leader and nothing could change that fact. Now Faye was going to start her reign by getting revenge on the people she hated most.

'Diana,' she said, 'I have a little surprise for you.'

THE
POWER

CHAPTER 1

'**D**iana, I have a little surprise for you,' Faye said.

Diana's emerald eyes, with their thick sooty lashes, were swimming already. She still hadn't recovered from the shocks of tonight, and her face was strained as she stared at Faye.

Well, there was worse to come.

Now that it was finally going to happen, Cassie felt a curious sense of freedom. No more hiding, no more lying and evading. The nightmare was here at last.

'I suppose I should have told you before, but I didn't want to *upset* you,' Faye was saying. Her eyes burned golden with a savage inner fire.

Adam, who wasn't stupid, glanced from Cassie to Faye and obviously came to a quick, if shattering, conclusion. He swiftly cupped a hand under Diana's elbow.

'Whatever it is can wait,' he said. 'Cassie ought to go and see her mother, and—'

'No, it can't *wait*, Adam Conant,' Faye interrupted. 'It's time Diana found out what sort of people she has around her.' Faye whirled to face Diana again, her pale skin glowing with strange elation against the midnight-dark mane of her hair. 'The ones you've *chosen*,' she said to her cousin. 'Your dearest friend – and *him*. The incorruptible Sir Adam. Do you want to know the reason you couldn't make it as leader? Do you want to know how naive you really are?'

Everyone was gathering close now, staring. Cassie could see varying degrees of bewilderment and suspicion in their expressions. The full moon shining from the west was so bright that it cast shadows, and it illuminated every detail of the scene.

Cassie looked at each of them: tough Deborah, beautiful Suzan with her perfect face marred by a puzzled frown, cool Melanie, and graceful, elfin Laurel. She looked at Chris and Doug Henderson, the wild twins, who were standing by the slinking figure of Sean, and at icily handsome Nick behind them.

Finally she looked at Adam.

He was still holding Diana's arm, but his proud, arresting face was tense and alert. His eyes met Cassie's and something like understanding flashed between them, and then Cassie looked away, ashamed. She had no right to lean on Adam's strength. She was about to be exposed for what she was in front of the entire Circle.

'I kept hoping they would do the decent thing and control themselves,' Faye said. 'For their own sake, if not yours. But, obviously—'

'Faye, what are you *talking* about?' Diana interrupted, her patience splintering.

'Why, about Cassie and Adam, of course,' Faye said, slowly opening her golden eyes wide. 'About how they've been fooling around behind your back.'

The words fell like stones into a tranquil pool. There was a long moment of utter silence, then Doug Henderson threw back his head and laughed.

'Yeah, an' my mom's a topless dancer,' he jeered.

'And Mother Teresa's really Catwoman,' said Chris.

'Come on, Faye,' Laurel said sharply. 'Don't be ridiculous.'

Faye smiled.

'I don't blame you for not believing me,' she said. 'I was shocked too. But you see, it all started before Cassie came to New Salem. It started when she met Adam down on Cape Cod.'

The silence this time had a different quality. Cassie saw Laurel look quickly at Melanie. Everyone knew that Cassie had spent several weeks on the Cape last summer. And everyone knew that Adam had been down in that area too, looking for the Master Tools. Cassie saw the dawning of startled understanding on the faces around her.

'It all started on the beach there,' Faye went on. She was obviously enjoying herself, as she always enjoyed being the centre of attention. She looked sexy and commanding as she wet her lips and spoke throatily, addressing the entire group although her words were meant for Diana. 'It was love at first sight, I guess – or at least they couldn't keep their hands off each other. When Cassie came up here she even wrote a poem about it. Now how did that go?' Faye tilted her head to one side and recited:

Each night I lie and dream about the one
Who kissed me and awakened my desire
I spent a single hour with him alone
And since that hour, my days are laced with fire.

'That's right; that was her poem,' Suzan said. '*I* remember. We had her in the old science building and she didn't want us to read it.'

Deborah was nodding, her petite face twisted in a scowl. 'I remember too.'

'You may also remember how strange they both acted at Cassie's initiation,' Faye said. 'And how Raj seemed to *take* to Cassie so quickly, always jumping up on her and licking her and all. Well, it's very simple really – it's because they'd known each other before. They didn't want any of *us* to know that, of course. They tried to hide it. But eventually they got caught. It was the night we first used the crystal skull in Diana's garage – Adam was taking Cassie home, I guess. I wonder how *that* got arranged.'

Now it was the turn of Laurel and Melanie to look startled. Clearly they remembered the night of the first skull ceremony, when Diana had asked Adam to walk Cassie home, and Adam, after a brief hesitation, had agreed.

'They thought they were alone on the bluff – but somebody was watching. Two little somebodies, two little friends of mine ...' Lazily, Faye worked her fingers, with their long, scarlet-tipped nails, as if stroking something. A flash of comprehension lighted Cassie's mind.

The *kittens*. The damned little bloodsucking kittens that lived wild in Faye's bedroom. Faye was saying the *kittens* were her spies? That she could communicate with them?

Cassie felt a chill at her core as she looked at the tall, darkly beautiful girl, sensing something alien and deadly behind those hooded golden eyes. She'd wondered all along who Faye had meant when she talked about her 'friends' who saw things and reported back to her, but she'd never imagined this. Faye smiled in feline satisfaction and nodded at her.

'I have lots of secrets,' she said directly to Cassie. 'That's only one of them. But anyway,' she said to the rest of the group, 'it was that night they got caught. They were – well, kissing. That's the polite way to put it. The kind of kissing that starts spontaneous combustion. I suppose they just couldn't resist their lustful passions any longer.' She sighed.

Diana was looking at Adam now, looking for a denial. But Adam, his jaw set, was staring straight ahead at Faye.

Diana's lips parted with the quick intake of her breath.

'And it wasn't the only time, I'm afraid,' Faye continued, examining her nails with an expression of demure regret. 'They've been doing it ever since, stealing secret moments when you weren't looking, Diana. Like at the Homecoming dance – what a *pity* you weren't there. They started kissing right in the middle of the dance floor. I guess maybe they went somewhere more private afterwards...'

'That's not true,' Cassie cried, realising even as she said it that she was virtually confirming that everything else Faye had said *was* true.

Everyone was looking at Cassie now, and there was no more jeering from the Hendersons. Their tilted blue-green eyes were focussed and intent.

'I *wanted* to tell you,' Faye said to Diana, 'but Cassie just begged me not to. She was hysterical, crying and pleading – she said she would just *die* if you found out. She said she'd do anything. And that,' Faye sighed, looking off into the distance, 'was when she offered to get me the skull.'

'*What?*' said Nick, his normally imperturbable face reflecting disbelief.

'Yes.' Faye's eyes dropped to her nails again, but she couldn't keep a smile from curling the corners of her lips. 'She knew I wanted to examine the skull, and she said she'd get it for me if I didn't tell. Well, what could I do?

She was like a crazy person. I just didn't have the *heart* to refuse her.'

Cassie sank her teeth into her lower lip. She wanted to scream, to protest that it hadn't been that way ... but what was the use?

Melanie was speaking. 'And I suppose you didn't have the heart to refuse the skull, either,' she said to Faye, her grey eyes scornful.

'Well ...' Faye smiled deprecatingly. 'Let's put it this way – it was just too good a chance to miss.'

'This isn't funny,' Laurel cried. She looked stricken. 'I still don't believe it—'

'Then how do you think she knew where to dig up the skull tonight?' Faye said smoothly. 'She stayed over at your house, Diana, the night we traced the dark energy to the cemetery. And she snuck around and figured out where the skull was buried by reading your Book of Shadows – but only after she stole the key to the walnut cabinet and checked there.' Gleeful triumph shone out of Faye's golden eyes; she couldn't conceal it any longer.

And nobody in the group could deny the truth of Faye's words any longer. Cassie *had* known where to dig up the skull. There was no way to get around that. Cassie could see it happening in face after face: the ending of disbelief and the slow beginning of grim accusation.

It's like *The Scarlet Letter*, Cassie thought wildly as she stood apart with all of them looking at her. She might as well be standing up on a platform with an A pinned to her chest. Helplessly, she straightened her back and tried to hold her chin level, forcing herself to look back at the group. I will not cry, she thought. I will not look away.

Then she saw Diana's face.

Diana's expression was beyond stricken. She seemed

simply paralysed, her green eyes wide and blank and shattered.

'She swore to be loyal and faithful to the Circle, and never to harm anyone inside it,' Faye was saying huskily. 'But she lied. I suppose it's not surprising, considering she's half outsider. Still, I think it's gone on long enough; she and Adam have had enough time to enjoy themselves. So now you know the truth. And now,' Faye finished, looking over the ravaged members of the Circle, and especially her deathly still cousin, with an air of thoughtful gratification, 'we'd probably better be getting home. It's been a long night.' Lazily, smiling faintly, she started to move away.

'No.' It was a single word, but it stopped Faye in her tracks and it made everyone else turn towards Adam.

Cassie had never seen his blue-grey eyes look this way before – they were like silver lightning. He moved forward with his usual easy stride. There was no violence in the way he caught Faye's arm, but the grip must have been like iron – Cassie could tell that because Faye couldn't get away from it. Faye looked down at his fingers in offended surprise.

'You've had your turn,' Adam said to her. His voice was carefully quiet, but the words dropped from his lips like chips of white-hot steel. 'Now it's mine. And all of you' – he swung around on the group, holding them in place with his gaze – 'are going to listen.'

CHAPTER

2

'You've told the story your way,' Adam said. 'Some of it's been close to the truth, and some of it's been just plain lies. But none of it happened exactly the way you told it.'

He looked around the Circle again. 'I don't care what you think of me,' he said, 'but there's somebody else involved here. And *she*' – he glanced at Cassie, just long enough for her to see his blue-grey eyes, still shining like silver – 'doesn't deserve to be put through this, especially not tonight.'

A few of the coven members, notably Laurel and Melanie, looked away, slightly ashamed. But the rest simply stared, angry and mistrustful.

'So what's your side of the story?' Deborah said, scowling. Her expression said she felt she'd been taken in, and she didn't like it.

'First of all, it wasn't like that when Cassie and I met. It wasn't love at first sight ...' Adam faltered for a moment, looking into the distance. He shook his head. 'It wasn't love. She *helped* me, she saved me from four outsider guys with a gun. The witch-hunting kind of outsiders.' He looked hard at Chris and Doug Henderson.

'But she didn't know—' Deborah began.

'She didn't know what I was, then. She didn't know what *she* was. Witches were something out of fairy tales to her. Cassie helped me just because I needed help. These guys were after me, and she stashed me in a boat and sent them all off running in the wrong direction down the beach. They tried to get her to tell where I was, they even hurt her, but she didn't give me up.'

There was a silence. Deborah, who admired physical bravery above all other qualities, looked quizzical, her scowl smoothing out a little.

Faye, though, was squirming like a fish trying to get off a hook, and her expression was unpleasant. 'How sweet. The brave heroine. So you just couldn't resist fooling around with her.'

'*Don't be a jerk, Faye,*' Adam said, giving Faye's arm a little shake. 'I didn't do anything with her. We just—' He shook his head again. 'I told her "thank you." I wanted her to know that I wouldn't forget what she'd done – remember, at the time I still thought she was an outsider, and I'd never known an outsider who did anything like that for one of us. She was just this nice outsider girl; sort of quiet and pretty, and I wanted to say "thanks." But when I was looking at her I suddenly felt – as if we were connected somehow. It sounds stupid now, maybe, but I could almost see this connection...'

'The silver cord,' Cassie whispered. Her eyes were full, and she wasn't aware she'd spoken aloud until she saw faces swing towards her.

Melanie's eyebrows went up and Diana looked startled too, maybe just at hearing Cassie break the silence she'd kept so long. Suzan's rosebud lips were pursed into an O.

'Yeah, I guess that was what it looked like,'

Adam was saying, staring off into the distance again. 'I don't know – it was just this confused impression. But I did feel grateful to her, and I would have liked her for a friend – how about that, an outsider friend?' There were murmurs of amusement and unbelief. 'And,' Adam said, looking straight at Diana, 'that's why I gave her the chalcedony rose you gave me.'

No murmurs this time. Grim silence.

'It was a token of friendship, a way to repay a debt,' Adam said. 'I figured if she ever got in trouble, I could sense it through the crystal and maybe do something to help. So I gave it to her – and that was *all* I did.' He looked at Faye defiantly, and then even more defiantly around the group. 'Except – yeah, right – I did kiss her. I kissed her hand.'

Laurel blinked. The Henderson brothers looked at Adam sideways, as if to say he was crazy but they guessed it was his own business what bits of girls he kissed. Faye tried to look scornful, but it didn't come off very well.

'Then I left the Cape,' Adam said. 'I didn't see Cassie again until I came back up here for Kori's initiation – which turned out to be Cassie's initiation. But there's one other important thing. In all the time I talked to Cassie I never told her who I was or where I was from. I never told her my name. So whatever she came up here and did – whatever *poems* she wrote, Faye – she didn't know who I was. She didn't know Diana and I were together. Not until that night when I showed up on the beach.'

'So I suppose that's a good reason for pretending you didn't know each other, for sneaking around behind everybody's back and meeting each other,' Faye said, on the offensive again.

'You don't know what you're talking about,' Adam

said tightly, looking as if he'd like to shake Faye again. 'We didn't sneak *anywhere*. The first time we ever talked alone was the night the skull ceremony in Diana's garage went wrong. Yeah, that night on the bluff when your little spies saw us, Faye. But d'you know what Cassie said to me in our first conversation alone since we'd met? She said she was in love with me – and that she knew it was wrong. Ever since she'd found out it was wrong, ever since she realised that I wasn't just some guy on the beach, but Diana's boyfriend, she'd been fighting against it. She'd even taken an oath – a blood oath – not to ever show anybody, by word or look or deed, how she felt about me. She didn't want Diana to find out and feel bad, or feel sorry for her. Does that sound like somebody who's trying to sneak around?'

The Circle looked back at him. Soberly, Melanie said, 'Let me get this right. You're saying there's nothing at all to Faye's accusations?'

Adam swallowed. 'No,' he said quietly. 'That's not what I'm saying. That night on the bluff ...' He stopped and swallowed again, and then his voice hardened. 'I can't explain what happened, except that it was my fault, not Cassie's. She did everything she could to avoid me, to keep out of my way. But once we were alone we were drawn together.' He looked at Diana without flinching, although the pain was evident in his face. 'I'm not proud of myself, but I never meant to hurt you. And Cassie is completely innocent. The only reason she was speaking to me at all that night was that she wanted to give me back the chalcedony rose – so I could give it back to you. In all of this, she's never been anything but honest and honourable. No matter what it cost her.' He stopped and his mouth turned grim. 'If I'd known she was being blackmailed by this snake—'

'I *beg* your pardon,' Faye interrupted, golden eyes flashing dangerously.

Adam returned the look, just as dangerous. 'That's what it was, wasn't it, Faye? Blackmail. Your little spies saw us that night – when we were saying *good-bye*, and swearing never to see each other alone again, and you decided to make the most of it. I knew there was something going on with you and Cassie after that, but I could never figure out what it was. Cassie was scared to death all of a sudden, but why she didn't just come to me and tell me what you were up to ...' His voice trailed off and he looked towards Cassie.

Cassie shook her head mutely. How could she explain? 'I didn't want you caught up in it too,' she said in a voice scarcely above a whisper. 'I was afraid you'd tell Diana, and Faye said if Diana found out...'

'What?' Adam said. When Cassie shook her head again he gave Faye's arm a little shake. '*What*, Faye? If Diana found out it would kill her? Wreck the coven? Is that what you told Cassie?'

Faye smirked. 'If I did, it was only the truth, wasn't it? As things turned out.' She wrenched away from Adam.

'So you used her love for Diana against her. You blackmailed her to make her help you find the skull, right? I'll bet it took some persuading.'

Adam was only guessing, but his guess was dead on target. Cassie found herself nodding. 'I found out where it was—'

'But *how?*' Diana interrupted, blurting it, speaking for the first time directly to Cassie. Cassie looked into the clear green eyes with the tears hanging on the dark lashes and spoke directly back.

'I did what Faye said,' she said tremulously. 'First I looked in the walnut cabinet – remember when I stayed overnight and you woke up with me in the room? When the skull wasn't there I thought I'd have to give up, but then I had a dream. It made me remember something I'd seen in your Book of Shadows, about purifying an evil object by burying it in sand. So I went and searched the beach and finally found the skull under that ring of stones.'

Cassie paused, looking at Faye, her voice growing stronger. 'Once I had my hands on it, though, I realised I *couldn't* give it to Faye. I just couldn't. But she had followed me and she took it anyway.'

Cassie took a deep breath, making herself meet Diana's eyes again, her own eyes begging Diana to understand. 'I know I shouldn't have let her have it. I should have stood up to her, then and afterwards, but I was weak and stupid. I'm *sorry* now – I wish I'd just come and told you in the beginning, but I was so afraid you'd be hurt ...' Tears were choking her voice now, and making her vision blur. 'And as for what Adam said – about it all being his fault – you have to know that isn't true. It was my fault, and at the Halloween dance I *tried* to make him kiss me, because I was so upset by then and I thought that nothing really mattered, since I was evil anyway.'

There was wetness on Diana's cheeks, but now she looked taken aback. 'Since *what?*'

'Since I was evil,' Cassie said, hearing the terrible, stark truth in the simple words. 'Since I was responsible for killing Jeffrey Lovejoy.'

The entire coven stared at her, appalled.

'Wait a minute,' Melanie said. 'Run that by me one more time.'

'Whenever anybody used the skull, it released dark energy, which went out and killed somebody,' Cassie said carefully and clearly. 'Faye and I were the ones who used the skull before Jeffrey was killed. If it wasn't for me, she couldn't have used it, and Jeffrey would still be alive. So, you see, I'm responsible.'

Animation was returning to Diana's eyes. 'But you didn't *know*,' she said.

Cassie shook her head fiercely. 'That's no excuse. There's no excuse for any of it – not even for doing worse things because I thought I was evil anyway and what did it matter? It *did* matter. I listened to Faye and I let her bully me.' And I kept the hematite, she thought, but there was no point in getting into that. She shrugged, blinking more tears away. 'I even let her make me vote for her for leader. I'm *sorry*, Diana – I'm so sorry. I don't know why I did it.'

'I do,' Diana said shakily. 'Adam said it already – you were scared.'

Cassie nodded. All the words she'd held back for so long were pouring out. 'Once I started doing things for her, I couldn't stop. She had more and more to blackmail me with. Everything just went more and more wrong and I didn't know how to get out of it...' Cassie's voice broke. She saw Faye, lip curled, step forward and try to say something, and she saw Adam shut her up with a single glance. Then she turned and saw Diana's eyes.

They were as luminous as peridot crystals held up to the light, liquid with unshed tears, but also with – something else. It was a look Cassie had never expected to see again, especially not directed at *her*. A look of pain, yes, but also of forgiveness and longing. A look of love.

Something broke inside Cassie, something hard and tight that had been growing since she had started to deceive Diana. She took a stumbling step forward.

Then she and Diana were in each other's arms, both crying, both holding on with all their strength.

'I'm so sorry, I'm so sorry for everything,' Cassie sobbed.

It seemed a long time before Diana drew back, and when she did she stepped away from the group, turning to look into the darkness. Cassie wiped her cheeks with the back of her hand. The moon, hanging low on the horizon, shone like old gold on Diana's hair.

There was absolute silence except for the distant roar and crash of waves on the beach. The entire group stood motionless, as if waiting for something that none of them could quite define.

At last Diana turned back to them. 'I think we've all heard enough,' she said. 'I think I understand, maybe not everything, but most of it. Listen, everybody, because I don't want to say this again.'

Everyone was quiet, their faces turned towards Diana expectantly. Cassie had the distinct feeling that a judgement was about to be rendered. Diana looked like a priestess or a princess, tall and pale, but resolute. There was a strange dignity about her, an aura of greatness and of certainty that belied the pain in her eyes.

I'm waiting to hear my punishment, Cassie thought. Whatever it was, she deserved it. She glanced at Adam and saw he was waiting too. His expression asked no favours, but Cassie knew what he must be feeling underneath it. They both stood before Diana, connected by their crime, glad to have it in the open at last.

'I don't want anybody to discuss what's happened tonight again,' Diana said, her voice soft and distinct. 'Not ever. Once I've finished talking we'll all consider the subject closed.' She looked at Adam, not quite meeting his eyes. 'I think,' she said slowly, 'that I know how it must have been for you. These things happen sometimes. I forgive you. And as for you, Cassie

– you're even less to blame. There was no way for you to have known. I don't blame either of you. All I ask—'

Cassie drew a shuddering breath and broke in. She couldn't hold back any longer.

'Diana,' she said, 'I want you to know something. All this time, underneath, I've been angry and jealous because Adam belonged to you and not me. Even up until tonight. But all that's changed now – truly. Now all I want is for you and Adam to be happy. Nothing is more important to me than you – and the promise I made.' For an instant it crossed Cassie's mind to wonder if Adam were *less* important, but she shoved the thought away and spoke earnestly, with utter conviction. 'Adam and I – we both made that promise. If you'll just give us another chance to keep it – just one more chance…'

Diana was opening her mouth, but Cassie went on before she could speak.

'*Please*, Diana. You've got to know that you can trust me – that you can trust us. You've got to let us prove that.'

There was a slight pause, then Diana said, 'Yes. Yes – you're right.' She took a deep breath and let it out, looking at Adam almost tentatively. 'Well, then, what if – if we just forget all about this for a while? Just – wipe the slate clean?'

A muscle in Adam's jaw jerked. Silently, he took the hand Diana extended towards him.

Diana held her other hand out to Cassie. Cassie took it and held on tightly to the slim, cold fingers. She wanted to laugh and cry at once. Instead she just gave Diana a wobbly smile. Looking at Adam she saw that he was trying to smile too, although his eyes were dark as storm clouds over the ocean.

'And that's *it*?' Faye exploded. 'Everything's all

right now, all sweetness and light? Everybody loves everybody and you're all going home holding hands?'

'Yes,' Adam snapped, giving her a hard look. 'As for the last, anyway. We're going home – it's past time for that.'

'Cassie needs to rest,' Diana agreed. The blank helplessness had left her entirely, and although she looked more fragile than Cassie had ever seen her before, she also looked determined. 'We all need that.'

'And we need to call a doctor – or somebody,' Deborah said unexpectedly. She inclined her head towards Number Twelve. 'Cassie's grandma...'

'Whose side are you on?' Faye snarled. Deborah just gave her a cool look.

Diana's fingers tightened on Cassie's. 'Yes. You're right, we'll call Dr Stern – and Cassie can come home with me.'

Faye gave a short bark of laughter, but nobody laughed with her. Even the Henderson brothers were serious, their slanted eyes thoughtful. Suzan twisted a lock of strawberry-blonde hair around her fingers, looking at Cassie's and Diana's intertwined hands. Laurel nodded encouragingly when Cassie glanced at her, and Melanie's cool grey eyes shone with quiet approval. Sean chewed his lip, looking uncertainly from one member of the group to another.

But it was Nick's expression that surprised Cassie most. His face, usually so unemotional, was clearly strained, as if there were some violent struggle going on beneath the surface.

There was no time to think about him now, though. No time even to think about Faye, who was seething uselessly, her plans to fracture the coven in ruins. Melanie was speaking.

'Do you want to go by my house first, Cassie? Great

Aunt Constance is looking after your mom, and if you want to see her...'

Cassie nodded eagerly. It seemed like a hundred years since she had seen her mother, since she had been inside that room filled with red light, looking at her mother's glassy, empty eyes. Surely her mother would be all right by now; surely she would be able to tell Cassie what had happened.

But when she three of them, Melanie, Cassie and Diana, who hadn't let go of Cassie's hand on the short drive to Number Four, went into the house, Cassie's heart sank. Melanie's great-aunt, a thin-lipped woman with severe eyes, led them silently into a downstairs guest room. One look at the ghostly figure on the bed sent chills of dismay through Cassie's bloodstream.

'Mom?' she whispered, knowing already there would be no answer.

God, her mother looked *young*. Even younger than she normally did, frighteningly young, unnaturally so. It was as if it weren't Cassie's mother on the bed there at all, but some little girl with dark hair and big haunted black eyes that vaguely resembled Mrs Blake's. A stranger.

Not someone who was going to be of help to Cassie.

'It's okay, Mom,' Cassie whispered, stepping away from Diana to put a hand on her mother's shoulder. 'Everything's going to be all right. You'll see. You're going to be just fine.'

Her throat ached, and then she felt Diana gently leading her away.

'You've both been through enough,' Melanie said once they were outside again. 'Let us take care of things with the doctor – and the police, if they have to come. You and Cassie get some sleep.'

The rest of the coven was waiting in the street, and

they nodded in agreement when Melanie said this. Cassie looked at Diana, who nodded too.

'Okay,' Cassie said. It came out faint and slightly hoarse and she realised how tired she was – bone-tired. At the same time she was light-headed, and the entire scene in front of her was assuming a dreamlike quality. It was just too strange to be standing out here in the wee hours of the morning, knowing that her grandmother was dead and her mother was in shock, and that she didn't have a house to go back to. Yet there were no adults on the street, no commotion, only the members of the Circle and an eerie stillness. Come to think of it, why *weren't* there any parents out here? Surely some of them must have heard what was going on.

But the houses on Crowhaven Road remained shuttered and silent. On the way to Melanie's house, Cassie thought she'd seen a light go off in Suzan's house and a curtain whisk back at the Hendersons'. If any adults were awake, they weren't getting involved.

We're on our own, Cassie thought. But Diana was beside her, and she could see Adam's tall form silhouetted against the headlights of the coven's parked cars. A sort of strength flowed into Cassie just at their nearness.

'We've got to talk tomorrow,' she said. 'There's a lot I've got to tell you – all of you. Things my grandmother told me right before ... before she died.'

'We can meet at lunchtime on the beach—' Diana began, but Faye's throaty voice cut her off.

'No, we can't. *I'm* the one who decides where the meetings are now, or had you forgotten?'

Faye's head was thrown back proudly, the silver crescent-moon diadem gleaming against the midnight-black of her hair. Diana opened her mouth, then shut it again.

'All right,' Adam said with deceptive calmness, stepping out of the glare of headlights to stand by Faye. 'You're the leader. So lead. Where do we meet?'

Faye's eyes narrowed. 'At the old science building. But—'

'Fine.' Adam didn't wait for her to finish; he turned his back on her. 'I'll drive you home,' he said to Diana and Cassie.

Faye looked furious, but the three of them were already moving away. 'By the way, Diana – happy birthday,' she called spitefully after them.

Diana didn't answer.

CHAPTER

3

'Jacinth! Are you in there? Jacinth!'

Cassie blinked in the bright sunlight. She'd seen this room before. It was her grandmother's kitchen – except that it wasn't. The walls of her grandmother's kitchen were sagging and dingy; these were straight and clean. Her grandmother's hearth was stained with the smoke of centuries; this hearth looked almost new and was a slightly different shape. The iron hook for hanging pots on shone.

It was the room in her dream, the dream she'd had the last time she spent the night at Diana's house. The low chair she was sitting in was the same. But this dream seemed to be picking up where the other had left off.

'Jacinth, have you fallen asleep with your eyes open? Kate is here!'

A feeling of anticipation and excitement filled Cassie. Kate; who was Kate? Without even knowing why, she found herself standing up, and she realised that she was wearing a dress that brushed the tips of her neat brocade shoes. The red leather Book of Shadows fell from her lap to the ground.

She turned towards the voice, towards what would have been the side door of her grandmother's house. In this house it seemed to be the front door. It was filled with sunlight, and there were two figures standing there. One was tall, with a silhouette like the engravings of Puritan women she'd seen in history books. The other was smaller, with shining hair.

Cassie couldn't see either of the figures' faces, but the smaller one was holding out eager hands to her. Cassie reached for them, stepping forward—

—and the dream changed. It was dark and she could hear the tortured scream of wood being ripped asunder. Salt spray stung her face and her eyes struggled vainly to pierce the darkness.

The ship was going down. Lost, all lost. And the Master Tools were lost as well – for now.

But only for now. The savage determination of the thought filled Cassie and she tasted bile at the back of her throat. Even as icy water rushed around her legs she felt the dream lose focus. She tried to hang on to it, but it melted and shifted around her, and the darkness of the turbulent, stormy night became the quiet darkness of Diana's room.

She was awake.

And relieved beyond reason just to be alive.

It wasn't really so dark in here. Dawn was brightening the curtains, turning the room grey. Diana was sleeping peacefully beside her. How *could* Diana be peaceful after all that had happened? After what Diana had learned about her best friend and her boyfriend, after losing the leadership of the coven, how could Diana sleep at all? But the dark lashes on Diana's cheek were still and serene and there was no bitterness in Diana's face.

She's so good. I could never be that good, Cassie thought. Not if I tried all my life. Still, just being near Diana made her feel better.

Cassie knew she wasn't going to sleep any more. She sat back against the headboard and thought.

God, she was glad to have things right with Diana again. And with Adam – Cassie was almost afraid to think of Adam, worried about what kind of pain it would bring. But although there was a deep-down ache at the picture of him, it was not unbearable, and the poison of jealousy and anger was truly gone. She honestly wanted him and Diana to be happy. She was a different person from the one who'd burned with the frustration of not being able to have him these last six weeks.

She'd done a lot of strange things in the last six weeks, so many that she hardly knew herself any more. I can't believe it, she thought; I went out and stole pumpkins with Chris and Doug in Salem. I drove that dog off Chris – that wasn't like me at all. I played Pizza Man with Faye. I went on that wild motorcycle ride with Deborah ... well, that wasn't so bad.

A lot of things she'd done in the last month weren't all bad. The lying and deception and guilt had been awful, but some of the changes had been good. She'd gotten closer to Deborah and Suzan, and she'd gained some insight into what made the Henderson brothers tick. Even Nick – she thought she understood him better now. And she'd found strength in herself she'd never thought she had. Strength to chase the shadowy thing in the cemetery – Black John? – after Jeffrey's death, strength to ask a boy to a dance, strength, in the end, to stand up to Faye.

She only hoped it was enough strength to stand up to the days ahead.

Cassie hadn't been to the old science building since Faye had lured her there and held her hostage, that first week of school. It was just as dark and unsafe-looking as she remembered. She had no idea why Faye had wanted them to meet here, except that this was Faye's territory, while the beach had always been Diana's.

It was strange to see Faye in Diana's place, standing in front of the group with all eyes on her. Faye was wearing ordinary clothes today, black leggings and a red and black striped sweater, but a mysterious aura of leadership still clung to her. As she paced, her star rubies flashed in the shafts of sunlight that came through the boarded-up windows.

'I believe it was Cassie who wanted this meeting called. She said there was a lot she had to tell us – right, Cassie?'

'About what my grandmother said before she died,' Cassie said steadily, looking Faye in the eyes. 'Before Black John killed her.' If she'd expected Faye to be abashed, she was disappointed; those hooded golden eyes remained level and arrogant. Apparently Faye took no responsibility for the actions of Black John, even though she was the one who'd arranged for him to be set free.

'Was it really Black John?' Suzan said doubtfully, putting an exquisitely manicured fingernail to her perfect mouth, as if thinking was a new and difficult exercise. 'Was he really there?'

'He was really there. He *is* really *here*,' Cassie said. Suzan wasn't as stupid as she acted, and sometimes she had surprising insights. Cassie wanted her on their side. 'He came out of that mound in the cemetery. It was his grave, I guess. When we brought the skull to the cemetery and released the dark energy, it gave him the strength to come back.'

'Back from the dead?' Sean asked nervously.

Before Cassie could answer, Melanie said, 'That mound couldn't have been Black John's grave, Cassie. I'm sorry, but it just couldn't. It's far too modern.'

'I know it's modern. It's not Black John's first grave; I don't even know if he had a grave in the 1600s. I guess not if he died at sea ...' There were startled looks from some of the group, but Cassie scarcely noticed. 'Anyway, it's not his grave from then. It's his grave from 1976.'

Laurel, who was pouring a thermos cup of herbal tea, sloshed hot liquid on the floor.

Faye stopped dead. *'What?'* she snarled.

Even Diana and Adam looked disconcerted, glancing at each other. But support came from an unexpected quarter.

'Just let her tell the story,' Deborah said. Thumbs hooked in her jeans pockets, she moved to where Cassie was sitting on an overturned crate, and stood beside her.

Cassie took a deep breath. 'I knew something was weird when I saw all those graves in the cemetery – graves of *your* parents, all killed in 1976. Diana said it was a hurricane, but it still seemed strange to me. I mean, why were only parents dead? Especially when I learned that you'd all been born just a few months before. With all those little babies, you'd think some of them would have died in an ordinary hurricane. That's not even to mention the weirdness of *all* of you being born within a one-month period.'

She was relaxing a little now, although it was difficult to talk with everyone looking at her. At least their eyes weren't glinting with enmity and suspicion today. Only Faye looked hostile, standing with her arms folded across her chest, her feline eyes narrowed.

'But you see, the explanation for all of it is really simple,' Cassie went on. 'Black John came back during the last generation, our parents' generation. Nobody knew it was him, and my grandmother said nobody could ever figure out how he came back, but it was Black John. He tried to make our parents into a coven when they were just a little older than us.'

'*Our* parents?' Doug asked, snickering. 'C'mon, Cassie, give us a break.' There were chuckles from others in the audience, and the expressions ranged from sceptical to troubled to openly mocking.

'No, wait,' Adam said, beginning to look excited. 'There are some things that that would explain. I know my grandmother wanders in her mind now and then, but she's said things to me about my parents – about us kids forming a coven – that just might fit.' His blue-grey eyes were snapping with intensity.

'Here's something else,' Deborah said, looking sideways at Nick. 'Cassie's grandma said my mom was going to marry Nick's dad, but Black John made her marry my dad instead. That might explain why my mom freaks when you even mention magic, and why she always looks kind of guilty when she says Nick is growing up to look just like his father. It might explain a lot.'

Cassie noticed Nick, who was standing apart from the group as usual, in a dark corner. He was staring at the floor so hard, his eyes seemed to be about to bore a hole through it. 'Yeah, it might,' he said so softly Cassie could barely hear the words. She wondered what he meant.

'It would explain why they yell at each other all the time, too – my parents, I mean,' Deborah was adding.

'All parents yell all the time,' Chris said with a shrug.

'All the parents around *here* are the ones who survived Black John,' said Cassie. 'They survived because they didn't go to fight him. My grandmother said that after eleven babies were born in one month, our parents realised what Black John was up to. He wanted a coven he could control completely, a coven of *kids* he could mould while they were growing up. You guys' – Cassie nodded around the group – 'were going to be his coven.'

The members of the Club looked at one another. 'But what about you, Cassie?' Laurel asked.

'I wasn't born until later. Neither was Kori, you know. We weren't part of Black John's plans; we were just regular kids. But you guys were going to be *his*. He arranged everything about you.'

'And the parents who didn't like that idea went to fight Black John,' Deborah put in. 'They killed him; they burned him and the house at Number Thirteen, but they died themselves doing it. The ones that are alive are the cowards who stayed at home.'

'Like *my* father,' Suzan said abruptly, looking up from her nails. 'He gets really nervous if you mention the Vietnam Memorial or the Titanic or anything about anybody dying to save other people. And he won't talk about my mom.'

Cassie saw startled looks around the Circle. There was a kind of recognition in many of the members' eyes.

'Like *my* dad,' Diana said wonderingly. 'He always talks about my mother being so brave, but he's never said exactly why. No wonder, if he didn't go, if he let her go alone.' She bit her lip, distressed. 'What a horrible thing to find out about your own father.'

'Yeah, well, I've got it worse,' Deborah said, looking grim. '*Both* my parents didn't go. And neither did yours,' she added to the Hendersons, who looked at each other and scowled.

'While those of us with no parents are lucky?' Melanie

asked, raising her eyebrows.

'At least you know they had guts,' Deborah said shortly. 'You and Adam and Laurel and Nick have something to be proud of. I'd rather be raised by a grandmother or a great-aunt than have parents who scream at each other all the time because they're so ashamed of themselves.'

Cassie was watching Nick again, and she saw something leave his face, some tension that had been there ever since she'd known him. It made him look different, softer somehow, more vulnerable. At that moment he raised his eyes and met hers, catching her in the act of watching him. Cassie wanted to look away, but she couldn't, and to her surprise there was no hostility in his gaze. His mouth crooked slightly in a wry, relieved smile, and she found herself almost smiling back in sympathy.

Then she realised Faye was looking at them. Turning back, she spoke quickly to the entire group.

'The ones who died were killed because our parents didn't all stick together. That's what my grandmother said, anyway. She said that *we* were the ones in danger now, because Black John's come to take us back. He still wants his coven, and now he's alive again – a living, breathing man. She said that he won't look burned and awful when we see him again, and we might not recognise him, but we have to be ready for him.'

'Why?' Adam asked, his level voice seeming loud in the sudden silence. 'Just what did she think he's going to do?'

Cassie lifted her hands. There was no longer a guilty secret between her and Adam, but every time she looked at him, she felt – a connection. A new connection, that of two people who'd been tried by fire and had come out stronger. There would always be an understanding between them.

'I don't know what he's going to do,' she told Adam. 'Fool us, my grandma said. Get us to follow him the way our parents did. But *how*, I don't know.'

'The reason I ask is because he may not want *all* of us,' Adam said, still quietly. 'You said he arranged for the eleven of us to be born – and if he joins the coven as its leader, that makes twelve. But you weren't one of the eleven, Cassie. Neither was Kori. And it looks like he got Kori out of the way.'

Diana drew in a sharp breath. 'Oh, my God – Cassie! You've got to leave. You've got to get out of New Salem, go back to California—' She stopped, because Cassie was shaking her head.

'I can't,' Cassie said simply. 'My grandma told me I had to stay and fight. She said that was why my mom brought me back, so I *could* fight him. I may be half outsider, but I guess I'm one kid he didn't plan, so maybe I have some kind of advantage.'

'Don't be modest,' Deborah broke in caustically. 'The old lady told us it was because your family was always the strongest. You've got the clearest sight and the most power, she said.'

'And I've got our Book of Shadows, now,' Cassie said, somewhat embarrassed, bending to take the red leather book out of her backpack. 'My grandmother had it hidden behind a loose brick in the kitchen fireplace. Black John wanted it, so there must be something in it that he's afraid of. I'm going to read it and try to find out what that something is.'

'What can the rest of us do?' Laurel asked. Cassie realised the question was directed at *her*; except for Faye, who was glowering, they were all looking at her expectantly. Flustered, she lifted her hands again and shook her head.

'We can talk to the old ladies in the town who're still alive,' Deborah suggested. 'That's my idea, anyway. Cassie's grandma said our parents have forgotten about magic, that they made themselves forget to survive. But I figure the old ladies might not have forgotten, and we can question them. Like Laurel's Granny Quincey, and Adam's grandma, old Mrs Franklin. Even your great-aunt, Mel.'

Melanie looked doubtful. 'Great Aunt Constance doesn't approve of the old ways *at all*. She's pretty – inflexible – about it.'

'And Granny Quincey is so frail,' Laurel said. 'As for old Mrs Franklin – well, she's not always all there.'

'To put it tactfully,' Adam said. 'Let's face it, my grandmother can get pretty loopy at times. But I think Deborah's right; they're all we've got, so we have to make the most of them. We can *try* to pump some parents for information, too ... what have we got to lose?'

'An arm and an eye, if it's my father you're pumping,' Suzan muttered, holding her fingers in a shaft of sunlight to examine her nails. But Chris and Doug Henderson grinned wildly and said they'd be happy to interrogate all the parents.

'We'll say, "Hey, remember that guy you fried like Freddy Krueger sixteen years ago? Well, he's back, so can you, like, give us any help in recognising him?"' Doug said with relish.

'Didn't your grandma say *anything* that might help?' Laurel asked Cassie.

'No ... wait.' Cassie straightened up, excitement stirring inside her. 'She said they identified Black John's body in the burned house because of his ring, a lodestone ring.' She looked at Melanie. 'You're the crystal expert; so what's lodestone?'

'It's magnetite, black iron oxide,' Melanie said,

her cool grey eyes narrowed thoughtfully. 'It's like hematite, which is iron oxide too, but hematite's blood-red when you cut it in thin slices. Magnetite is black and magnetic.'

Cassie tried to control her expression. Well, she'd known the hematite came from Black John's house; maybe it had even been his stone. She shouldn't be surprised that he wore a ring of something similar. Still, she felt a twinge of apprehension. She'd really better get rid of that piece of hematite. Right now it was sitting in a jewellery box in her bedroom, where she'd put it when Diana drove her over to her house to pick up her clothes this morning before school.

'Okay, we'll keep on the lookout for that,' Adam was saying, sparing Cassie the necessity of speaking. 'We can talk to the old ladies tomorrow – or maybe we should wait until after Cassie's grandmother's funeral.'

'All right,' Cassie murmured.

'You're making a lot of *suggestions*, Adam,' Faye said, stung into speaking at last. Her arms were still folded over her chest, and her honey-pale skin was flushed with anger.

Adam looked back without expression. 'Come to think of it, there was another suggestion I was going to make,' he said. 'I think we should retake the leadership vote.'

Faye lunged towards him, golden eyes blazing. 'You can't do that!'

'Why not? If all of us agree,' Adam said calmly.

'Because it's not in the traditions,' Faye hissed. 'You look at any Book of Shadows and you'll see! The vote is the vote; I won and it can't be changed now. *I'm* the coven leader.'

Adam turned to the others for help, but Melanie

was looking troubled and Diana was slowly shaking her head.

'She's right, Adam,' Diana said softly. 'The vote was fair, at the time. There aren't any provisions for changing it.' Melanie nodded her unwilling agreement.

'And I don't like you making all these plans without consulting me,' Faye went on, pacing again like a panther in a cage. Sparks actually seemed to flash from her eyes, the way they flashed from the red gems at her throat and on her fingers as she crossed patches of sunlight.

'Well, what do *you* want us to do?' Laurel said challengingly, tossing her long light-brown hair back. 'You were the one who wanted Black John out, Faye. You said he was going to help us, to give us his power. Well, how about it? What do you say now that he's here?'

Faye was breathing hard. 'He may be testing us—'

'By killing Cassie's grandma?' Deborah cut in harshly. 'Don't be stupid, Faye. I was there; I *saw* it. There's no excuse for murdering old ladies.'

Faye glared at her defecting ex-lieutenant. 'I don't know why he did that! Maybe he has some plans that we don't know about.'

'*That's* the truest thing you've ever said,' Melanie interrupted. 'He does have plans, Faye – to take us over. He's already killed four people, and if we annoy him I'm sure he'll be happy to kill us, too.'

Faye stopped pacing and smiled triumphantly. 'He can't,' she snapped. 'If Cassie is right – and I'm not saying she is, but *if* she is – then he needs us for his coven. So he can't kill us!'

'Well, he can't kill all of us, anyway,' Adam said dryly. 'He can only spare one.'

Silence fell. The members of the Circle glanced uneasily

at one another.

'Well, then, maybe you'd each better be sure *you're* not the one,' Faye said, smiling around at them. It wasn't quite her old, lazy smile; it was more a baring of teeth. Before anyone could say anything she turned around and stalked out of the room. They could hear her footsteps going rapidly down the stairs, then the slam of the science building's front door.

Cassie, Adam, and Diana looked at one another. Adam shook his head.

'We're in trouble,' he said.

'Oh, so is that what we figured out at this meeting?' said Deborah.

Diana leaned her forehead against her hand wearily. 'We need her,' she said. 'She *is* the coven leader, and we need her on our side, not on his. We'd better go talk to her.'

Slowly, the Club members got up. Outside, it was too bright, and Cassie squinted. Seventh period had just ended and people were flooding out of the school exits. Cassie scanned the crowds but couldn't see Faye.

'She's probably gone home,' Diana was saying. 'We'll have to go after her...'

Cassie didn't hear the rest. Among the milling students in the parking lot she had suddenly glimpsed a familiar face. A *strange* familiar face, one that didn't belong here, one that she had to rack her brains to identify. For God's sake, where had she seen that turned-up nose, that straw-coloured hair, those cold hazel eyes before? It was someone she'd known quite well, someone she'd been used to looking at day after day, but that she'd been only too happy to forget about when she came to New Salem.

A feeling of heat and humidity overcame Cassie. A

memory of sand underfoot, sweat trickling down her sides, suntan lotion greasy on her nose. A sound of lapping waves and a smell of overheated bodies and a sense of oppression.

Cape Cod.

The familiar girl was Portia.

CHAPTER
4

'**H**ey, watch out, Cassie,' Chris said, running into her as she stopped in her tracks. 'What's wrong?'

'I just saw someone.' Cassie could feel how wide her eyes were as she stared into the crowd. Portia had disappeared in a sea of bobbing heads. 'A girl I knew this summer ...' Her voice trailed off as her mind boggled at the task of explaining Portia to the Circle.

But Adam had seen her too. 'A witch hunter,' he said grimly. 'The one whose brothers carried a gun. They're seriously into it – not just as a hobby, but as an obsession.'

'And they've come *here*?' Deborah scoffed. Cassie looked back and forth between the dark-haired girl and Adam; obviously witch-hunting was something these people had encountered before. 'They ought to know better.'

'Maybe it was a mistake – or an accident. Maybe her parents moved and she was just transferred here or something,' Laurel said, ever the optimist.

Cassie shook her head. 'Portia doesn't make mistakes,' she murmured. 'And I pity the accident that tries to happen to her. Adam, what are we going to do?' She was almost more upset by this than she had been by the knowledge that Black John was loose somewhere in New Salem. *That* terror was mind-numbing, too much to deal with rationally. Fear of Portia was more familiar, and Cassie felt herself being sucked towards an old pattern of helplessness. She'd never been able to deal with Portia; she came out of every encounter tongue-tied and humiliated, defeated. Cassie shut her eyes.

I am not like that any more. I won't *be* like that, she thought. But dread churned in her stomach.

'We'll deal with her,' Adam was beginning bleakly when Doug leaned in, his tilted blue-green eyes sparkling.

'Hey, she's an enemy, right? Black John the Witch Dude said he wanted to help us destroy our enemies, right? So—'

'Don't even think about it,' Melanie cut in swiftly. *'Don't,* Doug. I mean it.'

Doug hunched his shoulders, but he looked at his twin sideways under his lashes.

'Bad magic,' Chris muttered, staring into the distance.

Cassie looked at Adam.

'Never,' Adam said reassuringly. 'Don't worry, Cassie. Never.'

Cassie was living with Diana now. 'Obviously you can't stay in that house alone,' Diana had said, and that afternoon she and Laurel and Melanie helped Cassie move her things. Adam and Deborah came too, for protection, pacing around the house restlessly, and most of the other Club members stopped by for one reason or another. Only Faye was conspicuously absent. No one had seen her since she'd disappeared from school.

The house itself wasn't too badly damaged, aside from the strange burned places on the floor and some of the doors. The official story, as decided on by the adults who'd come last night to take Cassie's grandmother's body away, was that there had been a fire and Mrs Howard had been frightened into a heart attack. The Club hadn't mentioned an intruder, and the police hadn't even cordoned the house off. How the police thought a hardwood floor had caught fire in such a strange pattern, Cassie didn't know. Nobody had asked her and she certainly wasn't going down to the station to volunteer anything.

The house seemed empty and echoing despite the Circle members bustling around it. There was an emptiness inside Cassie, too. She'd never have thought she would miss her grandmother so much – just a stooped old lady with coarse grey hair and a mole on her cheek. But those old eyes had seen a lot, and those knotted hands had been deft and kind. Her grandmother had *known* things, and she had always made Cassie feel better.

'I wish I had a picture of her,' Cassie said softly. 'My grandma.' Witches didn't like being photographed, so she didn't even have that.

'She was a pretty cool old broad,' Deborah said, slinging a tote bag over one shoulder and picking up a cardboard box full of books and CDs. 'You want anything else?'

Cassie looked around the room. Yes, everything, she thought. She wanted her four-poster bed with the dusty-rose canopy and hangings, and her damask-upholstered chairs, and her solid mahogany chest that was just the colour of Nick's eyes.

'That's bombé, that chest of drawers there,' she told Deborah. 'It was made here in Massachusetts, the only place in the colonies that produced that style.'

'Yeah, I know,' Deborah said, unimpressed. 'My house

is full of it. It weighs a ton and you can't take it. You want the stereo, or what?'

'No, I can use Diana's,' Cassie said sadly. She felt as if she were leaving her life behind. I'm only moving down the road, she reminded herself as Deborah left.

'Cassie, if you want to stop by and see your mom this afternoon, it's okay with Great Aunt Constance,' Melanie said, appearing in the doorway. 'Any time before dinner.'

Cassie nodded, feeling something twist in her chest. Her mother. Of course her mom was going to be all right; Melanie's great-aunt was willing to take care of her, and it would be better for her to stay at Melanie's house than to be taken – somewhere else. Say what you mean: an institution, she told herself fiercely. If the doctors saw her they'd want to put her in an institution or a hospital. But she doesn't belong there, and she's going to be just fine. She needs to rest a little, that's all.

'Thanks, Melanie,' she said. 'I'll come after we finish moving. It's nice of your aunt to take care of her.'

'With Great Aunt Constance it's not so much nice; it's duty,' Melanie said, turning to go. 'Great Aunt Constance believes in doing your duty.'

So do I, Cassie thought, pausing as she picked up a bundle of clothes from the bed. So do I. 'I just thought of something – I'll be down in a second,' she said.

What she'd thought of was the hematite One-handed, she opened the jewellery box on the dresser – and then stiffened. She stirred through the contents of the box with her fingers, but it was no use.

The piece of hematite was gone.

Panic swelled in Cassie's throat. She'd kept *meaning* to do something about the stone, but now that it was out of her hands she realised how dangerous she thought it really was.

This time, she told herself, you are not going to keep it a secret and worry and stew about it all by yourself. This time you're going to do what you should have done in the beginning, which is tell Diana.

Cassie went downstairs. Diana and Laurel were in the herb garden, salvaging things Laurel thought might be useful. Cassie squared her shoulders.

'Diana,' she said, 'I've got something to tell you.'

Diana's green eyes widened when Cassie explained about the hematite, how she'd found it, how she'd kept it a secret. No one had known about it except Deborah – and Faye.

'And now it's gone,' Cassie said. 'I don't think that means anything good.'

'No,' Diana said slowly. 'I'm sure it doesn't. Cassie, don't you see, when you were carrying the hematite, it affected you. It made you do things … were you wearing it at the Halloween dance when you tried to make Adam kiss you?'

'I … yes.' Cassie could feel the blood rising to her cheeks. 'But, Diana – I wish I could say the hematite made me do that, but it *didn't*. It was just me. I wanted to.'

'Maybe, but I'll bet you'd wanted to before and you didn't actually do it. Hematite might not force you to do things against your will, but it makes it easier to give in to things you normally wouldn't.'

'Like onyx. Surrender to your shadow-self,' Cassie whispered.

'Yes,' said Diana.

'It must be one of us who has it; one of the Circle,' Cassie said. 'Because I put it in the box this morning and nobody else has been by the house today. But *which* one of us?'

Diana shook her head. Laurel grimaced. 'I stick to plants,' she said. 'They're safer, as long as you respect them and know what you're doing. They don't influence you.'

At Diana's suggestion, the three of them searched Cassie's room again. But the hematite was nowhere to be found.

Cassie went to school on Thursday. It was strange to sit in her writing class and see life going on around her as usual. All these people – students counting the days until Thanksgiving vacation, teachers giving their lectures, the vice-principal walking through the halls and looking harried – had no idea what was loose in their community, just waiting to strike again. Of course, Cassie didn't know exactly, either. What form was Black John going to take now? What would he look like when she saw him next? But she knew there was danger.

Faye didn't show up for English. Cassie had to stay after class to explain to Mr Humphries why she'd been absent for two days. He was sympathetic and told her to take extra time for her next assignment, but it was hard to get away from him. Cassie was already late for algebra when she hurried into the third-floor bathroom. But once in a stall, she heard voices outside that made her freeze and forget the time.

They were carrying on a conversation that had obviously been going for a while.

'And then she was supposed to go back to California,' the first voice was saying. Cassie had heard it too many times not to recognise it. Portia. 'But that was obviously a lie too, if it's the same Cassie I knew.'

'What did you say she looked like?' asked the other voice. A strident, contentious voice. Cassie recognised Sally Waltman.

'Oh, she's just a little nonentity. She's completely average, average height, a little taller than you...'

A throat-clearing sound from Sally.

'Not that you're *short*, of course. You're – petite. Anyway, she's got a fairly slim build, and everything about her is just ordinary: ordinary brownish hair, ordinary little face, ordinary clothes – *not* anything to write home about. Overall, she's unutterably dreary—'

'It's not the same Cassie,' Sally interrupted curtly. 'This one had every guy at Homecoming dance following her around with his tongue hanging out. Including *my* boyfriend – and look where it got him. She looks ordinary at first, maybe, but there are all sorts of colours in her hair; it changes depending on the light. I'm serious. And I'm sure it's just an act, but she's the kind that looks all fragile and sweet, the kind guys are just dying to take care of – and *then* she starts ordering them around. And she gets away with it, probably because she opens those great big eyes and pretends she thinks she's inadequate. The 'Oh, I'm just the girl next door, but I'll do my *best*' routine – they lap it up.'

Cassie opened her mouth indignantly, then closed it again.

'And she's got eyes to kill for,' Sally was going on bitterly. 'Not the colour, so much – they're sort of greyish blue – but they're so big and *sincere* it's disgusting. They always look like they're full of tears just ready to spill. Drives the guys crazy.'

'It *is* the same girl,' Portia said positively. 'Only when I knew her she had the sense not to flaunt herself. She knew her place then.'

'Well, right now her place is with the most popular clique in school. They all think they're so wonderful; they think they can do anything. Including kill people.'

'Well, not any more,' Portia said with satisfaction. 'Things around here are about to change dramatically – for the better. You know, I'm *glad* my mom decided to move here after the divorce. I thought it would be terrible, but it's all turning out for the best.'

Cassie held herself carefully still. So Sally and Portia were joining forces. Now if they would just be so obliging as to describe a little of their plans...

But the sound of running water drowned out the next few sentences, and then she heard Sally say, 'I'd better get to calculus. Want to meet for lunch?'

'Yes, and I think you should come over to my house at Thanksgiving vacation,' Portia said. 'I think you'll like my brothers.'

Cassie stood protectively surrounded by the rest of the Circle. It was Saturday and the burial was almost over.

This wasn't the old burying ground, the one which had been 'vandalised' (that was the official story) the night her grandmother died. It was the modern cemetery where Kori had been buried. Modern in New Salem terms, that is: the oldest graves were from the 1800s. Cassie wondered why the parents killed by Black John in 1976 hadn't been buried here. Maybe someone had felt the old graveyard was more appropriate.

People were coming up to her, saying how sorry they were, asking about her mother. The official story on her mother was that she was in shock over the death of Cassie's grandmother and too ill to come. Cassie told them her mother was going to be fine.

Faye had showed up, to Cassie's surprise. Her lacy black dress was beautiful, if a little too clinging to be appropriate at a funeral. Her red lips and nails were the only touches of colour about her.

'So sorry,' a familiar voice said coolly, and Cassie looked up to see Portia. Sally was right behind her; those two seemed joined at the hip these days.

'What a surprise to see you here,' Portia added, her hazel eyes fixed on Cassie's. Cassie remembered them; mean as snakes' eyes, she thought. They seemed to have a mesmerising effect, and Cassie felt the crushing sense of helplessness start to descend.

She fought it, and tried to speak, but Portia was going on. 'I didn't realise you had family up here. But maybe now that you don't you'll be going back to California...?'

'No, I'm staying.' To Cassie's frustration, she couldn't think of anything else to say. She'd come up with a devastatingly witty retort tonight, undoubtedly.

But she wasn't alone in New Salem. Adam said, 'Cassie still has family here,' and moved to Cassie's side.

'Yeah, we're all brothers. All life is, like, linked,' Chris said, coming up on Cassie's other side. He stared at Portia out of his strange blue-green eyes. Doug joined him, grinning his mad grin.

Portia blinked. Cassie had forgotten what the Henderson brothers looked like to people who didn't know them.

But Portia recovered quickly. 'That's right – they say all you people are related. Well, maybe someday soon you'll meet *my* family.' She looked at Adam. 'I'm sure they'd enjoy that.' She turned on her heel and walked away.

Cassie and Adam exchanged a glance, but before they could say anything, Mr Humphries had stepped up.

'It's been a beautiful service,' he told Cassie. 'We'll all miss your grandmother.'

'Thank you,' Cassie said. She managed a smile for him; she liked Mr Humphries, with his neat little salt-and-pepper beard and his sympathetic eyes behind gold-rimmed glasses. 'It was nice of you to come.'

'I hope your mother is feeling better soon,' said Mr Humphries, and then he moved on. Ms Lanning, Cassie's American-history teacher, came up to talk then, but Cassie's attention lingered on Mr Humphries. A tall man with dark hair had joined him, and Cassie heard the rumble of a deep voice, followed by Mr Humphries's lighter, quicker tones.

'—introduce me?' the dark man was saying.

'Why, certainly,' Mr Humphries said. He turned back to Cassie, bringing the dark man with him. 'Cassie, I thought you might want to meet our new principal, Mr Jack Brunswick. He's interested in getting to know his students as soon as possible.'

'That's right,' the tall man said, in deep, pleasant tones. He reached out and took Cassie's hand in a firm grip. His own hand was large and strong. She glanced down at it as she opened her mouth to say something polite, but then froze, paralysed, feeling her heart pound like a trip-hammer while the blood drained out of her face.

'I don't think she's feeling well – this must have been a long day...' Ms Lanning was saying, but her voice seemed to come from a distance. She took hold of Cassie's arm.

But Cassie couldn't let go of the dark man's hand with its strong, well-made fingers. All she could see was the signet ring on his index finger, carved with a symbol that reminded her of the inscriptions on Diana's silver bracelet – Faye's silver bracelet now. The stone in the ring was black and reflective, with a metallic lustre. It looked like hematite, but Cassie knew it wasn't. It was a lodestone.

Then, at last, Cassie looked up at the new principal, and she saw the face she'd seen during the skull ceremony in Diana's garage. The face that had rushed at her, faster and faster, bigger and bigger, trying to escape from the crystal skull. A cruel, cold face. For an instant she seemed to see the crystal skull itself superimposed on the principal's face, its bone structure clearly visible. The hollow eyes, the grinning teeth—

Cassie swayed on her feet. Ms Lanning was trying to support her; she could hear Adam's alarmed voice, and Diana's. But she could see nothing except the darkness of the new principal's eyes. They were like glassy volcanic rock, like the ocean at midnight, like magnetite. They were swallowing her up...

Cassie. The voice was in her mind.

Rushing blackness surrounded her and she fell.

Darkness. She was on a ship – no, she wasn't. She was fighting, struggling in icy water. Cassie clawed out, trying to get to the surface. She couldn't *see*—

'Take it easy! You're safe. Cassie, it's all right.'

A wet cloth fell away from Cassie's eyes. She was in Diana's living room, lying on the couch. It was dim because the curtains were drawn and the lamps were off. Diana was leaning over her, and the long, silvery cascade of Diana's hair was falling down like a shield between Cassie and the world.

'Diana!' She clung to the other girl's hand.

'It's all right. You're okay. You're okay.'

Cassie let out her breath, leaning back against the couch, her eyes meeting Diana's.

'Jack Brunswick is Black John.' It was a flat statement.

'I know,' Diana said grimly. 'After you went down we all saw the ring. I don't think he expected us to recognise him so fast.'

'What happened? What did he do?' Cassie was envisioning chaos at the cemetery.

'Not much. He left as we were carrying you to my

car. Adam and Deborah went after him, but they weren't obvious about it. They're going to try to follow him. Nobody else – none of the adults – realised anything was wrong. They just figured you were exhausted. Mr Humphries said maybe you'd better take some time off from school.'

'Maybe we'd all better,' Cassie whispered. Her head was spinning. Black John in charge of the school. What in the name of God was he planning?

'You said Adam went after him?' she asked, and Diana nodded. Cassie felt a pang of anxiety – and frustration. She wanted Adam *here*, so she could talk to him. She needed him. . . .

'Hey, everything okay in there?' Chris and Doug were hanging in the doorway, as if it were a lady's boudoir that they weren't allowed inside of.

'She's all right,' Diana said.

'You sure, Cassie?' Chris asked, venturing a few steps in. Cassie nodded wanly, then suddenly thought of Sally's words in the bathroom. *She's the kind guys are just dying to take care of.* That certainly wasn't true . . . was it? Sally had warped everything; she'd had it all wrong.

'Come on, you two, there's double-fudge cake in the kitchen,' Diana said to the brothers. 'Everybody in the neighbourhood's been dropping food off, and we need help eating it.' Cassie thought it was strange that Diana was leaving her, then she saw that Chris and Doug hadn't been alone.

Nick was standing in the hallway outside the living room. When Diana ushered the Henderson brothers out, he came in, walking slowly.

'Uh . . . hi, Nick,' Cassie said.

He gave her an odd, fleeting smile and sat on the arm of

the couch. His customary mask of stone was gone today. In the dim room, Cassie thought he looked little tired, a little sad, but maybe that was only her imagination.

'How're you doing?' he said. 'You had us scared for a minute there.'

Nick, scared? Cassie didn't believe it. 'I'm fine, now,' she said, and then she tried to think of something else to say. It was the same as it had been with Portia: when she really needed it, her mind wouldn't work.

The silence stretched out. Nick was looking at the scrolls and flowers on the upholstery of the couch. 'Cassie,' he said finally, 'I've been meaning to talk to you.'

'Oh, have you?' Cassie said faintly. She felt very strange; hot and embarrassed and at the same time weak. She didn't want Nick to go on – but some part of her did.

'I realise this isn't exactly the perfect moment,' he said ironically, transferring his gaze to the wallpaper. 'But the way things are going we may all be dead before the perfect moment comes.' Cassie opened her mouth, but no sound came out, and Nick was going on, relentlessly, inevitably, his voice low but perfectly audible. 'I know you and Conant were pretty attached to each other,' he said. 'And I know you thought a lot of him. I realise I'm hardly the perfect substitute – but like I said, the way things are going maybe it's stupid to wait for perfection.' Suddenly he was looking directly at her and Cassie saw something in his mahogany eyes she'd never seen before. 'So, Cassie, what do you think about it?' Nick said. 'About you and me?'

CHAPTER

5

Cassie opened her mouth to speak, but Nick was going on.

'You know, when I first saw you I thought you were just ordinary,' he said. 'Then I started noticing things about you – your hair, your mouth. The way you kept on fighting even when you were scared. That night when Lovejoy was killed you were scared to death, but you were the one who suggested we look for the dark energy, and when we were out at the burying ground you kept up with Deborah.' Nick stopped and grinned ruefully. 'And with us guys,' he said.

Cassie felt an answering smile tug at her own lips; quickly suppressed it. 'Nick, I . . .'

'Don't say anything yet. I want you to know that I – felt bad about how I treated you when you came to ask me to the dance.' His jaw was tight, and he looked steadily at one particular flower on the upholstery of the couch. 'I don't know why I did it – I've just got a lousy temper, I guess. I've had it so long I don't even think about it any more.' Nick took a deep breath before continuing, 'See, I've always hated living with Deb's parents; I always felt like I *owed* them something. It put me in a permanent bad mood, I guess. I felt like my mom and dad screwed up somehow, getting themselves killed in a hurricane so their kid had to be supported by other people. It made me hate them – and my aunt and uncle, too.'

Nick stopped and shook his head thoughtfully. 'Yeah, especially Aunt Grace. She talks about my dad all the time, goin' on and on about how reckless he was, how he didn't care who he left behind, that kind of crap. It made me sick. I never figured it could be because she missed him.'

Cassie was fascinated. 'Is that why you don't like magic?' It was a blind guess, but he looked at her, startled.

'I don't know – I suppose it could have something to do with it. I resented the rest of the coven because I felt like they all had a better deal than me. They all had at least a grandparent, and I just had my dead parents that screwed up. And they were all so damn *cheerful* about it – like Conant. He—' Nick paused and glanced up at Cassie wryly. 'Well, maybe the less said about him, the better. Anyway, I know the truth now. My parents didn't screw up, and if *I* screw up I can't blame them any more. I've got only one person to blame – me. So I'm sorry about the way I acted.'

'Nick, that's okay. You did take me to the dance.'

'Yeah, after you came back and asked again. That took guts. And after I took you we went to Number Thirteen and you got hurt.' The corner of Nick's mouth turned down. 'I couldn't do anything about that. It was Conant who saved you.'

A memory of the smoky thing at the Halloween ceremony, the dark form that had risen out of the Samhain fire, flickered through Cassie's mind. She shoved it away, feeling panic rise in her chest. She didn't want to think about Black John now – frightening though he had been as a smoky figure, he was more frightening by far as a man. His eyes...

'Cassie.' Nick's strong fingers were wrapped around her wrist. 'It's okay. You're okay.'

Cassie gulped a deep breath and nodded, her awareness returning to the dim room. 'Thanks,' she whispered. It felt good to have Nick's hand on her arm: warm fingers, firm grip. It steadied her. And, God, she'd needed somebody to hang on to, for so long ... She remembered sitting in Adam's car, aching with the need to hold him, to be held. And knowing that she couldn't, that she never could. Cassie had that same ache now, and Adam was completely lost to her. How long did she have to live with the empty feeling?

'I know,' Nick was saying in a low voice, 'that you're not in love with me. I know I'm not him. But, Cassie, I like you. I like you a lot, more than any girl I've ever seen. You're so decent to people, you're not hard, but inside you're tough as Deb. Tough as me, maybe.' He laughed shortly. 'You haven't kept a grudge against anybody in the Club, no matter how they treated you in the beginning. Deb was really surprised about that. And in the end you've made them all respect you. The Henderson brothers never fell for a girl before, but they don't know if they're on their heads or their feet any more. I think they're going to make you a pipe bomb for Christmas.'

Cassie couldn't help laughing with him. 'Well, I guess that's one way to get rid of the problem.'

'Even Faye respects you,' Nick said. 'She wouldn't have tried so hard to destroy you otherwise. Look, Cassie, I can't explain what it is about you – you're good but you're tough. You can take it. And you've got the most gorgeous eyes I've ever seen.'

Cassie felt the blood rising to her face. She could feel his eyes on her, and *she* was the one forced to study the wallpaper. The hot, strange feeling inside her was stronger every minute.

She was thinking about that first week of school, when Deborah and the Henderson brothers had been teasing her, playing keepaway with her backpack – and suddenly a brown arm had reached into her field of vision, catching the backpack, saving her. Nick. And about how nice he'd been in the boiler room when she'd found Jeffrey's body, how he'd held her and said, 'Steady, steady.' His arms had been solid and comforting then. Nick wasn't intimidated by anything. She liked Nick.

But liking wasn't enough.

Cassie found herself shaking her head. 'Nick – I'm so sorry. I can't lead you on...'

'I said I knew you weren't in love with me. But if you just want to give it a try – I'll be there when you need somebody. We could have some fun,' he added, as lightly as she'd ever heard Nick speak. 'Get to know each other.'

Cassie thought about how annoyed she'd been a while ago that Adam wasn't here at Diana's. She didn't have the right to demand Adam like that – and it was dangerous. *I'll be there when you need somebody*. How could Nick know how important that was to her?

She looked up at him, and in a voice she herself could barely hear, she said, 'Okay.'

The mahogany eyes widened slightly in surprise – which by Nick's normally expressionless standards translated into astonishment. A wondering smile curved his lips a little. He looked so happy that Cassie felt herself drawn into it. Why could she never resist smiling back at him?

'I didn't think you'd go for it,' he said, still wonderingly.

Cassie laughed, but blushed harder. 'So why did you ask?'

'I figured it was worth asking, even if you told me to get lost.'

'Nick.' Cassie felt something strange. 'I wouldn't ever tell you to get lost. You're – well, you're really special.' She didn't know how to say what she meant, and the words caught in her throat anyway. Her vision was blurring, swimming. She blinked to clear it and felt tears spill. And then Nick moved towards her and somehow she was in his arms, crying on his shoulder. Nothing had ever been so comforting as that grey wool-clad shoulder.

She sniffled and she could feel him leaning his cheek against her hair. 'Let's just give it a try for a while,' he said softly. And Cassie nodded and let herself rest in his arms.

It was dark when she let Nick out the front door. Diana was upstairs; Chris and Doug had left a long time ago. Cassie felt uncertain and shy as she tapped on Diana's door.

'Come in,' Diana said, and Cassie did, remembering the first time she'd tapped on this door and come into this room, the day Diana had rescued her from Faye in the science building. Then, Diana had been sitting at the window seat, surrounded by a whirling crowd of rainbows. Now Diana was sitting at the desk with a pile of papers in front of her.

'So what happened?' she said, turning around.

Cassie could feel the heat in her cheeks. 'I – we – we decided that we would give it a try. Being – well, sort of being together, I mean.'

Diana's lips parted. She looked into Cassie's eyes, as if searching for something there. 'You *what*?' she said, and then she caught herself. She looked at Cassie for another long moment. 'I see,' she said slowly.

'You're not mad?' Cassie was trying to figure out what was going on behind those emerald-green eyes.

'Mad? How could I be mad at you? I'm just – surprised, that's all. But don't worry about it. Nick's a nice guy, and I know you won't hurt him. You know how special he is.'

Cassie nodded, but she was startled to hear her own words on Diana's lips. She hadn't known *Diana* knew.

'No, I think it's a good thing,' Diana said firmly, pushing the papers out of the way.

Cassie breathed a sigh of relief. Then she looked at the papers Diana had been examining when she came in. They were old and yellowing, covered with thick strokes of black writing in columns. The writing had some odd curlicues in it and little punctuation that Cassie could see, but it was legible.

'What are these?'

'Black John's personal papers. Letters and things – we gathered them all up when we started looking for the Master Tools. I was looking through them to see if maybe I could find some weakness that we can use against him, to fight him. That's how we found out where to look for the crystal skull in the first place; he wrote a letter about it to one of Sean's ancestors and we found it in Sean's attic. Not giving the exact location of the island, of course, but giving some clues.'

'I didn't realise he would trust anybody enough to give them clues.'

'He didn't. Apparently, he was planning to go back and get the skull, either to use it or to put it somewhere safer, but he died before he could do it.'

'He drowned,' Cassie murmured, turning over a

small rectangular paper in her fingers. It was printed *Massachusetts-Bay Colony, 8 dollars.* Good grief, it was money, money from the 1600s.

'You said that before,' Diana said eyeing Cassie thoughtfully. 'I wondered then how you knew.'

'What? Oh, I guess one of you told me.' Cassie tried to think. 'Maybe Melanie.'

'Melanie couldn't have told you. None of us could have, Cassie, because none of us ever knew it. You're the first person who's suggested he died at sea.'

'But ...' Bewildered, Cassie searched her mind, trying to think where she'd come up with the idea. 'But then how ...' Suddenly she knew. 'My dreams,' she whispered, backing up to the bed. 'Oh, Diana, he's been in my dreams. I *dreamed* about drowning, about being on a ship that was going down. But it wasn't me, it was him. It was Black John.'

'Cassie.' Diana came over and sat down beside her. 'Are you sure it was him?'

'*Yes.* Because it happened again today, when I saw him at the cemetery. I looked into his eyes – and then I felt myself falling. Drowning. There was salt water all around me, and it was cold. I could taste it.'

Diana put her arms around Cassie's heaving shoulders. 'Don't think about it any more.'

'I'm all right,' Cassie whispered. 'But why would he make me go through that? Why would he put it in my head? Is he trying to kill me?'

'I don't know,' Diana said, her voice unsteady. 'Cassie, I told you before, you don't have to stay here—'

'I *do*, though.' Cassie thought of her grandmother, and words echoed in her mind. *There's nothing frightening in the dark, if you just face it.*

The ocean was dark, dark as midnight underwater, and

cold as hematite. But I can face that, Cassie thought. I refuse to be afraid of it. I refuse. She pushed the fear away from her and slowly felt the trembling inside her steady.

My line has the sight and the power, she thought. I want to use that power to stand up to him. To face him.

She drew away from Diana. 'I think you've got the right idea tonight,' she said, nodding at the papers on the desk. 'You go through those, and your Book of Shadows, and I'll keep going through mine.' She looked at the window seat where the red leather-covered book lay beside a block of multicoloured Post-it notes and a scattering of felt-tip pens and highlighters.

'Have you found anything interesting so far?' Diana asked as Cassie settled into the window seat with the book on her lap.

'Nothing about Black John. In the beginning the spells seem to be pretty much the same as yours. But everything in it's interesting, and who knows what's going to turn out to be useful in the end,' Cassie said. She was determined to get familiar with the range of spells and amulets in the book, to learn as many as possible of them and to at least know where to find the rest. Still, it was a project that would take years, and they didn't have years. 'Diana, I think we'd better talk to the old ladies in town – soon. Before – well, before anything happens so we *can't* talk to them.' She met Diana's eyes grimly.

Diana blinked, taking in Cassie's meaning, and then nodded. 'You're right. He's already killed four people, at least. If he thinks they're a threat …' She swallowed. 'We'll talk to them tomorrow. I'll tell Adam when he calls – he's supposed to call me when he and Deborah get through shadowing Black John.'

'I hope Black John doesn't know he's being shadowed,' Cassie said.

'I hope so too,' Diana said quietly, and bent her head over the papers again.

The meeting was held the next day on the beach. Faye didn't have a chance to veto the location because Faye wasn't there.

'She's with *him*,' Deborah said briefly. 'I followed her this morning – Adam and I flipped for it last night. She met him at that same coffee shop where they met yesterday—'

'Hang on, hang on,' Laurel said. 'You're getting ahead of yourself. What coffee shop?'

'I'll tell it,' Adam said, in response to Diana's look. 'Yesterday we went out of the cemetery and followed – Mr Brunswick. That's a joke, by the way.'

Diana nodded. 'I used to do a little oil-painting, and Brunswick is a kind of paint,' she told Cassie and the group. 'Black paint.'

'Very funny,' said Cassie. She was sitting beside Nick, a new position, and one that made her slightly self-conscious. She was very aware of him, of his arm beside her. If she leaned a little to the right, she could touch him, and it was comforting. 'I wonder what he did with the real person who was supposed to be principal,' she said.

'I don't know.' Adam couldn't have helped but notice who she was sitting by, and the new expression in Nick's eyes, a sort of protectiveness. Right now Cassie could see his blue-grey gaze flicker towards Nick, looking him up and down narrowly. It wasn't a friendly look. 'I don't know how he managed to get the position. I don't know *why* he would want it, either.' He glanced at Nick again and opened his mouth, but Diana was talking.

'Go on with the story. Go on, Adam. Tell us what happened when you followed him yesterday.'

'Huh? Oh, right. Well, he left alone, in a grey Cadillac, and we followed; Deborah on her bike and me in my jeep. He drove into town and went to the Perko's Koffee Kup there – and guess who drove up a few minutes later?'

'Wearing a black lace mini-dress and looking *really* perky,' Deborah put in.

'Faye,' Diana whispered, looking sick. 'How *could* she?'

'I dunno, but she did,' Deborah said. 'We watched her through the window, and she went to his booth. He's a living, breathing man, all right – he was drinking coffee. They talked for about an hour. Faye was prancing and tossing her head like a little filly in a show. And he seemed to like it – anyway, he was smiling at her.'

'We waited until they left, then Deb followed her and I followed him,' Adam said. 'He drove to a summer cottage on the mainland – I guess he's rented it. He stayed there all night, I think; I finally left around one in the morning.'

'Where did Faye go?' Melanie asked Deborah.

Deborah made a face. 'I don't know.'

'Why not?'

'Because she lost me, okay? Riding a Harley isn't exactly inconspicuous. She started going through red lights and suddenly making U-turns, and in the end she lost me. You want to make something out of it?'

'Deb,' Cassie said. Deborah scowled at her, then rolled her eyes and shrugged.

'Anyway, this morning I waited outside her house, and she went back to meet him. They had a booth at the back, though, not near a window. So I went inside, but I really couldn't see what was going on. I *think* she gave him something, but I don't know what.'

'Wonderful,' Suzan said, and Deborah glared at her.

'I mean, wonderful that she's – what do you call it? In

league with him. Is anybody going to eat that doughnut?' Suzan daintily shook off powdered sugar and bit in.

Laurel murmured something about white sugar being worse than rat poison, but she didn't have the energy to say more.

'It's *good*,' Suzan said indistinctly. 'The only thing it's missing is cream filling.'

'I think we'd better go talk with the old ladies,' Cassie said. 'With Adam's grandmother, I mean, and Laurel's grandmother and Melanie's great-aunt.'

'Today's a good day,' Melanie volunteered. 'Every Sunday afternoon they get together and have lunch at our place: a kind of tea, you know, with sandwiches and little cakes and stuff.'

'That's right,' Cassie said. 'My grandmother used to go too.'

'Cakes?' said Suzan, looking interested. 'Why didn't you say so? Let's go.'

'Right – no, wait,' Diana said. She looked around the group. 'Look, it's probably pointless to ask this, but did any of *you* take the piece of hematite out of Cassie's room?' Everyone stared at her, then at each other. Everyone except Cassie and Laurel. Heads were shaken, and all the faces wore the same look of puzzlement.

'Somebody took the hematite?' Deborah asked. 'The piece you found at Number Thirteen?' Cassie nodded, unobtrusively studying the other members of the Circle. Adam was frowning, the Henderson brothers looked blank. Sean looked nervous, but then Sean always looked nervous. Melanie seemed troubled, Nick was slowly shaking his head, and Suzan was shrugging.

'I didn't think anybody would admit to it,' Diana said. 'But I suspect that's because the person who took it isn't here. She's at Perko's Koffee Kup.' Diana sighed. 'All right.

Let's go to Number Four.'

Cassie had been getting quite familiar with Melanie's house since her mother had been taken to stay there. The house was in the Federal style, very similar to Cassie's grandmother's, but in much better repair. The white clapboard walls were freshly painted and everything inside had a shipshape, tidy look. Great Aunt Constance was sitting in the front parlour with old Mrs Franklin, Adam's grandmother, and Laurel's Granny Quincey. She didn't look at all pleased to see the eleven of them crowding in the parlor door.

'Great Aunt Constance? Can we talk to you?'

The elderly woman turned a cool, disapproving eye on Melanie. She was thin and regal, and in her high-cheekboned face Cassie could detect some resemblance to Melanie's classic beauty. Her hair was still very dark, but maybe she dyed it.

'Are you here to see your mother?' she said, spotting Cassie in the group. 'She's fast asleep right now; I really don't think she should be disturbed.'

'Actually, Aunt Constance, we came to talk to you,' Melanie said. She looked at the other women in the parlour. 'To all three of you.'

A line appeared between Great Aunt Constance's eyebrows, but the short plump woman sitting on the sofa said, 'Oh, let them in, Connie. Why not? There you are, Adam. What kept you out so late last night, hm?'

'I didn't realise you noticed, Grandma,' Adam said.

'Oh, I notice more than people think,' Mrs Franklin chuckled, picking up a cookie and popping it into her mouth. Her grey hair was piled untidily on her head in braids, and there was a disorganised air about her that contrasted with the austere white and gold parlour. Cassie liked her.

'What's going on, Laurel?' a quavery voice asked, and Cassie looked at Granny Quincey, a tiny woman with a face like a dried apple. She was actually Laurel's great-grandmother, and she was so little and light she looked as if a puff of wind would blow her away.

'Well—' Laurel looked at Adam, who spoke up.

'Actually, it has something to do with what my grandmother asked me. What I was out doing last night. And it has to do with something that happened a long time ago, right around the time all of us kids were born.'

Great Aunt Constance was really frowning now, and Granny Quincey's lips were pursed together. Old Mrs Franklin was chuckling, but she was looking around the room in a way that made Cassie wonder if she'd really heard her grandson.

'Well?' Great Aunt Constance said sharply. 'Explain yourself.'

Adam glanced back at the rest of the Circle, all of whom were beaconing their support, silently electing him spokesman. He took a deep breath and turned back to the old women.

'What I was out doing was shadowing our new high-school principal, Mr Jack Brunswick,' he said. The name elicited no reaction. 'I think you might have known him under a different name.' Utter silence.

'The name we're all most familiar with is Black John,' said Adam.

The silence was shattered as Great Aunt Constance stood so abruptly that one of the fragile willow-patterned tea cups dashed to the floor.

'Get out of this house! Get out!' she said to Adam.

CHAPTER 6

'**A**unt Constance!' Melanie gasped.

'You heard me,' the dark-haired woman said to Adam. She looked at the rest of the group. 'Get out of here, all of you! I don't like that kind of joke, especially now. Haven't you made enough trouble with your meddling? Poor Alexandra in the guest room, and Maeve scarcely in the ground ... Melanie, I want them out of the house!'

Laurel and Granny Quincey were both fluttering. 'Oh dear, Oh dear,' Granny Quincey was saying, raising hands that looked like little bird claws, and 'Oh, please, Miss Burke,' Laurel was beseeching, almost in tears.

'You have no respect at all,' Aunt Constance said, breathing hard. Her eyes were as bright as if she had a fever.

'Young people never do, Constance,' Adam's grandmother said, chuckling. 'Why, I remember when we were their age, the mischief we used to get up to ... oh, me.' Still laughing and shaking her head, Adam's grandmother popped another cookie in her mouth.

'Grandma, please listen. It's not a joke,' Adam began helplessly, but it was no use. There was too much noise;

everyone was talking at once. Over it all Great Aunt Constance continued to order them out, telling Melanie to forget about the mess on the floor and just *go*. Granny Quincey was twittering and making calming gestures, which everybody ignored. Old Mrs Franklin was smiling at them all benevolently. Diana was pleading with Melanie's aunt to listen, but to no avail.

'For the last time!' Aunt Constance cried, flapping a hand as if to shoo Diana and the Club out the door.

'Miss Burke!' Cassie yelled. She felt close to tears herself, although Nick had been quietly trying to escort her out since the shouting had started. Cassie didn't want to go; she thought she understood what Great Aunt Constance was talking about when she mentioned the kids' meddling. 'Miss Burke,' she repeated, forcing her way forward again. She found herself directly in front of Great Aunt Constance.

'I'm sorry,' Cassie said, and it was suddenly quiet enough that she could hear the unsteadiness in her own voice. 'It's my mom who's in your guest room, and you know how grateful I am that you're taking care of her. And it's my grandmother who's in the ground. But who do you think did that to them? It wasn't the Club. My grandmother told me before she died that he had planned all along to come back, and that she always knew he would manage to do it. It's true that it's partly the Circle's fault he's back – it's partly *my* fault. And we're sorry, more sorry than you can know. But he really is here.' She paused a moment, then added in almost a whisper, 'Really.'

Aunt Constance was breathing very quickly through her nose. She drew herself up more regally than ever, her lips a thin red slash across her face.

'I'm afraid I can't believe any of what you're saying.

It is simply im—impossible—' The woman's expression changed, twisting in pain. She gave a gasp and clutched at her chest.

'Aunt Constance,' Melanie cried, rushing to her. It took both her and Adam to help the rigid woman to a chair.

'Should I call a doctor?' Diana asked.

'No!' Aunt Constance said, lifting her head. 'It's nothing. I'm all right now.'

'It's not nothing, Constance,' a quavery voice said, and Cassie saw Granny Quincey getting off the sofa to come stand beside the chair. 'It's your heart telling you the truth. I think we'd better listen to these children.'

There was a silence while Melanie's aunt looked at Melanie, then at Adam, then at Cassie. Cassie forced herself to return the piercing gaze.

Aunt Constance's eyes shut and she slowly leaned back in the chair.

'You're right,' she said, without looking at anyone. 'Come in, all of you, and find somewhere to sit down. Then you can tell your story.'

'So finally we decided we'd better talk to you three, since you were the ones who might remember him from the last time,' Diana said. 'We thought of asking our parents, too—'

'Don't go to your parents,' Aunt Constance said flatly. She had sat and listened to the whole tale, her expression getting grimmer and grimmer. An aura of bleak horror hung in the room. 'They wouldn't understand,' she said, and her gaze settled on Cassie emptily, making Cassie think of her mother's blank eyes. 'They won't remember. Dear God, how I've wished that *I* could forget too...'

'What's past is past,' Granny Quincey said.

'Yes,' said Great Aunt Constance. She straightened. 'But

I don't know how you think three old women are going to help you – against *him*.'

'We thought that you might remember something about him, some weakness; something we can use to fight him,' Adam said.

Aunt Constance slowly shook her head. Granny Quincey was frowning, her face pursed into hundreds of wrinkles. Old Mrs Franklin wore a very pleasant expression; Cassie couldn't tell if she'd been following the story or not.

'If he can come back from the dead, he can't have many weaknesses,' Aunt Constance whispered harshly. 'And he was always clever at manipulating. You say that Faye Chamberlain is on his side?'

'We're afraid so,' Adam said.

'That's bad. He'll use her to get at you, at *your* weaknesses. Lure her away from him if you can. But how?' Aunt Constance's brow lined in concentration. 'The hematite – take that from her. It's very dangerous; he can use it to influence her mind.' Diana glanced at Cassie, as if to say, *I told you*. Aunt Constance was going on. 'And you say the skull is gone now? Are you sure?'

'It's gone,' Adam said.

'It looked like it exploded when Faye was holding it, just before we were all knocked out,' Cassie said. 'Something exploded *out* of it, anyway. And we couldn't find a trace of it afterwards.'

'Well ... there's no way to use that against him, then. And you, Cassie, you haven't found anything in your grandmother's Book to help you?'

'Not yet. I haven't gotten all the way through it, though,' Cassie admitted.

Aunt Constance was shaking her head. 'Power, you need power to use against him. You're all too young to fight him – and we're too old. And in between our ages are nothing but fools. There's no power strong enough around here...'

'There was once,' Granny Quincey said in her reedy voice.

Aunt Constance looked at her, and her expression changed. 'Once ... yes, of course.' She turned to the Circle. 'If the old stories are true, there once was a power strong enough to destroy Black John.'

'What power?' Laurel asked.

Aunt Constance countered with a question. 'How did Adam happen to find the skull, exactly?'

'It wasn't an accident,' Diana said. 'He was out looking for the Master Tools ...' She stopped. 'The Master Tools,' she whispered.

'Yes. The ones that belonged to the original coven, the real Salem witches. Our ancestors who founded New Salem after the witch hunters drove them out of Salem Village.'

Cassie was speaking out loud before she thought. 'But just what *were* the Master Tools, exactly?'

It was Granny Quincey who answered. 'The symbols of the witch leader, of course. The diadem, the bracelet, and the garter.'

'The ones we use are just imitations,' Melanie said. 'They *are* just symbols. The original coven's were very powerful; real tools to be used. But, Aunt Constance' – she turned back to her aunt – 'it was Black John who hid the Master Tools. Adam's been looking for them for years, from here to Cape Cod. How can we find them now?'

'I don't know,' the woman said. 'But you've got one thing wrong there. Black John didn't hide them, the original coven did. They hid the tools *from* him, so he wouldn't be able to use them. They knew that with the power of the skull and the tools together, he would be invincible. That's what *my* grandmother told me, anyway.'

'They wouldn't have taken the tools far to hide,' Granny Quincey added. 'That's just sense. Black John was a traveller, but our ancestors weren't. They were peaceable, home-loving people.'

'You came for our advice – well, that's mine,' Aunt Constance said. 'Find the Master Tools. If you all stand together, using those, you may have a chance against him.' Her lips were a thin line again.

'All right,' Adam said slowly. 'We understand.'

Cassie let her breath out, trying not to feel disappointed. It was good advice, but she'd hoped – for what? For her own grandmother, she supposed. She wanted her grandmother, who had been so wise, and had somehow always made Cassie feel as if she were stronger than she'd thought.

'And keep reading that book your grandma gave you!' Granny Quincey said suddenly, looking right at Cassie. Cassie nodded and the old woman gave her a wrinkled but oddly intense smile.

Mrs Franklin was smiling too, patting her knees and looking around as if she'd forgotten something.

'What's tomorrow?' she said.

There was a pause. Cassie wasn't sure if Adam's grandmother was speaking to them or to herself. But then she repeated, 'What's tomorrow?' looking at them encouragingly.

'Uh – our birthday,' Chris offered.

But Diana looked startled. 'I think – I think it's the night of Hecate,' she said. 'Is that what you mean?'

'That's right,' old Mrs Franklin said comfortably. 'Oh, when I was young, we would have done a ceremony. I remember ceremonies under the moon, when there were Indians in the shadows ...'

Glances were exchanged. Mrs Franklin couldn't possibly remember that; there hadn't been Indians around here for centuries.

But Diana was getting excited. 'You think we should have a ceremony?'

'*I* would, dear,' Mrs Franklin said. 'A girls' ceremony. We girls always had our secrets, didn't we, Connie? And we stuck together.'

Diana looked a little puzzled, then nodded slowly, determinedly. 'Yes. *Yes*. It would be good for the girls to get together – *all* the girls. And I think I know what kind of ceremony to have. It's not the right time of year, but that doesn't matter.'

'I know you'll enjoy it, dear,' Mrs Franklin said. 'Now let me see – Cassie!'

Cassie looked at her, startled.

'Cassie,' Adam's grandmother said again. Her head was on one side, and she was sighing, the way you do when somebody shows you a picture of a smiling baby. 'Dear me, you are a pretty little thing, though you don't look at all like your mother. Still—' She broke off suddenly and looked around. 'Hm?'

Great Aunt Constance was looking more severe than ever, her snapping eyes right on Mrs Franklin. 'Edith,' she said, in a flat voice.

Mrs Franklin looked at Granny Quincey, who was also staring at her with great concentration.

'Why – I was only going to say I could see a bit of her mother in her expression,' she said, and nodded at Cassie pleasantly. 'You try not to worry so much, dear. It'll all come right in the end.'

Aunt Constance relaxed almost imperceptibly. 'Yes.

That's all, Melanie; you'd better take your friends away.'

And that was that. The eleven of them got up and said thank you and good-bye politely, and then they were outside the big white house in the thin November sunlight.

'Whew!' said Cassie. 'Adam, do you know what was going on there at the end?'

'Sorry,' Adam said, grimacing. 'She gets like that sometimes.'

'It wasn't her so much as the other two,' Cassie began, but Deborah broke in, impatient.

'So what's this night of Hecate thing?'

'It's the night of the crone,' Diana said. 'That's what Hecate stands for.'

'The crone?' Suzan echoed in distaste, and Cassie knew what she meant. The word conjured up an unpleasant image – a stooped, wrinkled figure holding up a poisoned apple.

'Yes.' Diana looked at Cassie. 'It's not a bad thing, Cassie. Crone just means old woman – it's the last stage in a woman's life. Maiden, mother, then crone. Crones are wise and – well, tough. Not physically, maybe, but mentally. They've seen a lot; they've been through it, and they know things. They're the ones who pass things on to us.'

'Like my grandmother,' Cassie said, understanding dawning. Of course – that stooped, wrinkled figure was the very picture of her grandmother. Not a poisoned apple, then, she thought. If her grandmother offered anything to anybody, it was help. 'Fairy tales give us the wrong idea,' she said.

'Right.' Diana nodded firmly. 'When I'm old I hope I'm a crone like your grandmother.'

'Whatever you want,' Doug said, rolling his eyes.

'They're all trying to help,' Melanie said. 'Even Aunt Constance. But what are we going to do for the night of Hecate, Diana?'

'It's a night for fortune-telling and prophecies,' Diana said, 'and we have to find a crossroads where we can celebrate it. Hecate was the Greek goddess of crossroads – they're supposed to symbolise transformation. Starting on a new passage of life. It could be old age, or death, or some other kind of change.'

'I think we're all at a crossroads,' Melanie said soberly.

'I do too.' Diana looked at Adam. 'I think your grandmother was right; this is something we girls should do. But that'll leave you guys alone...'

Adam grinned. 'Oh, I guess we could manage to amuse ourselves for one night without you. Maybe Chris and Doug have some ideas.' He spoke easily; Cassie had noticed that all the guys in the Circle were undisturbed by the girls' rights and privileges. They didn't feel threatened; they seemed to know that they were just as important, in a different way.

'But I think you should be very careful,' Nick said, without a trace of humour in his voice. Chris and Doug were punching each other, arguing about how they wanted to celebrate their birthday. When Nick spoke they shut up.

'I think you'd better find a crossroads right near here,' Nick went on, speaking to Diana and Cassie. 'And that we'd better not be too far away.'

Cassie looked into his face, saw the concern behind the careful control in his eyes. She took his hand, felt his strong fingers interlace with hers.

'We'll be careful,' she promised quietly. She saw Deborah's sharp glance at their linked hands, saw a knowing grin flash across the biker girl's face. Chris was poking Doug, who was glowering indignantly. Melanie's normally cool grey eyes were wide, and Laurel and Suzan were smiling.

Cassie couldn't help but notice that Adam was *not* smiling. He didn't smile again the rest of the day.

That night, Cassie had dreams. Swirling, formless dreams that seemed to have something to do with Books of Shadows. She and Diana had been up late, reading and studying. They hadn't found anything helpful. But in Cassie's dreams she felt she was on the verge of a momentous discovery.

She caught a glimpse of the sunlit room again. Just a swift bright flash that melted almost instantly into darkness. She found herself awake, staring around Diana's bedroom as if she might find it here.

'Cassie,' Diana murmured. 'You okay?'

'Yes,' Cassie whispered. She was glad when Diana went still again. Diana was the one who'd insisted Cassie sleep with her, worried about Cassie having nightmares. But if Cassie really started disturbing Diana she couldn't let herself stay here any more. She was enough trouble to Diana without keeping her up all night.

Actually, Cassie had slept very peacefully in the Meade house. It wasn't like Number Twelve, which had groaned and popped so much in settling that Cassie had been constantly jolted awake. Some difference in the way the houses were made, she supposed. The additions to Diana's house were much newer; perhaps they'd used better materials.

Cassie lay for a while in the warm darkness, listening to Diana's soft breathing. Where was Black John tonight? she wondered. Out there on the mainland in his rented cottage? Or here, on the island of New Salem?

For some reason thinking of New Salem as an island upset her. She felt – isolated, somehow: besieged. As if Black John could cut all of them off from the rest of the world and cast them adrift on the ocean.

Don't be silly, she told herself. But the threads of panic churning in her stomach wouldn't be stilled. She wondered suddenly if her mother wouldn't be better off in an institution – away from here. Anywhere away from here.

There's no reason for him to hurt her. It's us he hates, she thought desperately.

But he had come after her grandmother. Why? For the Book of Shadows?

I'm the one who has the Book of Shadows now, she realised with a sick lurch of heart. What if he decides to come and take it?

The thought grabbed hold of her imagination. She could feel the bed quiver with the pounding of her heart. What if Black John were to come here, now? He was a living, breathing man – but he was also a witch. Was he bound by the rules of other men? Or could he come sliding in here like a shadow, crawling along the floor towards the bed?

I have to stay calm. I have to. If I crack up, it's all over. For Mom, for the coven, for everyone. It's going to take all of us to fight him. I can't be the weak link.

'There is nothing frightening in the dark if you just face it,' she whispered to herself between clenched teeth. 'There is nothing frightening in the dark if you just face it.'

Burning tears spilled out of her eyes, but she kept on whispering her grandmother's phrase. On and on until at last she fell asleep.

* * *

The next school day began with an assembly. Faye hadn't been in her normal seat in writing class again, but as Cassie filed into the auditorium she was astonished to see the dark-haired girl up by the stage.

Faye was standing quietly, almost demurely – for Faye. She was wearing a tailored suit and looked like a very smart, very sexy secretary. Her mane of dark hair was piled up softly on her head, and she was carrying a stack of papers and a clipboard. All she needed was a pair of horn-rimmed glasses and she could have been some billionaire's girl Friday.

Cassie couldn't believe it.

She looked around the auditorium and caught sight of Suzan and Sean, who both had the same remedial-English class first period. She jerked her chin at them and they split off from their class and joined her. Suzan's blue eyes were enormous.

'Did you see Faye? What's she doing up there?'

'I don't know,' Cassie said. 'Nothing good.'

'She *looks* good,' Sean said, wetting his lips quickly. 'She looks great.'

Cassie glanced at Sean, really noticing him for the first time in a long time. Since she'd danced with him at the Halloween dance, maybe. It was so easy to overlook Sean; in a crowd he just seemed to blend in. But here, with only him and Suzan beside her, Cassie focussed.

I should pay more attention to him, she thought. An image skittered through her mind: Sean as he had appeared the first time she'd seen him. Shiny eyes, shiny belt engraved with his name. Standing by his locker full of Soloflex ads, grinning at her. Something about the picture disturbed her profoundly, but she couldn't think what.

The last of the junior and senior classes were coming

into the auditorium. Cassie saw the Henderson brothers and Deborah sitting down with their history class. There was Diana and Melanie and Laurel from British Literature, and Sally Waltman, too, with the now-familiar straw-coloured head of Portia Bainbridge next to her. She saw Adam and his chemistry class, but didn't spot Nick.

'Looks like Faye's doing a little extracurricular activity,' a voice behind her murmured, and Cassie turned gratefully. Nick nodded at the guy who was occupying the seat there, and the guy scrambled up and left. Cassie hardly noticed the occurrence, it was so common. The kids from Crowhaven Road indicated what they wanted, and the outsiders gave it to them. Always. It was the way things worked.

Nick sat in the vacated chair and took out a pack of cigarettes. He opened it, shook one forward. Then he noticed Cassie.

Cassie was staring at him with her eyebrows lifted, her best Diana expression on. Disapproval radiating from her like heat waves.

'Ah,' Nick said. He glanced at the cigarettes, then at her again. He tapped the protruding cigarette back into place and tucked the pack in his pocket.

'Bad habit,' he said.

'Testing, one, two, three ...' It was Faye's voice over the microphone. Cassie turned quickly.

'It's on,' Faye said, with a smile Cassie could only describe as kittenish. Faye moved away from the lectern, and the tall man also standing onstage walked up to it. He adjusted it, his eyes on the crowd of seated students.

'Good morning,' he said, and his voice sent waves of darkness crashing through Cassie. Every muscle in her body tightened defensively, ready to obey some deeply buried instinct to fight or flee. Just his voice, she thought dazedly, how can someone's voice alone do that?

'As some of you already know, I'm Mr Brunswick, your new principal.'

CHAPTER

7

There was a scattering of applause, hesitant, dying away quickly. Already the atmosphere in the auditorium was uncertain, alert. The usual whispers and fidgets snuffed out like candle flames, until the great room was utterly still. All eyes were on the stage.

He's a handsome man, Cassie thought, fighting the pounding in her brain that was telling her to run, run. Why did she react so violently to his presence? It was like her reaction on the night of her initiation, when Adam had produced the crystal skull. Cassie had taken one look at it and felt horror creep up her spine – to her, it seemed surrounded by a halo of darkness. It had only been later that she realised not all the coven members could see what she saw.

As Cassie looked around now, she could tell by the expressions of the other students that they didn't feel the darkness emanating from the new principal. To her, he cast a shadow across the entire auditorium. To them, he simply seemed powerful, impressive.

'I realise there has been some turmoil at New Salem High School recently,' he was saying, his eyes moving slowly up and down the rows of students. Cassie got the odd impression that he was memorising each one of them. 'But you'll be happy to know that's over now. The – unfortunate occurrences – that have plagued this school are behind us. It's time for a brand-new start.'

'Turmoil' meaning two students and one principal dead, Cassie thought. Since *you* killed all three of them, I guess you can decide when it's over. At the same time she wondered exactly how he'd managed the murders from his grave. Did the dark energy itself do it? she wondered. She wanted to whisper the question to Nick or Suzan – or Sean, her mind added hastily, guiltily – but it was hard to turn her head away from the man on the stage.

'I've heard reports that the last administration's attitude towards discipline was somewhat – lenient. A policy of, shall we say, *permissiveness* which was undoubtedly intended to be benign.' The principal glanced towards the teachers lining the auditorium walls, as if to intimate that he knew they might use other words to describe that policy, but there was no point in speaking ill of the dead. 'Certain activities were allowed which were detrimental not only to the students they affected, but also to the very spirit of formal education. Certain groups were afforded special privileges.'

What is he talking about? Cassie thought. It's like a politician; lots of fancy words and no meaning. But something inside her was sinking in dismay.

'Well, the policy has changed now, and I think in the end most of you will be pleased with the changes. There's a new hand on the tiller of this boat.' The principal held up one hand with a slight, self-deprecating smile.

Then he started talking again. Afterwards Cassie could never remember exactly what he said, but she remembered his voice, deep, authoritative. Commanding. There were buzzwords scattered through his speech: 'tough love,' 'old-fashioned discipline,' 'punishment fitting the crime'. She could feel the response from the audience: dark, dark. Like something swelling and growing in the crowd. It frightened her almost more than Black John himself. It was as if he were feeding and cultivating some horrible power inside the students. They should have hated him, but instead they were enthralled.

The rules. The rules must be obeyed. Students who didn't obey the rules would be *sent to the office ...*

'I think it's time for the handout now,' Jack Brunswick added in a soft aside, and Faye and several other girls moved down from the stage, passing out papers. Cassie watched the principal as he watched the audience, standing at ease, commanding their attention effortlessly even when he wasn't speaking. Yes, handsome, she thought. He looked something like a young Sherlock Holmes: deep-set eyes, hawk nose, firm mouth. His voice even had traces of an English accent. Cultured, thought Cassie. Cultured – and full of conviction.

More like a witch hunter than a witch.

Faye reached Cassie's row, thrust a sheaf of papers at her. Cassie whispered 'Faye!' and was rewarded by a swift flash of golden eyes before Faye moved on. Bewildered, Cassie took one handout and passed the rest to Suzan. It was three pages long and covered with small type.

Prohibited Actions – Type A. Prohibited Actions – Type B. Prohibited Actions – Type C.

It was a list of rules. But so many rules, line after line after line. Her eyes caught words here and there.

Wearing clothing inconsistent with the serious and dignified purpose of formal education ... using a locker or being in the corridors at any time other than the passing period between classes ... possession or use of squirt guns ... littering ... running in the halls ... chewing gum ... failing to comply with an order from any teacher or hall monitor ...

Hall monitors? Cassie thought. We don't have hall monitors. Her eyes skimmed on.

Public displays of affection ... failing to recycle styrofoam lunch trays ... placing feet on seats or chair backs ...

'They can't be serious,' Suzan whispered. There was a faint whistle from Nick.

'You'll have time in class to go over these guidelines and become thoroughly familiar with them,' the new principal said. In the corner of Cassie's eye she saw rows of heads lifting. The rustling of paper stilled.

'Right now I'd like to ask for volunteers to be hall monitors. This is a position of great responsibility, so please think carefully before you raise your hand.'

Hands flew up all over the auditorium. The students at New Salem High had never volunteered so fast for anything. Cassie saw Portia, rigid and trembling like a hound dog pointing in the air. Sally, in the next seat, was waving madly, like a third-grader dying to get called on by the teacher. The room was like one giant Nazi salute.

Black John's eyes moved up and down, scanning them, examining each one.

Then Cassie realised that Sean's hand was going up.

'Sean!' she hissed. The auditorium was so quiet she didn't dare speak loudly. Suzan glanced at Sean, then shrank back from him. He was out of Nick's reach. 'Sean!' she said.

He didn't seem to hear her. His shiny eyes were fixed on the stage. His face was eager, tense.

Desperation tingled in the palms of Cassie's hands. She reached across Suzan to grab his left arm, and

with all the power she could summon up, thought:
Sean!

She felt it go out of her like a blast of heat, just as she'd
felt it when she was facing the pumpkin-patch dog. A
burst of pure power. Sean's head snapped towards her,
his expression full of astonishment.

'*Put your hand down*,' she whispered, feeling shaky
and exhausted in the aftermath. Sean looked at
his hand as if he'd never seen it before and hastily
snatched it down. He gripped the seat of his chair, eyes
still sideways on Cassie.

Now Suzan was cringing away from *her*, Cassie realised.
Both the strawberry-blonde and Sean looked scared.
Cassie looked towards the stage and saw the new principal
looking directly at her, his lips curved in a faint smile.

Great. *He* likes it, and my own friends are afraid of
me.

Black John continued to gaze at her steadily for a
moment, then turned the slight smile on the rest of the
auditorium.

'Very good. Those of you who've been chosen will
please remain after the assembly to learn about your new
duties. The rest are dismissed. Good morning.

Hairs lifted on the back of Cassie's neck. 'Chosen?'
she whispered, looking around. There hadn't been any
selection. But some of the students who'd had hands
up were moving to the stage in a quiet, orderly manner.
Portia and Sally were among them.

Don't you see? You've got to see now how strange
this is, Cassie thought, twisting to look at Mr Humphries
standing in the aisle. But Mr Humphries didn't seem to
find anything unusual about the proceedings. He looked
calm and rather pleased as he motioned his class out.
Tranquillised, Cassie thought, shivering. Hypnotised.

Black John was still standing at the lectern. She could feel his eyes on her back as she walked out of the auditorium.

Cassie fell back as her writing class walked down the hall, slowing to stay with Nick and Suzan and Sean. Suzan and Sean looked at her oddly, but Nick put his arm around her.

'That was pretty good,' he said softly. Cassie felt better, until she noticed he didn't have his handout.

'I left it on the seat,' he said, and Cassie's heart sank a little further.

That's littering,' she said. 'And littering's a Type-A offence. Nick, we've got to be careful – he's out to get us.'

'No kidding,' Adam said, joining them. His blue-grey eyes flickered once over Nick's arm around Cassie's shoulders, but his expression didn't change. 'Have you read over the Prohibited Actions, Type C?'

Cassie hadn't. She thumbed to the last page of the handout and looked. 'Skateboarding, roller-skating, or bike riding ... playing or wearing radios on school grounds ... smoking or using tobacco products ... these are supposed to be worse than Type-B offences like using drugs or fighting?'

'They seem to be a little specifically directed,' Adam said grimly.

And then Cassie knew. She remembered her very first day of school at New Salem High, nearly being knocked off her feet by the Henderson brothers – only at the time she didn't know it was the Henderson brothers. She'd only seen two crazy guys with heavy-metal T-shirts and dishevelled blond hair, rollerblading down the halls and listening to Walkmans.

She swallowed hard. 'They're for *us*,' she whispered.

Adam met her eyes, nodding.

'Smoking,' Cassie said. She clutched Nick's hand, turning to look him full in the face. 'Nick, please, you've got to be careful. He wants to get us and we're not ready to confront him yet ... Nick!' She had a terrible feeling about this. Nick hated authority, took any rules as a challenge. Right now she didn't see any sign of him changing, by his expression. 'Nick!'

'Punishment for Type-C offences is getting sent to the office,' Adam said. 'He *is* trying to get us, Nick. He's playing his own little game.'

'Nick, I want you to promise me you'll try not to get in trouble,' Cassie said. 'Please, Nick. You have to promise.'

Nick looked down at her slowly. Cassie tightened her grip on his hand, returning the intensity of his gaze. Please, she was thinking. For me, please.

Nick's brow furrowed and he turned away.

'Okay,' he said, nodding slightly, eyes on the ceiling. 'Okay, I'll try – not to get caught.'

Cassie's muscles relaxed. 'Thank you,' she whispered, just as Diana, Melanie, and Laurel came up, faces bleak.

'Did you get that stuff in the beginning, about the previous administration allowing certain activities to go on?' Melanie asked. 'That was *us* he was talking about. The Club and its special privileges. He said all that was going to change now.'

Cassie spoke softly. 'He was telling them we're not in power any more. He was as good as giving them permission to...'

Her voice died away. She and the other members of the Club looked at one another silently.

'Everybody get your guns. Sounds like it's open season

for witches,' Nick said finally. He put his arm around Cassie again.

'Let's get out of here,' Suzan said.

'We can't,' said Laurel. 'Leaving school grounds without permission is an offence.'

'*Everything* is an offence,' Suzan said.

'Where are Chris and Doug?' Cassie asked sharply. 'And Deborah?'

Everyone looked around. Aside from Nick, the Henderson brothers and the biker were the ones most likely to get into trouble.

'They have history first period, but I think their class went back without them,' Sean volunteered. 'I think they're still in the auditorium.'

'Come on,' said Adam briefly.

Chris and Doug were just outside the auditorium. They were in the centre of a group of outsider students and they were getting ready to fight.

'—not gonna get away with it any more,' one of the outsider boys was carolling triumphantly.

'Oh, yeah?' Chris yelled back.

'Yeah! Your days are over, man! You're gonna get *sent to the office*.'

'Didn't take them long to catch on,' Nick murmured in Cassie's ear.

'You're all going to get sent to the office,' Adam said, pushing between the outsiders to get to Chris and Doug. He faced them, holding up the handout like a magic talisman. 'Fighting's a Type-B offence. You'll *all* go down for it.'

There was a moment of uncertainty, then the outsiders drew back, eyeing each other.

'We'll see you later,' they decided finally, and turned down the hall. Doug tried to go after them.

'Any time, any place,' he yelled as Nick caught him and held him still. 'Leggo of me!' he snarled at Nick.

'We can't afford a confrontation yet,' Diana told him. 'Good job,' she added to Adam.

'It worked – this time,' Adam said. 'If I'm right about what he's doing, they'll eventually figure out that the rules are mainly against *us*. They may not get in trouble for fighting, but we will.'

To Cassie's vast relief Deborah came around the corner at that moment. 'Deb, where have you been?'

'Watching the hall monitors get their orders. They're giving them badges like SS men.'

'It *is* like the Nazis,' Cassie said.

'He's organising a witch hunt,' said Adam.

'I wonder if he's done it before,' Suzan said.

Cassie started to say, 'What do you mean?' but stopped in the middle of it and stared at her. Suzan, who looked so – fluffy, so brainless, who even now was groping in her purse for a compact, had done it again.

'And Faye is working for him—' Diana was saying. Cassie interrupted.

'No, wait, listen. Did you hear what Suzan just said? Don't you get it? *I wonder if he's done it before*. You know, I'll bet he has.'

'In 1692,' Adam said slowly. 'In Salem. How could we be so stupid?'

'Huh?' said Chris.

I think they're saying that Black John could have organised the Salem witch hunt,' Diana said. 'But—'

'Not organised, maybe, but contributed, helped it along,' Cassie said. 'Made sure it didn't just die out, fed the hysteria. Like he was feeding it today.'

'But *why*?' asked Laurel.

There was a silence, then Adam lifted his head, his

frown clearing. His voice was grim. 'To get the coven to leave. To follow *him*. They couldn't hang around in that atmosphere any more, so they followed him to New Salem, with all their tools – including the Master Tools.'

'You told me that he was a leader of the original coven,' Cassie said. 'But I wonder if he was a leader before the coven moved to New Salem – or only after.'

The faces of the Circle members were very sober.

'I think he's trying to do the same thing again,' Adam said. 'Turn everybody against us so we don't have anywhere else to go – but to him. He's the only one who can defend us.'

'He can go to hell,' Deborah said, as if this ought to be obvious.

'Yeah, well, I'm sure he doesn't think we're going to come crawling to him right now,' Nick murmured. 'Things may look a little different in a couple of weeks.'

'I think we'd better have a talk with Faye,' Diana said.

They lay in wait for Faye by the back entrance of the auditorium, where Deborah thought she was most likely to come out. When she did she had the clipboard on her arm.

'Alone at last,' Nick said, and they surrounded her, the eleven of them, forcing her to a stop. Looking at the faces of the Circle members right then, Cassie was reminded of the way Faye, Deborah, and Suzan had looked when they had caught her spying on them in front of the school. Beautiful, focussed, and deadly. Dangerous.

Faye looked around at them and tossed her head. It didn't work as well with her hair gathered up in a bun.

'Get out of my way. I have work to do,' she said.

'For him?' Adam asked tightly. Diana laid a hand on his arm and spoke herself.

'Faye, we know you can't talk now. But we're going to have a ceremony tonight, because it's the night of Hecate—'

'And our birthday,' Chris put in, aggrieved.

'—and we want you to be there.'

'*You're* going to have a ceremony?' Faye said, looking less like a rich man's girl Friday and more like her old self, the black panther. 'You can't. I'm the coven leader.'

'How can you be the coven leader when you're never even with the coven? We're going to have this ceremony tonight, Faye, at the crossroads of Crowhaven and Marsh Street. With or without you. If you're there, you're welcome to lead it.'

Faye looked for backing from Deborah and Suzan, her age-old supporters. But the biker's petite face was set in a hard scowl and Suzan's china-blue eyes were blank. No help was coming from that quarter.

'Traitors,' Faye said contemptuously. Her beautiful, sulky mouth pinched, but she said, 'I'll be there – to *lead* the ceremony. Now you'd better get out of here before a hall monitor spots you.'

She turned and stalked away.

They all managed to get through that day without serious trouble, although Suzan received a detention for not throwing away a cupcake wrapper. Not for leaving it at a table or anything, just for not throwing it away as soon as she was done eating. It was a Type-A infraction.

That night they celebrated the Henderson brothers' birthday quietly, at Adam's house. Chris and Doug were extremely disappointed. They wanted a beach party with skinny-dipping. 'And all kinds of wildness,' Chris said. Adam said it was this or nothing.

Faye showed up around ten, wearing the black raw-silk shift she'd worn the night of the leadership vote. 'In my day it was white,' old Mrs Franklin chuckled, leading her into the untidy living room with its comfortable, shabby furniture. 'But times change.'

Faye didn't even answer her. 'I'm here,' she said with a haughty glance around. 'Let's go.'

Cassie studied the silver diadem nestled in Faye's midnight-dark hair, the silver bracelet on Faye's rounded arm, and the garter, made of green leather lined with sky-blue silk, on Faye's thigh. She wondered what the real ones, the ones used by the original coven, looked like.

There wasn't much talking as the seven girls walked slowly down Crowhaven Road. Diana and Faye were in the lead, and Cassie heard Diana speaking in a low voice. The blonde girl was carrying a white bag that held the things necessary for casting a circle and beginning a meeting.

They reached the crossroads. 'It has to be a junction where three roads diverge,' Diana had said, 'to symbolise the three stages of womanhood: maiden, mother, and crone.' Here Marsh Street met Crowhaven Road running north and south.

'Do we have to be right *in* the road?' Suzan said now. 'What if somebody comes driving up?'

'We get out of the way, fast,' said Laurel.

'I think we're safe,' Diana said. 'There aren't many cars this late. Come on, you guys, it's cold.'

'It's my ceremony,' Faye reminded her, taking out the ritual black-handled knife.

'I never said it wasn't,' Diana said quietly. She stepped back to watch Faye cast the circle. Cassie felt blood burning in her own face as she stood behind Diana, watching Faye do what Diana had always done, what Diana would still be doing – if not for Cassie. She wanted to whisper something to Diana but instead she just made the promise in her own heart.

Somehow I'll make things right. Faye won't be the leader forever. Whatever I have to do, I'll see to that, she thought. She added, almost absently, I swear by Earth, Water, Fire, and Air.

CHAPTER
8

Faye drew a circle on the road with the black-handled knife. Then she went around the circle with water sprinkled from a cup, then with a long stick of incense, then with a lighted candle. Symbolising the elements Cassie had named: Earth, Water, Air, and Fire. The sweet, pungent smell of the incense drifted to Cassie on the cool night air.

'All right, come inside,' Faye said. They filed into the circle through a gap which faced north-east, and sat down around the inner perimeter. It was strange to see only the faces of girls around the circle, Cassie thought.

'Do you want to explain or shall I?' Diana asked Faye, her hand on the white bag. There was still something inside it.

'Oh, you can *explain*,' Faye said negligently.

'All right. We each take a candle, you see, and light it, and put it in a circle in the middle. And we each say a word, naming one of the aspects of womanhood. Not the stages, you know, like maiden, mother, and crone, but a quality. A—'

'Virtue,' Melanie helped her out.

'Right. A virtue. Something that women have. Then, when we get all of them together, we show the candles to the elements and get their blessing. It's an affirmation of what we girls are, sort of; a celebration.'

'I think that's lovely,' Cassie said softly.

'All right; let's do it. Who wants red, or do I need to ask?' Diana took a red candle out of the bag. Very faintly, Cassie thought she caught the warm, spicy scent of cinnamon.

'Me. I'm red,' Faye said. She turned the candle over in her hands, examining its smooth waxiness. She held it upright and cupped a hand swiftly around the wick. Cassie saw the flame spring into being, shining through Faye's fingers so they looked like pink shells, turning Faye's long red nails into jewels.

Diana, who had been holding a pack of matches towards Faye, put them down.

'Passion,' Faye said throatily, smiling her old, slow smile around the group as she dripped wax on the road and stuck the candle in it.

'Is that a virtue?' Melanie asked sceptically.

Faye raised an eyebrow. 'It's an aspect of womanhood. It's the one I want to celebrate.'

'Let her have it,' Laurel said. 'Passion's okay.'

The red candle burned like a star.

'Next comes orange,' said Diana. 'Who wants that?'

'I'll take it,' Suzan said. The orange candle was close to the titian of Suzan's own hair. Suzan sniffed at it.

'Peaches,' she said, and Cassie could smell the sweet, voluptuous fragrance from where she sat. 'All right: beauty,' Suzan said. She lit her candle in the conventional manner, with a match.

'Beauty *definitely* isn't—'

'Well, it's not a virtue, but it's something women have,'

Cassie argued. Melanie rolled her eyes. Suzan stuck the orange candle in its own wax on the road, beside the red one.

'Here, let me go next. *I* know how to do this,' Deborah said. She snatched up the white sack and rummaged in it, coming out with a yellow candle.

'Matches,' she said commandingly to Suzan, who put them in her outstretched palm. Deborah lit the yellow candle.

'Courage,' she said, clearly and distinctly, tilting the candle so a transparent stream of yellow wax ran onto the road. Cassie smelled a clean lemony sharpness and thought that it smelled like Deborah, like courage. The flame of the yellow candle lit Deborah's dark hair and flickered madly off her leather jacket as it burned by the other two.

'Okay, green,' Diana said, retrieving the bag.

'Me,' said Melanie, and took the dark green candle. She was sitting right beside Cassie and Cassie leaned in to smell the wax when Melanie did. It was scented with something woodsy: pine, Cassie decided. Like a Christmas tree.

'Wisdom,' said Melanie, her cool grey eyes steady as she lit the wick. She breathed in the scent for a moment, then placed the green candle on the road. The four burning candles formed a semicircle.

'Now blue,' said Diana. Cassie felt a jolt of nervousness and excitement. Blue was her favourite colour, and she wanted it, but she wasn't quite sure she ought to speak out. Still, Diana and Laurel weren't saying anything, and she remembered that Laurel liked amethysts and often wore purple. Cassie cleared her throat.

'I'll take it,' she said, and reached for the pale blue candle Diana offered. She was very pleased to have it, to represent blue in the coven's rainbow – but she hadn't thought of anything to say. What's blue like? she asked herself, sniffing at the candle to gain time. What virtue do girls have that I want to celebrate?

She couldn't quite identify the scent, which was sweet but sharp. 'It's bayberry,' Melanie told her, as Cassie kept sniffing. 'A smell with a history. The colonists all used to make bayberry candles.'

'Oh.' Maybe that was why it smelled familiar. Maybe her grandmother had burned bayberry candles – her grandmother had done a lot of old-fashioned things. Cassie knew what virtue she wanted to celebrate now.

'Inspiration,' she said. 'That's imagination – or like the flash of an idea, you know. When my grandmother was helping make my muse outfit for Halloween, she said that's what the muses were for. They gave people inspiration, the ability to think of new things, to have brilliant ideas. And they were female, the muses.'

Cassie hadn't meant to make a speech, and she looked down, embarrassed. I didn't get the matches, she realised – and then she had an inspiration. Cupping her hand around the candlewick as Faye had, she concentrated hard, thinking of fire, bright leaping fire – then she *pushed* with her mind, the way she had with the Doberman and with Sean. She felt the power leave her like a blast of heat and focus on the wick and suddenly a flame shot up, so high that she had to jerk her hand away to keep from getting burned.

'An idea – just like that,' she said, a little shaken, and she dripped wax on the road to stick the blue candle in. The other girls were looking at her wide-eyed, except Faye, whose eyes were narrow and hooded.

Deborah grinned. 'I guess we've got more than one

fire-handler around here,' she said. Faye looked even less amused.

'Ah – purple,' Diana said, giving herself a little shake and taking a lavender candle from the bag.

'That's me. How did you *do* that, Cassie? All right; I'm going on with the ceremony. I just wanted to know,' Laurel said. She looked at her candle. 'I don't know how to get mine into one word,' she said. 'I wanted, to do environmental awareness – sort of like, *connectedness* to all things. We're a part of the earth and we should care about all the other things that live here with us.'

'What about "compassion"?' Melanie said quietly. 'That would cover it, I think.'

'That's good; compassion.' Laurel lit the purple candle.

'What's it smell like?' Suzan whispered as Laurel stuck the candle in the road between Cassie's blue candle and Faye's red one, completing the rainbow circle.

'It's sweet and floral; I think it's supposed to be hyacinth,' Laurel whispered back.

'Wait,' Cassie said. 'If it goes there, what about Diana? Don't you get a candle, Diana?' She felt jealous on Diana's behalf, she wanted the blonde girl to have a turn too.

'Yes: white goes in the middle, and I'm the only one left to do it.' And it's perfect, Cassie thought, watching Diana take out the vanilla-scented white candle and hold it up. Diana represented white as surely as Faye did red.

It showed in the virtue Diana named, too. 'Purity,' she said simply, lighting the white candle with a match and reaching into the circle of candles to place it in the centre. Anybody else would have sounded ridiculous saying it, but Diana looked like the embodiment of purity sitting there, her beautiful face lit by the candles, her silky straight hair of that impossible colour falling down her back. Her expression was serious and unself-conscious. When Diana said purity she *meant* purity, and not even Faye dared to snicker.

The circle of candles was pretty; seven tongues of flame leaping and dancing in the night air; seven scents mingling into one delicious composite fragrance. Eddies in the breeze seemed to bring the smell of cinnamon to Cassie, then a whiff of pine, then the sharpness of lemon.

'Passion, beauty, courage, wisdom, inspiration, compassion, and purity,' Laurel ticked off, pointing to the candles that represented each.

'Let us all ...' Diana prompted, nudging Faye.

'Let us all have all of them,' Faye said. 'Earth, Water, Fire, Air, witness. Not that we don't have them already,' she added, regarding the glowing circle with a satisfied smile. Laurel's eyes twinkled at Cassie from across the flames and Cassie let her own eyes twinkle back.

'Well, anyway, we have all of them if you count all of *us*,' Deborah said, and grinned. Diana smiled her gentle smile. For a moment, all the girls were smiling at each other over the candles, and Cassie felt as if they were a part of something bigger. Each of them contributed something important, and together they were more than just the sum of the parts.

'Now we're supposed to let them burn all night,' Melanie said, nodding at the candles.

'What if somebody runs them over?' Suzan asked pragmatically.

'Well, I guess if we don't see it, it doesn't matter,' Diana said. 'Wait, though, there's something else I wanted to do. It's not part of the night of Hecate, but it's another Greek thing, the Arretophoria. It means the trust festival.' She reached into the white bag again. 'The Greek priestesses of Athena used to do this. It's where one of the older members of the group – that's me – gives a box to the youngest member – that's you, Cassie. You have to go bury the box somewhere without looking at what's inside it. It's supposed to be a dark and perilous journey you go on, but I think Nick's right and you'd better stick around here. Just take it off the road somewhere and bury it.'

'And that's all?' Cassie looked at the box Diana had given her. It was made of some light-coloured wood, carved all over with tiny, intricate figures: bees and bears and fish. Something inside it rattled. 'I just bury it?'

'That's all,' Diana said, handing Cassie the last item from the white bag: a small trowel. 'The point is that you don't look inside it. That's why it's called the trust festival; it's a celebration of trust and responsibility and friendship. Someday later we'll come back and dig it up.'

'Okay.' Carrying the box and trowel, Cassie stepped outside the circle and walked away from the group, leaving the little dancing points of flame behind.

She didn't want to bury the box close to the road. For one thing, the soil was hard and strewn with gravel; it wouldn't be easy to dig here; she'd just be scratching at the surface. Besides, this close someone might see the ground had been disturbed and dig the box up before its time.

Cassie kept walking east. She could hear the whispering of the sea from that direction and feel a faint, salty breeze. She climbed over some large rocks, and the beach stretched out before her, deserted and somehow eerie. Lacy white waves were lapping quietly at the shore.

A yellow moon, just over half full, was rising above the ocean. The mourning moon, Cassie remembered. It was just the colour of Faye's eyes. In fact, it looked like a jaundiced, ancient eye, and Cassie had the uncomfortable sense of being spied on as she stuck the trowel into the cold dry sand and began to dig.

That was deep enough. The sand scooped out by the trowel was caked now, and she hoped the moisture wouldn't ruin Diana's box. As Cassie put the wooden box in the hole, moonlight glinted off the brass hasp. It wasn't locked. For just an instant, she had the temptation to open it.

Don't be *stupid*, she told herself. After all you and Diana have been through, if you can't do a little thing like bury a box without looking inside...

Nobody would know, the voice in her mind countered defensively.

I would know, Cassie told the voice. So there. She dumped sand on the box decisively, scooping with both the trowel and her hand to cover it faster.

It was sometime while she was covering the box that she noticed the blackness.

It's just a shadow, she thought. The moon was high enough now to throw a long shadow behind an outcrop of rock which was closer to the water than Cassie. Cassie watched it out of the corner of her eye as she smoothed the sand over the buried box. There, now you'd never know anything was hidden here. The shadow was stretching closer, but that was just because the moon was rising...

Wrong, Cassie thought. She stopped in the middle of brushing sand off her hands and looked at it.

Shadows get *shorter* as the moon gets higher. Just like the sun, she thought. But this one was definitely closer to her.

The whispering of the ocean was suddenly loud.

I should have listened to Diana. I should have stayed near the group, Cassie thought. Slowly and casually, she glanced over her shoulder. The rocks she'd climbed over seemed far away, and there was no sign of the circle of candles behind them. No sound either, except the waves. Cassie felt exposed and very much alone.

Don't act scared. Get up and go, she told herself. Her heart was knocking against her ribs. As she stood, the shadow moved.

Oh *God*. There was no way to pretend that was normal. The shadow wasn't even attached to the rock any more. It was just a blackness on the sand, flowing like water, moving towards her. It was alive.

Go, go! Cassie's mind screamed at her. But her legs wouldn't obey. They were locked, paralysed. She wasn't going anywhere.

Cassssie. Her head jerked up; she looked for the person who had spoken. But it wasn't a person. It was the waves.

Casssssssie.

I want to get out of here, Cassie thought. Her legs still wouldn't move.

The blackness flowed like tar, rippling towards her. It divided, pouring itself on either side of her, encircling her.

Casssssssie.

The shadow was whispering to her with Black John's voice. It eddied around her, a formless darkness like smoke. As she looked down at it, Cassie seemed to see snakes in it, and black beetles, all crawling loathsome things. It was around her, but it didn't want to kill her. It wanted to get into her mind.

She could *feel* it trying. A pressure as it swirled around her feet. All she could think was, thank God I don't still have the hematite.

I should have listened; why didn't I listen? she thought then. The girls wouldn't miss her for a while. Too long. She wanted to scream, but her throat was as paralysed as her legs. She could only stand there and watch the rippling blackness swirl around her feet.

Push with your mind, she thought, but she was too frightened. She couldn't scare away this darkness the way she had the Doberman. She wasn't strong enough.

Please help me, she thought.

And then, in a rush, it was all she was thinking. Oh please somebody help me, somebody please come, I can't get out of this myself, oh please *somebody*—

Cassssssie, the whisper came. The waves and the darkness and the watching moon all seemed to be saying it.

Help me . . .

'Cassie!' It was a shout, not a whisper, and behind it Cassie heard a dog barking. At the sound, Cassie's mind was flooded with images of safety, of comfort. She looked around frantically. Her legs still wouldn't move.

'I'm here!' she shouted back. Even as she called, she felt herself released. The black was edging away, retreating to the rock. Merging with the real shadow there.

'Cassie!' The voice was familiar, loved.

'I'm here,' Cassie called again, stumbling towards it. The visions of comfort and safety and closeness were still whirling inside her, pulling her. She followed them. Just as she reached the rocks, strong arms caught her up, held her tightly. She felt the warmth of a human body against her.

Over Nick's shoulder, she met Adam's eyes.

The moon was shining full in his face, turning those eyes odd colours, blue-violet like the bottom of a flame. Like the sky before some strange storm. She thought she could see silver reflecting in his pupils. Raj bounded up beside him, still barking. The German shepherd's tail was waving frantically as he headed for Cassie. Adam caught him by the ruff and held him back.

'Are you okay? Are you hurt?' Nick said in her ear.

'No. I'm all right,' she whispered. She didn't know what she was saying.

'You shouldn't have gone off by yourself,' Nick said angrily. 'They shouldn't have let you do it.'

'It's okay, Nick.' She hung on to him with all her strength and buried her face in his shoulder just as Adam turned, leading the reluctant Raj away. Then she clung there, knowing he could feel her shaking.

'Cassie.' He stroked her back soothingly.

Cassie pulled back slightly. Adam was gone. She looked at Nick in the moonlight, at the clean carven handsomeness of his features with their hint of coldness. Except his eyes weren't cold now.

Passion, she thought and brought up Faye's red candle in her mind. Then she kissed him.

She'd never really kissed anybody besides Adam, but she guessed she knew how to do it well enough. Nick's mouth was warm, and that was nice. She felt how startled he was, and then instantly felt the surprise swept away by something deeper, sweeter. She felt him kissing her back.

She kissed not to think. Kissing was good for that. Suzan had been dead wrong about Nick. He wasn't an iguana. Little lines of fire ran along Cassie's nerves, tingling her fingers. She felt warm all over.

Eventually, they both broke it. Cassie looked up at him, her fingers still intermeshed with his.

'Sorry,' she said unsteadily. 'I was just scared.'

'Remind me to get you scared frequently,' Nick said. He looked slightly dazed.

'We'd better go back. Black John was here.'

She had to give Nick credit; he didn't yell *'What?'* and shake her. He cast a quick, hunting look around, switching his grip on her so that he was holding her arm with his left hand and his right hand was free.

'He's gone now,' she said. 'There was a shadow that came out from that rock, but it's not there any more.'

'After this, nobody goes out alone,' Nick said, guiding her towards the rocks they had to climb to get back to the crossroads.

'I think he was trying to get into my mind,' Cassie told the others when they were all back at Adam's house again. She sat beside Nick, holding tightly to his hand. 'To influence me, or take me over, or whatever. I didn't know how to stop him. If you guys hadn't come, he would have done it.'

'Nobody should be out by themselves any more,' Nick said, with a hard glance at Diana. It was unlike Nick to say anything at meetings, but now his voice was decisive, not to be argued with.

'I agree,' said Melanie. 'Moreover, I think we should do something to defend ourselves, to put up some kind of shield against him.'

'What did you have in mind?' Adam asked her. He was sitting on the arm of Diana's chair, his face calm, his voice steady.

'Some kind of crystal might help. Amethyst, maybe. It should help us to focus and fight against him, against any psychic attack. Of course, if anyone were simultaneously wearing another crystal that he could use against them – like hematite – it wouldn't do any good.' Melanie was looking at Faye.

Faye made an impatient gesture. 'As I've already told my interfering cousin, I don't have any stupid hematite.

I don't have to steal other people's crystals.'

'All right; we won't argue,' Diana said. 'Melanie, do you have enough amethysts at your place? Or can you lend us some, Laurel? I think we should get them ready immediately, so everybody can wear them home tonight.'

'Yes, and keep them on all the time,' Melanie said. 'When you take a bath, when you go to sleep, at school, whatever. But wear them under your clothes; don't let him see the crystals, if possible. They'll be more effective that way.'

'What a way to end a party,' Doug groused, as he picked up his jacket.

'Think of it as a party favour,' Nick replied unsympathetically. 'A memento.' He squeezed Cassie's fingers quickly with a sideways glance, as if to say he knew what *he* would be remembering.

Cassie felt warmed by that. But as they were leaving for Melanie's house she asked casually, 'By the way, why *did* you guys come after me?'

'Yeah, did you get bored with the party or something? Found out you couldn't deal all by yourselves, so you had to find us girls?' Deborah put in, her dark eyes flashing at Chris.

Chris looked at her oddly. 'No, we were dealin' fine. It was Adam who told us to come. He said Cassie was in trouble.'

CHAPTER
9

Cassie's piece of amethyst was quite large. It was a pendant, hanging from the claws of a silver owl with outspread wings, and it felt cool against Cassie's chest under her blue and white sweater. She checked in Diana's mirror to make sure it didn't make a bump and then touched it nervously. Cassie had had three stones so far: the chalcedony rose Adam had given her, the quartz necklace Melanie had put around her neck at the Homecoming dance, and the piece of hematite she'd found at Number Thirteen. She hadn't kept any of them long. The chalcedony she'd had to give back to Adam, the quartz had been lost that same night at the burying ground, and the hematite had been stolen. She just hoped nothing was going to happen to this amethyst.

Clouds had gathered in the night, and the sky was steely-grey as Diana drove them to school that morning. And school these days was about as bleak as the weather. Hall monitors, wearing badges and wintry expressions, stood in every corridor waiting for someone to break the rules. Which usually didn't take very long; there were so many rules that it was impossible not to break one or two just by being alive.

'We almost got sent up for wearing a noise-makin' device,' Chris said as they were walking down the hall at lunchtime.

Cassie tensed. 'What did you do?'

'Bribed him,' Doug said with a wicked grin. 'We gave him a Walkman.'

'*My* Walkman,' Chris said, aggrieved.

'I wonder what the penalty for bribing a hall monitor is?' Laurel mused as they reached the cafeteria.

Cassie opened her mouth, but the words froze on her lips. Through the glass windows of the cafeteria she could see something that wiped all thought from her mind.

'Oh *God*,' said Laurel.

'I don't believe it,' Diana whispered.

'I do,' Adam said.

In the very centre of the cafeteria was a wooden structure that Cassie recognised from her history books. It was made in two parts, which when closed held a person's wrists and neck securely in place, protruding through holes from the other side.

The stocks.

And they were occupied.

There was a guy inside them, a big husky guy Cassie recognised from her algebra class. He'd danced with her at Homecoming, and he'd been overly familiar with his hands. He liked to talk back to teachers, too. But she'd never seen him do anything deserving of *this*.

'He won't get away with it,' Diana was saying, her green eyes blazing with intensity.

'Who, the principal?' Deborah asked. She and Suzan and Nick were standing by the cafeteria door, waiting for the others. 'He already has. He was taking some parents on a guided tour a few minutes ago and they came through here ... he *showed* it to them, for God's sake. Said it was part of a "tough love" programme. Said other schools made troublemakers stand on tables so everybody could look at them, but that he thought the stocks were more humane because you could sit down. He almost made it sound *reasonable*. And they were just nodding and smiling – they ate it up.'

Cassie felt queasy. She was thinking of the Witch Dungeon at Salem, where she and Chris and Doug had scuttled through narrow corridors lined with tiny dark cells. The stocks gave her the same sick feeling in her stomach. How can people do this to other people? she thought.

'—passing it off as part of our heritage,' Nick was saying, his lip curled in disgust, and Cassie knew he felt the same way.

'Can we talk about it while we eat?' Suzan asked, shifting from one foot to the other. 'I'm starving.'

But as they made their way towards the back room – the private domain of the Club for the last four years – a short figure with rusty hair stepped in front of them.

'Sorry,' Sally Waltman smirked. 'That room is for hall monitors only, now.'

'Oh, yeah?' said Deborah.

Two guys with badges appeared from nowhere and stood on either side of Sally.

'Yeah,' one of them said.

Cassie looked through the glass windows of the back room – there was no crowd of hangers-on standing in front of it today – and saw Portia's tawny head. She was surrounded by girls and guys who were looking at her admiringly. They all wore badges.

'You'll just have to sit somewhere else,' Sally was

telling the Club. 'And since there aren't enough seats at any one table, you'll have to break your group up. What a shame.'

'We'll go outside,' Nick said shortly, taking Cassie's arm.

Sally laughed. 'I don't think so. No more eating out front. If you can't find a place to sit in here, you stand.'

Cassie could feel Nick's muscles cord. She held on to his arm tightly. Diana had a similar hold on Adam, whose blue-grey eyes were like chips of steel, fixed on the guys beside Sally.

'It's not worth it,' Diana said quietly, with forced calm. 'It's what he wants. Let's go stand over there.'

Sally looked disappointed as they all started to move to the wall. Then triumph flashed in her eyes.

'*He's* in violation already,' she said, pointing to Doug. 'He's wearing a radio.'

'It's not on,' Doug said.

'It doesn't have to be. Just wearing it is a Type-A offence. Come with me, please.' The two guys surged forward to help Doug come.

'Nick, don't. Wait—' Cassie gasped, getting in front of him. A fight in the cafeteria was all they needed.

Doug's eyes were glittering wildly. He looked mad enough to hit Sally, not to mention the two guys.

'Bring him,' Sally said in an exultant voice. The guys reached for Doug. Doug's fist jerked back. And then a throaty voice cut through the confusion.

'What's going on here?' Faye said, her amber eyes smouldering. She was wearing another of the little business suits; this one black and yellow.

Sally glared at her. 'They're refusing to comply with the orders of a hall monitor,' she said. 'And *he's* wearing a radio.'

Faye reached over and unhooked the Walkman from Doug's belt. 'Now he's not,' she said. 'And I'm telling them to go eat somewhere else – outside, maybe. On *my* authority.'

Sally was sputtering. Faye chuckled and led the Club out of the cafeteria.

'Thanks,' Diana said, and for a moment she and Faye looked each other in the eye. Cassie thought of the candles burning in a circle on the road. A new stage of life – was Faye entering a new stage of life? Coming back to the coven?

But Faye's next words undeceived her. 'You know, there's no reason that you *can't* eat in the back room,' she said. 'You can all become hall monitors. That's what he wants—'

'He wants to take us over,' interrupted Deborah scornfully.

'He wants to join with us. He's one of us.'

'No, he's not, Faye,' Cassie said, thinking of the shadow under the rock. 'He's nothing like us.'

Faye gave her a strange glance, but all she said was, 'There's a hall monitors' meeting in C-207 last period. Think about it. The sooner you join him, the easier things will be.' She tossed Doug's Walkman back to him with a negligent gesture and walked away.

Lunch was uncomfortable; it was cold in the front yard of the school, and nobody but Suzan had much of an appetite. Sean showed up late, after all the excitement was over. They discussed plans to fight Black John, but as always they came back to the single issue of power. They needed power to fight him effectively. They needed the Master Tools.

Everyone had a different idea of where to search. Adam proposed the beach – especially around Devil's

Cove, where Mr Fogle, the former principal, had been killed by a rock slide. Deborah thought maybe the old burying ground. 'It's been here since the 1600s,' she said. 'The original coven could easily have hidden things there.' Melanie and Diana discussed the possibility of making a crystal pendulum designed to seek out traces of 'white energy' the tools might be giving off.

Cassie sat quietly, close to Nick, not saying much. She had the stupid, desperate urge to forget all of this and bury her head in his shoulder. She didn't know New Salem as well as the others – how could she come up with a reasonable place to search? And she had such a feeling of dread, of evil things just waiting to happen.

We're going to lose, she thought, listening to the worried voices of the others. We're just kids, and he's got centuries of experience. We're going to lose.

The feeling of dread got worse as the day went on. She ran into Nick as she was walking to her last class and he stopped in the hall.

'You look awful,' he said.

'Thanks.' Cassie tried a wry smile for him.

'No, I mean you're so pale – you feeling okay? Do you want to go home?'

'Leaving school grounds without permission,' Cassie quoted automatically, tiredly, and then she was in his arms.

Nick said, 'They can take their permission and—'

Cassie just clung to him. Nick was so good to her; she wanted to love him. She would *make* herself love him, she decided. Maybe they should go back to Crowhaven Road; go someplace where they could be alone. Nick didn't like doing this kind of thing where people could see.

'Hold me,' she said. He did. Then he kissed her.

Yes. Just go with it. Be part of Nick – that was safe. Nick would take care of her. She could stop thinking now.

'Well, well, well ... looks like a Type-A violation to *me*,' an officious voice said. 'Public displays of affection, inappropriate to the serious and dignified purpose of formal education. What do you say, Portia?'

Nick and Cassie broke apart, Cassie flushing.

'I think it's just too revolting,' Portia Bainbridge said.

Behind her was a gaggle of hall monitors, on their way to the meeting, apparently. There were maybe thirty of them. Cassie's heart was suddenly beating hard and fast.

'And it's *her* fault,' Portia went on, looking down her aristocratic nose at Cassie. 'I heard her initiate it. Let's take her in.'

'That's right, the little flirt,' Sally said. Cassie remembered Sally's voice in the bathroom; the anger in it, the viciousness. *This one had every guy at Homecoming dance following her around with his tongue hanging out – including my boyfriend*. She'd come to think of herself so differently since she'd overheard Sally talking about her that day.

Nick was looking at the group of monitors, his face cold – like the old Nick, the one Cassie had first met. Cold as ice. 'Take her where? The penalty for a Type-A offence is supposed to be detention. Or don't you read your own rules?' he said.

'*We* decide what the penalties are—' Portia began, but Sally interrupted.

'She was refusing to cooperate with a hall monitor at lunchtime,' she said. 'That's what we're taking her in for. Mr Brunswick gave us special instructions. We're going to take her to the office – she can talk to *him*.'

'Then you can take both of us,' Nick said. His arm tightened on Cassie.

There were too many of them. Cassie's eyes skimmed over the crowd of hall monitors, seeing not a friendly face among them. All seniors, all kids who hated witches. And Faye wasn't here now.

'Nick,' she said, her voice soft and careful over the thumping of her heart, 'I think I'd better go with them.' She glanced back at Sally. 'Can I just say good-bye to him?'

Looking sardonic, Sally nodded. Cassie put her arms around Nick's neck.

'Get the others,' she whispered in his ear. 'The monitors will be in their meeting – you'll have to find a way to get me out.'

As he drew back, Nick's mahogany eyes met hers in acknowledgement. Then, with an expressionless look at Sally, he stood aside.

The group of monitors surrounded Cassie and escorted her down the hall, treating her like a mass murderer. She had a wild impulse to giggle, but as they reached the office the urge disappeared in a flood of sheer dread and anxiety.

He planned this, she thought. Maybe not this specifically, today. But he knew he'd get us somehow, one by one. She tried to ignore the little voice whispering, *he knew he'd get you. It's you he's after*.

Because she was an outsider – or because she didn't fit in with his plans. A vision of Kori flashed through her mind: Kori lying stiff and motionless with a broken neck at the bottom of the hill. She'd seen what happened to people who didn't fit in with Black John's plans.

'Maybe if you bat your eyes at him he'll let you off,' Sally whispered spitefully and pushed her in the office door.

Cassie didn't answer. She couldn't.

She hadn't been in this office since she'd gone to Mr Fogle to complain that Faye was persecuting her. It looked the same, except that there was a crackling fire in the fireplace now. And the man behind the desk was different.

Don't look at him, Cassie thought, as the door swung shut behind her, but she couldn't help it. Those black eyes held hers from the instant she glanced towards the desk. That hawklike face betrayed no sign of surprise that she was there.

The principal put a slim gold-plated pen on the desk with a barely audible click.

'Cassandra,' he said.

Cassie's knees felt weak.

It was the voice of the shadow. A dark, liquid voice. So quiet, so insidious – so *evil*. Under his hematite-black eyes she felt naked, exposed. As if he were looking at her mind. Looking for a crack to get in.

'Mr Brunswick,' she said. Her voice sounded strange to her own ears. Polite, but distant.

He smiled.

He was wearing a black turtleneck and a black jacket. He stood, resting his fingertips on the desk.

'So brave,' he said. 'I'm proud of you.'

It was the last thing she expected. Cassie just stared at him. Her fingers flew automatically to the bump of the amethyst pendant under her sweater.

His eyes followed the movement. 'I wouldn't bother,' he said, smiling faintly. 'That crystal is much too small to be effective.'

Cassie's hand dropped slowly. How had he known? She felt so confused, so off-balance. She stared at the man in front of her, trying to connect him with the burned creature that had crouched over her grandmother in the kitchen, with the seventeenth-century wizard who had led a frightened coven to New Salem. How was he here at all, that was the question. What was the source of his power?

'And amethyst is a weak stone, a stone of the heart,' he was going on softly. 'Purity of purpose, Cassie; that's the secret. Purity and clarity. Never forget your purpose.'

She had the strange feeling he was answering her question. Oh God, why didn't Nick come? Her heart was pounding so hard ... she was *frightened*.

'Let me demonstrate,' the dark man said. 'If you would give me that pendant? For a moment only,' he added, as Cassie stood motionless.

Slowly, Cassie reached around the back of her neck. With cold fingertips she undid the silver chain and removed it. She didn't know what else to do.

Slowly, precisely, he took it.

Suddenly, wildly, Cassie thought of a magician about to do a trick. Nothing up *those* sleeves, she thought. Only flesh that shouldn't be there in the first place.

Still holding the necklace in the air, the principal turned away from Cassie. The fire leaped and crackled and Cassie felt her pulse in her throat and fingertips. I can't stand much more of this, she thought. Nick, where are you?

'You see,' the principal said, in a voice that seemed oddly distorted, 'amethyst is a stone riddled with impurities. For power, quartz is always my choice ...' He began to turn around.

No, thought Cassie. Everything had gone into slow motion, as if she were watching one frame after another of a video. A video played on a very superior machine, each frame crisp and bright and sharp-edged, with no blurriness. Cassie didn't even know where the *No* had come from, except that something deep in her own brain was screaming in protest, trying to warn her. Don't look, oh, don't look.

Cassie wanted to stop the action, to freeze the frame. But she couldn't. It was taking forever, but the dark man was still turning. He was facing her.

She saw the elegant black jacket, the black turtleneck sweater. But above the turtleneck was a monstrosity that forced tears from her eyes and clogged the scream in her throat. The man had no face.

No hair, no eyebrows, no eyes, no nose. No mouth, only a grinning outline of clenched teeth. Even that, even the stark bones which faced her, were as clear as water.

Cassie couldn't scream, couldn't breathe. Her mind was out of control.

Oh God, oh God the skull isn't gone no wonder we couldn't find it, it didn't explode at all because it's in his head, oh Diana oh Adam it's in his *head*...

'You see, Cassandra,' came the inhuman voice from behind those clenched teeth, 'purity plus clarity equals power. And I have more power than you children have ever dreamed of.'

Oh God I won't believe this I won't believe this is happening I don't want to see any more...

'My spirit is not confined to this body,' the voice went on calmly, with terrible lucidity. 'It can flow like water wherever I direct it. I can focus its power anywhere.'

The hollow eye sockets tilted down, towards the amethyst pendant which hung from a perfectly normal-looking hand. Firelight flickered deep inside the crystal. Then Cassie felt it – an outrush of power like the one she'd sent to scare the dog and to warn Sean and to light the match. Only this was much stronger, much more concentrated than her feeble bursts had been. She could almost *see* it, like a blaze of light.

The amethyst pendant shattered.

The silver owl swung, but nothing hung from its claws now. The crystal was gone.

Cassie's ears caught the tinkle as bits of it fell. But she didn't really notice the sound consciously. She was blind and deaf with panic.

'Now, Cassandra,' the voice was beginning again, and then it was interrupted by a noise so loud that even Cassie couldn't ignore it. A *roar* was coming from the front yard of the school, a sound like a pep rally, only angry. Shrill screams rang out against the background of deep shouting.

The principal dropped the silver chain and strode over to the window which overlooked the front of the school.

And Cassie's brain woke up. It wanted only one thing, to get out of here. With the dark man's attention distracted, she dived for the door.

She ran straight through the office without looking at the secretaries. There was chaos in the second-floor halls. Everyone was flooding out of classrooms. 'It's a fight!' some guy on the stairs was yelling. 'Come on!'

It's like a riot; they can't control everybody at once, Cassie realised dimly. She was still running. She ran down the stairs and then down a hallway, instinctively heading for the centre of the confusion.

'Cassie, wait!'

Not a man's voice, but a threatening one. Faye. Cassie paused for an instant, looking around desperately for Nick or Diana or Adam.

'Cassie, stop, for pity's sake. No one is trying to hurt you. I've been running after you all the way from the office.'

Warily, Cassie edged backwards. The hall was deserted now. Everyone was outdoors.

'Cassie, just *listen* to me. He's not trying to murder you, I promise. He wants to *help* you. He likes you.'

'Faye, you're insane!' Cassie's control broke, and she screamed the words. 'You don't know what he is! Everything you see about him is an illusion. He's a monster!'

'Don't be ridiculous. He's one of us—'

'Oh, my God, oh, my *God*,' Cassie said. Reaction was setting in and her knees were shaking so badly that she had to lean against the wall. She slid down, tearing a poster about the Thanksgiving football game. 'You didn't see him. You don't know.'

'I know you're being a baby. *You* didn't even stay to listen to what he had to say to you. He was going to explain everything—'

'Faye, wake up!' Cassie cried. 'For God's sake, will you please wake up and *look* at him? He's nothing that you think. You're completely blind.'

'You think you know so much about it.' Faye stood back, arms crossed over her chest. She tilted her chin up and looked down at Cassie with heavy-lidded, queerly triumphant eyes. Her blood-red lips curved in a smile. 'You think you know everything – but you don't even know what his name was when he was here last. When he came to our parents and he lived at Number Thirteen.'

The strength of terror Cassie had felt moments earlier was gone, and the ground suddenly felt very unstable. She pressed a hand against the floor. Faye was still looking at her with those strange, triumphant eyes. 'No,' Cassie whispered.

' "No" you don't know? Or "no" don't tell you? But I want to tell you, Cassie, and it's time you did know. The name he used last time was John Blake.'

CHAPTER

10

Cassie stared, beyond speech, beyond thought. Not believing – but inside her, something knew.

'It's true. He's your father.'

Cassie just sat.

'And he wants you to be happy, Cassie. He wants you to be his heir. He's got a lot planned for you.'

'And what are you?' Cassie cried, outraged, pushed beyond the limits of her endurance. 'My new stepmother?'

Faye chuckled – that infuriating, lazy, self-satisfied chuckle. 'Maybe. Why not? I've always liked older men – and he's only about three centuries older.'

'You're disgusting!' Cassie couldn't find the right words. None were bad enough, and she didn't want to believe that any of this was actually happening. 'You're – you—'

'I haven't *done* anything yet, Cassie. John and I have a – business relationship.'

Cassie felt as if she were gagging. For herself, for Faye… 'You call him John?' she whispered.

'What do you think I should call him? Mr Brunswick?

Or what he called himself the last time he was here, Mr Blake?'

Everything was spinning around Cassie now. The pale green cinderblock walls were whirling. She wanted to faint. If only she could faint she wouldn't have to think.

But she couldn't. Slowly, the spinning steadied, she felt the floor solid beneath her. There was no way to escape this. There was no choice but to deal with it.

'Oh, God,' Cassie whispered. 'It's true. It's really true.'

'It's true,' Faye said quietly, with satisfaction. 'Your mother was his girlfriend. He told me the whole story, how she fell in love with him when he went over to Number Twelve to borrow some matches. They never *did* get married, apparently – but I'm sure he didn't begrudge her his name.'

It was true ... and that had been what Cassie's grandmother was trying to tell her when she died. 'I have one more thing to tell you,' she'd said, and then Laurel had come in. The last words had only been a whisper, 'John' and something else Cassie couldn't make out. But she could recall the shape of her grandmother's lips trying to make it. It had been 'Blake'.

'Why didn't she try to tell me before?' Cassie whispered raggedly, hardly aware she was speaking aloud. 'Why wait until she was dying? *Why?*'

'Who, your grandma? She didn't want to upset you, I suppose,' Faye said. 'She probably thought you'd be – disturbed – if you knew. And maybe' – Faye leaned forward – 'she knew it would bring you closer to him. You're his own flesh and blood, Cassie. His daughter.'

Cassie was shaking her head, blind, nauseated. 'The other old women – they must have known too! God, everybody who knew him must have known. And *nobody* told me. Why didn't they tell me?'

'Oh, stop snivelling, Cassie. I'm sure they didn't tell you because they were afraid of how you'd react. And I must say it looks as if they were right. You're falling apart.'

Great Aunt Constance, Cassie was thinking. *She* must have known. How could she stand to look at me? How can she stand to have my mother in her house?

And Mrs Franklin had been *going* to tell her, she realised suddenly. Yes. That had been what that last-minute scene in Aunt Constance's parlour had been all about. Adam's grandmother had been about to tell, about to say something to Cassie about her father. Granny Quincey and Aunt Constance had stopped her. They were all in a conspiracy of silence, to keep the truth from Cassie.

Probably not the parents, Cassie thought slowly, feeling very tired. They probably didn't remember anyway. They'd made themselves forget everything. But Aunt Constance had warned the Circle against stirring up those old memories, and her gaze had settled on Cassie when she did it.

'Just think about it, Cassie,' Faye was saying, and that husky voice sounded reasonable now, not gloating or triumphant. 'He only wants the best for you; he always has. You were born as part of his plans. I know you and I have had our problems in the past, but John wants us to get along. Won't you just give it a try? Won't you, Cassie?'

Slowly, painfully, Cassie made her eyes focus. Faye was kneeling in front of her. Faye's beautiful, sensual face seemed lit softly from within. She really means it, Cassie thought. She's sincere. Maybe she's in love with him.

And maybe, Cassie mused dizzily, I *should* think about it. So many things have changed since I came to New

Salem – I'm not at all the person I used to be. The old, shy Cassie who never had a boyfriend and never had anything to say is gone. Maybe this is just another change, another stage of life. Maybe I'm at the crossroads.

She looked at Faye for a long moment, searching the depths of those amber eyes. Then, slowly, she shook her head.

No.

Even as she thought it, chill white determination flooded her. That was one road she would never take, no matter what happened. She would never become what Black John – what her *father* – wanted.

Without a word, without looking back, Cassie got up and walked away from Faye.

Outside, the mêlée was still going on. Cassie scanned the front entrance of the school and saw the weak November sun shining on a cascade of fair hair. She headed for it.

'Diana...'

'Cassie, thank God! When Nick told us you were alone in his office ...' Diana's eyes widened. 'Cassie, what's wrong?'

'I have to tell you something. At home. Can we go home now?' Cassie was holding on to Diana's hand.

Diana stared at her for another moment, then shook herself. 'Yes. Of course. But Nick will be looking for you. He had the idea that we should start a fight on the first floor as a diversion; just grab a bunch of people and start swinging. All the guys did it, and Deborah and Laurel. They're all looking for you.'

Cassie couldn't face any of them, especially Nick. Once he knew what she really was – what he'd held in his arms, what he'd kissed...

'Please, can't you just tell them I'm okay, but I need to go home?' Suzan was standing nearby; Cassie nodded at her. 'Can't Suzan just tell them?'

'Yes. All right. Suzan, tell everybody I've taken Cassie home. They can stop the fight now.' Diana led Cassie down the hill to the parking lot. They had barely reached Diana's car, though, when Adam appeared, running.

'The fight's breaking up – and I'm coming with you,' he said. Cassie wanted to argue, but she didn't have the strength. Besides, Diana might need Adam there when Cassie told her the whole story.

Cassie nodded at Adam and he got in the car without further discussion. They drove to Diana's house and went up to Diana's room.

'Now tell us what happened before I have a heart attack,' Diana said.

But it wasn't that easy. Cassie went over to the bay window, where sunlight was striking the prisms hanging there so that wedges of rainbow light bobbed and slid over the walls. She turned to look at the black and white prints on either side of the window; Diana's collection of Greek goddesses. There was proud Hera, queenly with her mane of pitch-black hair and her hooded, untamed eyes; there was Aphrodite, goddess of beauty, with her soft bosom exposed; there was fierce Artemis, the virgin huntress afraid of nothing. And here, on the other side, was Athena, the grey-eyed goddess of wisdom, and Persephone, fresh-faced and elfin and surrounded by blooming flowers. Last of all, in colour, was the print of a goddess older than the Greek civilisation, the great goddess Diana, who ruled the moon and stars and night. Diana, Queen of Witches.

'*Cassie!*'

'Sorry,' Cassie whispered, and slowly turned to face her Diana. Who just now looked sick with suspense.

'I'm sorry,' she said, more loudly. 'I just don't know

how to say this, I guess. But I know now why I was born so much later than all of you ... or, actually, no, I don't.' She pondered that a moment. 'Not why I was so late. Unless he knew by then the coven was going to try to throw him out, so he thought he'd better have a back-up ...' Cassie thought it over and shook her head. Adam and Diana were staring at her as if she'd gone crazy. 'I guess I don't know everything. But I'm not half outsider, like we thought. That isn't why he's been after me; it's a completely different reason. We thought Kori and I spoiled his plans somehow ... oh, *God*.' Cassie stopped, feeling a pain like jagged glass shoot through her. Her eyes filled. 'I think – God, it must be. I know why Kori died. Because of *me*. If she hadn't died, she would have joined the coven instead of me, and he didn't want that. *She* was the one he hadn't planned on. So he had to get rid of her.' Another spasm of pain almost doubled Cassie over. She was afraid she might be sick.

'Sit down,' Adam was saying urgently. They were both helping her to the bed.

'Don't ... you don't know yet. You might not want to touch me.'

'Cassie, for God's sake tell us what you're talking about. You're not making any sense.'

'Yes, I am. I'm Black John's daughter.'

In that instant, if either of them had loosened their grip on her or recoiled, Cassie felt she might have tried to jump out the window. But Diana's clear green eyes just widened, the pupils huge and bottomless. Adam's eyes turned silver.

'Faye told me, and it's true.'

'It's not true,' Adam said tightly.

'It's not true, and I'll kill her,' Diana said. This, from gentle Diana, was astonishing.

They both went on holding Cassie. Diana was holding her from one side and Adam was on the other side, holding both of them, embracing their embrace. Cassie's shaking shook all three.

'It is true,' Cassie whispered, trying to keep some grip on herself. She had to be calm now; she couldn't lose control. 'It explains everything. It explains why I dreamed about him – him and the sinking ship. We're – connected, somehow. It explains why he keeps coming after me, like when we called him up at Halloween, and last night on the beach. He wants me to join him. Faye's in love with him. Just like my mother was.'

Cassie shuddered. Adam and Diana just kept hanging on to her. Neither of them even flinched when she looked them in the face.

'It explains my *mother*,' Cassie said thickly. 'Why he went to our house that night when he came back, when we let him out of the grave. He went to see her – that's why she's like she is now. Oh, Diana, I have to go to her.'

'In a minute,' Diana said, her own voice husky with suppressed tears. 'In a little while.'

Cassie was thinking. No wonder her mother had run away from New Salem, no wonder there had always been helpless terror lurking at the back of her mother's eyes. How could you not be terrified when the man you loved turned out to be something from a nightmare? When you had to go away to have his baby, someplace where no one would ever know?

But she'd been brave enough to come back, and to bring Cassie. And now Cassie had to be brave.

There's nothing frightening in the dark if you just face it. Cassie didn't know how she was going to face this, but she had to, somehow.

'I'm okay now,' she whispered. 'And I want to see my mom.'

Diana and Adam were telegraphing things over her head.

'We're going with you,' Diana said. 'We won't go in the room if you don't want, but we're going to take you there.'

Cassie looked at them: at Diana's eyes, dark as emeralds now, but full of love and understanding; and at Adam, his fine-boned face calm and steady. She squeezed their hands.

'Thank you,' she said. 'Thank you both.'

Great Aunt Constance answered the door. She looked surprised to see them and a little flustered, which surprised Cassie in turn. She wouldn't have thought Melanie's aunt ever got flustered.

But as Cassie was going into the guest room, Granny Quincey and old Mrs Franklin were coming out. Cassie looked at Laurel's frail great-grandmother, and at Adam's plump, untidy grandmother, and then at Aunt Constance.

'We were – trying one or two things to see if we could help your mother,' Aunt Constance said, looking slightly uncomfortable. She coughed. 'Old remedies,' she admitted. 'There may be some good in them. We'll be in the parlour if you need anything.' She shut the door.

Cassie turned to look at the figure lying between Aunt Constance's starched white sheets. She went and knelt by the bedside.

Her mother's face was as pale as those sheets. Everything about her was white and black: white face, black hair, black lashes forming crescents on her cheeks. Cassie took her cold hand and only then realised she didn't have the first idea what to say.

'Mother?' she said, and then: 'Mom? Can you hear me?'

No answer. Not a twitch.

'Mom,' Cassie said with difficulty, 'I know you're sick, and I know you're scared, but there's one thing you don't have to be scared of any more. I know the truth. I know about my father.'

Cassie waited, and she thought she saw the sheets over her mother's chest rise and fall a little more quickly.

'I know everything,' she said. 'And ... if you're afraid I'll be mad at you or anything, you don't have to be. I understand. I've seen what he does to people. I saw what he did to Faye, and she's stronger than you.' Cassie was holding the cold hand so tightly she was afraid she was hurting it. She paused and swallowed.

'Anyway, I wanted to tell you that I know. And it'll all be over soon, and I'm going to make sure he doesn't ever hurt you again. I'm going to stop him somehow. I don't know how, but I will. I promise, Mom.'

She stood up, still holding the soft, limp hand in hers and whispered, 'If you're just scared, Mom, you can come back now. It's easier than running away; it is, really. If you face things they're not as bad.'

Cassie waited again. She hadn't thought she was hoping for anything, but she must have been, because as the seconds ticked by and nothing happened her heart sank in disappointment. Just some little sign, that wasn't much to ask for, was it? But there was no little sign. For what seemed like the hundredth time that day, warmth filled Cassie's eyes.

'Okay, Mom,' she whispered, and stooped to kiss her mother's cheek.

As she did, she noticed a thin string of some kind of

fibre around her mother's neck. She pulled, and from the collar of her mother's nightgown emerged three small golden-brown stones strung on the twine.

Cassie tucked the necklace back in, waited one more second, and then left.

Can I face it if my mother dies like my grandma? she wondered as she shut the bedroom door. She didn't think so. But she was beginning to realise that she might have to.

In the parlour, Adam and Diana were drinking tea with the women.

'Who put the crystals around my mother's neck? And what are they?'

The old women looked at each other. It was Great Aunt Constance who answered.

'I did,' she said. She cleared her throat. 'They're tiger's eyes. For keeping away bad dreams – or so my grandmother always said.'

Cassie managed a small smile for her. 'Oh. Thank you.' Maybe Melanie's affinity for minerals ran in the family. She didn't bother to tell Aunt Constance what Black John could do to those stones if he tried.

'Bad dreams are a nuisance,' old Mrs Franklin said as Adam and Diana got up to leave. 'Of course, good dreams are something else again.'

Cassie looked at Adam's grandmother, whose disordered grey hair was coming uncoiled as she happily crunched cookie after cookie. Cassie had never known anybody who liked to eat so much, except Suzan. But there was more to Mrs Franklin than you'd think at first sight.

'Dreams?' Cassie said.

'Good dreams,' Adam's grandmother agreed indistinctly. 'For good dreams, you sleep with a moonstone.'

Cassie thought about that all the way home.

She and Diana had dinner quietly, just the two of them, since Diana's father was still at his law office. Adam had gone to talk to the rest of the Circle.

'I can't tell them,' Cassie had said. 'Not tonight – tomorrow, maybe.'

'There's no reason you should have to,' Adam replied, his voice almost harsh. 'You've been through enough. *I'll* tell them – and I'll make them understand. Don't worry, Cassie. They'll stick by you.'

Cassie couldn't help but worry. But she put it aside, because she had other things to think about. She'd made a promise to her mother.

She lay in bed reading her grandmother's Book of Shadows. *Her* Book of Shadows. She was looking for anything about crystals and dreams.

And there it was: *To Cause Dreams. Place a moonstone beneath your pillow and all night you will have fair and pleasant dreams which may profit you*. She also found a passage about crystals in general. Big crystals were better than little crystals; well, she knew that already. Melanie had said so, and Black John had demonstrated it today beyond question.

She put the book down and went to Diana's desk.

There was a white velvet pouch there, lined with sky-blue silk. Diana had long ago given Cassie permission to open it. Cassie took the pouch to the bed and poured the contents out on a folded-over section of the top sheet. The stones formed a kaleidoscopic array against the white background.

Blue lace agate – Cassie picked up the triangular piece and rubbed its smoothness across her cheek. She saw light yellow citrine – Deborah's stone, good for raising energy. And here was cloudy orange carnelian, which Suzan had once used for raising the passions of the entire football team. Here was translucent green jade, which Melanie used for calm thought, and royal purple amethyst – Laurel's stone, a stone of the heart, Black John had said. There were dozens of others, too: warm amber, light as plastic; dark green bloodstone speckled with red; a wine-coloured garnet; the pale green peridot Diana had used to trace the dark energy.

Cassie's fingers sorted through the clinking treasure until she found a moonstone. It was translucent, with a silvery-blue shimmer. She put it on the nightstand by her side of the bed.

Diana came in, fresh from her bath, and watched Cassie putting the stones back into the pouch.

'Find anything in your Book of Shadows?' she asked.

'Nothing specific,' Cassie said. She didn't want to explain what she was doing, even to Diana. Later, if it worked. 'I'm beginning to think my grandmother didn't mean there was anything specific in the book about Black John,' she added. 'Maybe she just wanted me to be a good witch, a *knowledgeable* witch. Maybe she'd thought that way I'd be smart enough to beat him.'

Diana got in bed and turned off the light. There was no moon; the bay window remained dark. It was peaceful, somehow, with the two of them lying in bed – like a sleepover. It made Cassie think of the old days, when she and Diana had first decided to be adopted sisters.

'We need to find a way to kill him,' she said.

A sleepover with a grim and bloodthirsty purpose. Diana was silent for a moment and then said calmly, 'Well, we know two things that *can't* kill him – Water and Fire. He drowned the first time when his ship went down, and he burned the second time, when our parents burned the house at Number Thirteen. But he didn't stay dead either time.'

Cassie appreciated the 'our parents'. *Her* mother hadn't been trying to burn anybody, she'd bet.

'He said his spirit didn't need to stay in his body,' she said. 'I think he can make it go different places. Maybe when he died, he just sent his spirit somewhere else.'

'Like into the crystal skull,' Diana said. 'And it stayed there until we brought it and his body together. Yes. But what can we *use* against him?'

'Earth ... or Air,' Cassie mused. 'Though I don't see how Air could kill anybody.'

'I don't either. Earth could mean crystals ... but we don't have a crystal big enough to use against him.'

'No,' Cassie said. 'It sounds like it's the Master Tools or nothing. We've got to find them.'

She could feel Diana nodding in the darkness. 'But how?'

Cassie reached over and felt for the moonstone. She put it under her pillow.

Maybe it's not the size, but how you use them, she thought. 'Good night, Diana,' she said, and shut her eyes.

CHAPTER

11

From the start, this dream was clearer than the others. Or maybe it was Cassie that was clearer; more calm, more aware of what was happening. Salt water slapped her face; she swallowed some. It was so cold she couldn't feel her hands or feet.

Going down. She was going to drown ... but not die. With the last of her will she sent her spirit to the place prepared for it ... to the skull on the island. Some of her power had been left in the skull already; now she herself would go to join it. And someday, when the time was right, when enough of her body diffused through the sea and washed up on the island, she would live again.

Good dreams, I wanted good dreams, Cassie thought frantically as the water closed over her head.

A shifting...

Sunlight blinded her.

'You and Kate may go play in the garden,' the kind voice said.

Yes. She'd made it. She was here.

The garden was in back. Cassie turned to the back door.

'Jacinth! What have you forgotten?'

Cassie paused, confused. She had no idea. The tall

woman in Puritan dress was looking down at the floor. There, on the clean pine boards, lay the red leather Book of Shadows. Cassie remembered now; it had dropped off her lap when she stood up.

'I'm sorry, Mother.' The word came so naturally to her lips. And her eyes had adjusted – but she couldn't figure out where the book was supposed to go. Somewhere special ... where? Then she saw the loose brick in the fireplace.

'Much better,' the tall woman said, as Cassie slid the book into the hole and plugged it up with the brick. 'Always remember, Jacinth: we must never grow careless. Not even here in New Salem, where all our neighbours are our own kind. Now run along to the garden.'

Kate was already going out the door. In the sunshine outside, Cassie noticed that Kate's hair was just the colour of Diana's: not really gold, but a paler colour like pure light. Kate's eyes were golden too, like sunshine. She was altogether a golden girl.

'Sky and sea, keep harm from me,' she laughed, twirling, looking over the herb bushes to the blue expanse of the ocean beyond the cliff. There was no wall in this time – it hadn't been built yet. Then she darted forward to pick something.

'Just smell this lavender,' she said, holding out a bunch to Cassie. 'Isn't it sweet?'

But Cassie was hovering by the open door. Two other people had come into the kitchen; Kate's mother and father, she guessed. They were talking in low, urgent voices.

'...news just came. The ship went down,' the man was saying.

There was an exclamation of joy and surprise from

Jacinth's mother. 'Then he is dead!'

The man shook his head, but Cassie didn't hear the next few words. She was afraid to be caught listening and sent away. '... the skull ...' she heard, and '... can never tell ... come back...'

'And this jasmine,' Kate was singing. 'Isn't it wonderful?' Cassie wanted to tell her to shut up.

Then she heard words that raised the hair on her arms, even in the hot sunshine. '... hide them,' Kate's mother was saying. 'But where?'

That was it. Where, *where*? If this dream had any meaning, it was to tell Cassie this. Kate was trying to put an arm around her waist, to get her to smell the jasmine, but Cassie grabbed her hand to hold her still and strained to listen.

The adults were arguing softly: exclamations of worry and disagreement came to Cassie's ears. 'Could we not ...?' 'No, not there ...' 'But where, then?' 'Oh, mercy, my bread is burning!'

And then, soft laughter. 'Of course! We should have thought of it earlier.'

Where? Fending Kate off, Cassie twisted to try and look into the kitchen.

'Jacinth, what's wrong with you?' Kate cried. 'You're not listening to a word I'm saying. Jacinth, look at me!'

Desperately, Cassie stared into the dark kitchen. It was too dark. The dream was fading.

No. She had to hang on to it. She had to see the end. Grandmother, help me, she thought. Help me see...

'Jacinth!'

Darker and darker—

Long skirts rustling, moving out of the way. And just a glimpse...

'The old hiding place,' Jacinth's mother said in a satisfied voice. 'Until they are needed again.'

Darkness took Cassie.

She woke confused.

At first, she couldn't remember what she'd been looking for in the dream. She remembered the dream, though. Who was Jacinth? An ancestress? One of her great-great-great-great-great-grandmothers, she supposed. And Kate?

Then she remembered her purpose.

The Master Tools. The members of the first coven had hidden them from Black John, because they'd known he might come back. Cassie had gone into the dream to find out where, and she had succeeded.

She'd wondered why Black John had come after her grandmother the night he was released. Not just for the Book of Shadows, she realised now; not just because he'd known her mother and grandmother before. He'd wanted something else from her grandmother. He'd wanted the Master Tools.

But her grandmother hadn't known where they were. Cassie felt sure that if she had, the old woman would have told *Cassie*. All her grandmother had known was that her own grandmother, Cassie's great-great-grandmother, had told her the fireplace was a good place to hide things. And now, because of the dream, Cassie knew that the loose brick had already been a hiding place in Jacinth's time.

But there had only been one loose brick, and nothing but the Book of Shadows had been stored behind it. Cassie knew that, and she knew that the original coven had been looking for a long-term solution, a place to put the Master Tools 'until they were needed' by some future generation. Not just a loose brick, then. Cassie thought about the glimpse of the hearth she'd gotten between the women's skirts in the last second of her dream. The fireplace had been a different shape than it was in modern days.

Cassie lay for a few moments in the velvet darkness. Then she rolled over and gently shook Diana's shoulder.

'Diana, wake up. I know where the Master Tools are.'

They woke Adam by throwing pebbles at his window. The three of them went to Number Twelve armed with a pickaxe, a sledgehammer, several regular hammers and screwdrivers, a crowbar, and Raj. The German shepherd trotted happily along beside Cassie, looking as if this kind of expedition in the wee hours was just what he liked.

The waning moon was high overhead when they got to Cassie's grandmother's house. Inside, it seemed even colder than outside, and there was a stillness about the place that dampened Cassie's enthusiasm.

'There,' she whispered, pointing to the left side of the hearth, where bricks had been added since the time of her dream. 'That's where it's different. That's where they must have bricked them up.'

'Too bad we don't have a jackhammer,' Adam said cheerfully, picking up the crowbar. He seemed undisturbed by the chill and the silence, and in the sickly artificial light of the kitchen his hair gleamed just the colour of the garnets in Diana's pouch. Raj sat beside Cassie, his black and tan tail whisking across the kitchen floor. Looking at the two of them made Cassie feel better.

It took a long time. Cassie grazed her knuckles helping to chip the ancient mortar away, using a screwdriver like a chisel. But at last the bricks began to drop onto the cold ashes of the hearth, as one after another was pried out. .

Each was a different colour; some red, some orange, some almost purple-black.

'There's definitely something in here,' Adam said, reaching inside the hole they'd made. 'But we'll have to get rid of a few more bricks to get it out ... There!' He started to reach again, then looked at Cassie. 'Why don't you do the honours? It's okay, there's nothing alive inside.'

Cassie, who didn't want to encounter a three-hundred-year-old cockroach, nodded at him gratefully. She reached inside and her hand closed on something smooth and cool. It was so heavy she had to use both hands to lift it out.

'A document box,' Diana whispered, when Cassie set the thing on the floor in front of the fireplace. It looked like a treasure chest to Cassie, a little treasure chest made of leather and brass. 'People used them to store important documents in the 1600s,' Diana went on. 'We got Black John's papers and things out of one like it. Go on, Cassie, open it.'

Cassie looked at her, then at Adam leaning on his pickaxe, his face decorated with soot. Her fingers trembled as she opened the little box.

What if she'd been wrong? What it it wasn't the Master Tools in here at all, but only some old documents? What if—

Inside the box, looking fresh and untouched as if they'd been buried yesterday, were a diadem, a bracelet, and a garter.

'Oh,' breathed Diana.

Cassie knew the diadem that the Circle always used was silver. The one in the box was silver too, but it looked softer, somehow; more heavy and rich, with a deeper lustre. Both it and the bracelet looked *crafted*; there was nothing machine-made about them. Every stroke of the bracelet's inscriptions, every intricate twist of the diadem's circlet, showed an artist's hand. The leather of the garter was supple, and instead of one silver buckle, it had seven. It was heavy in Cassie's hand.

Wordlessly, Diana reached out one finger to trace the crescent moon of the diadem.

'The Master Tools,' Adam said quietly. 'After all that searching, they were right here under our noses.'

'So much power,' Diana whispered. 'I'm surprised they sat here so quietly. I'd have thought they'd be kicking up a psychic disturbance—' She broke off and looked at Cassie. 'Didn't you say something about it being hard to sleep here?'

'Creaks and rattles all night long,' Cassie said, and then she met Diana's eyes. 'Oh. You mean – you think...'

'I don't think it was the house settling,' Diana said briefly. 'Tools this powerful can make all sorts of strange things happen.'

Cassie shut her eyes, disgusted with herself. 'How could I have been so stupid? It was so simple. I should have guessed...'

'Everything's always simple in hindsight,' Adam said dryly. '*Nobody* guessed where the tools were, not even Black John. Which reminds me: I don't think we'd better tell Faye anything about this.'

The two girls looked at him, then Diana nodded slowly. 'She told Black John about the amethyst. I'm afraid you're right; she can't be trusted.'

'I don't think we should tell *anyone*,' Cassie said. 'Not yet, anyway. Not until we decide what we're going to do with them. The fewer people who know about this, the safer we are.'

'Right,' said Adam. He began replacing the bricks in the

fireplace. 'If we leave everything looking fairly normal, and find a good place to hide that box before morning, no one should ever know we've found them.'

'Here.' Cassie dropped the garter back in the chest and put the chest into Diana's hands. 'Faye's got the other ones; these are yours.'

'They belong to the coven leader—'

'The coven leader is a jerk,' Cassie said. 'These are *yours*, Diana. I found them and I say so.'

Adam turned from his brick-replacing, and the three of them looked at each other in the light of the cold, quiet kitchen. They were all dirty; even Diana's beautiful cheekbones bore grey smudges. Cassie was still sore and exhausted from what had been one of the longest and most horrible days in her life. But at that moment she felt a warmth and closeness that swept the pain and fatigue away. They were – connected, all three of them. They were part of each other. And tonight they had won. They had triumphed.

If Diana hadn't forgiven us, where would we be? Cassie wondered, as she looked down at the hearth again.

I'm glad you're the one who has him; I really am, she thought then. Glancing up, she saw that Diana had tears in her eyes, almost as if she knew what Cassie was thinking.

'All right. I'll accept them for now – until it's time to use them,' Diana said.

'This is finished,' Adam said. They gathered up their tools and left the house.

It was when they were driving back to Adam's that they saw the silhouette beside the road.

'Black John,' Cassie hissed, stiffening.

'I don't think so,' Adam said, pulling over. 'Too little. In fact, I think it's Sean.'

It was Sean. He was dressed in jeans and a pyjama top and he looked very sleepy.

'What's going on?' he said, his small black eyes darting under heavy lids. 'I saw a light over at Cassie's house, and then I saw a car coming out of the driveway ... I thought you guys were Black John.'

'It was brave of you to come out alone,' Cassie said, remembering her vow to be kinder to Sean, and pushing away a flicker of uneasiness. Diana and Adam were consulting each other with their eyes, and Sean was looking from their dirty faces to the tools on the jeep's floor, to the hump under Adam's jacket.

'I think we'd better tell him,' Diana said. Cassie hesitated – they'd agreed not to tell anyone – but there didn't seem to be any choice. She nodded slowly, reluctantly.

So Sean climbed in the back and was sworn to secrecy. He was excited about the Master Tools, but Adam wouldn't let him touch them.

'We're going to find somewhere to hide them now,' Adam said. 'You'd better go back to bed; we'll see you tomorrow.'

'Okay.' Sean climbed out again. He started to shut the door, then stopped, looking at Cassie. 'Oh, hey – you know that stuff about Black John being your father? Well, uh, I just wanted to say – it's okay by me. I mean, you should see *my* father. That's all.' He slammed the door and scuttled off.

Cassie felt her throat swell, tears stinging behind her eyes. She'd forgotten about Adam having told them all; she'd have to face the rest of the Circle in the morning. But for now, Sean had made her feel glad and humble.

I've *really* got to be nicer to him in the future, she thought.

They hid the tools in Adam's cellar. 'As long as we don't

use them nobody should be able to trace them,' Diana said. 'That's what Melanie and I decided, anyway. But they're dangerous, Adam. It's risky to have them.' She looked at him soberly.

Then let somebody besides you two take a little risk,' he said gently. 'For once.'

Cassie went to bed for the second time that night, tired but triumphant. She put the moonstone back on the dresser; she'd had enough dreams for now. She wondered if she'd ever see Kate again.

'I don't care if her father's Adolph Hitler.' Deborah's voice, never soft, rang out clearly from downstairs. Cassie stood just inside the door of Diana's room, hanging on to the doorjamb. 'What's it got to do with *Cassie*?'

'We know, Deborah, but hush, can't you?' That was Melanie, a good deal more modulated, but still audible.

'Why don't we just go upstairs an' get her?' Doug said reasonably, and Chris added, 'I don't think she's ever comin' down.'

'She's probably scared to death of all of you,' Laurel scolded, sounding like a cub-scout den mother with a recalcitrant pack on her hands. 'Suzan, those muffins are for *her*.'

'Are you sure they're oat bran? They taste like dirt,' Suzan said calmly.

'You've got to go down sometime,' Diana said from behind Cassie.

Cassie nodded, leaning her forehead briefly against the cool wall by the door. The one voice she hadn't heard belonged to the one she was most worried about – Nick. She squared her shoulders, picked up her backpack, and made her legs move. Now I know how it feels to walk out to face the firing squad, she thought.

The entire Circle – except Faye – was gathered at the foot of the stairs, gazing up expectantly. Suddenly Cassie felt more like a bride descending the staircase than a prisoner. She was glad she was wearing clean jeans and a cashmere sweater Diana had loaned her, dyed in soft swathes of blue and violet.

'Hi, Cassie,' Chris said. 'So I hear – yeeouch!' He staggered sideways from Laurel's kick.

'Here, Cassie,' Laurel said sweetly. 'Have a muffin.'

'Don't,' Suzan whispered in Cassie's ear.

'I picked these for you,' Doug said, thrusting a handful of damp greenery at her. He peered at it doubtfully. 'I think they're daisies. They looked better before they died.'

'Want to ride to school on my bike?' Deborah said.

'No, she doesn't want to ride to school on your bike. She's going with me.' Nick, who had been sitting on the wooden deacon's bench in the hallway, stood up.

Cassie had been afraid to look him in the face, but now she couldn't help it. He looked cool, unruffled as always, but in the depths of his mahogany eyes there was a warmth that was for her alone. In taking her backpack, his strong, deft fingers squeezed her hand, once.

That was when she knew it was going to be all right.

Cassie looked around at the Club. 'You all – I don't know what to say. Thank you.' She looked at Adam, who had made them understand. 'Thank you.'

He shrugged, and only someone who knew him well would have noticed the pain at the edge of his smile. His eyes were dark as storm clouds with some repressed emotion. 'Any time,' he said, as Nick started to steer her to the door.

On the way, Cassie glanced back at Doug. 'What happened to your *face*?'

'He's always been that ugly,' Chris assured her.

'It was the fight,' Doug said, touching his black eye with something like pride. 'But you should see the other fifty guys,' he yelled after her.

'Are we all in trouble for fighting?' Cassie asked Nick, outside.

'Nah – they don't know who started it. They'd have to punish the whole school.'

Which, as it turned out, the principal did. The Thanksgiving football game was cancelled, and there was a good deal of ill feeling among the students. Cassie just prayed nobody found out where the ill feeling ought to be directed.

'Can we keep things quiet until Thanksgiving vacation next week?' Diana asked at lunch. Cassie and Adam were the only ones who knew exactly why she wanted things kept quiet – so they'd have time to decide how best to use the Master Tools – but the others agreed to try. No one except Doug and Deborah was really interested in more fighting at the moment.

'I'm afraid, though. I'm afraid he'll come after us anyway. He could have the hall monitors pick us up for no reason,' Cassie said to Diana afterwards.

It didn't happen. A strange peace, a sort of bizarre tranquillity, engulfed New Salem High. As if everyone were waiting, but no one knew what for.

'Don't go alone,' Diana said. 'Wait a minute and I'll go with you.'

'I know exactly where the book is,' Cassie said. 'I won't be in the house more than a minute.' She'd been meaning to lend *Le Morte D'Arthur* to Diana for a long time. It was one of her favourite books, and her grandmother had a beautiful copy from 1906. 'I can pick up some dried sage for the stuffing while I'm at it,' she said.

'No, don't. Don't do anything extra; just come back as quick as you can,' Diana said, pushing a strand of damp hair off her forehead with the back of a greasy hand. They'd been having a strenuous but rather interesting time, trying to stuff a Thanksgiving turkey.

'Okay.' Cassie drove to Number Twelve. They were late with the turkey; the sun was low in the sky.

Just in and out, Cassie told herself as she hurried through the door. She found the book on a shelf in the library and tucked it under her arm. She wasn't really uneasy – the last week had been so quiet. The Circle had celebrated Suzan's birthday undisturbed two days ago, on the twenty-fourth.

You see, I told you, she thought to Diana as she came out of the house. Nothing to worry abou—

She saw the car, a grey *BMW*, sitting beside her grandmother's white Rabbit. In that split second, she was already starting to act, to jump back through the doorway, but she never got the chance. A rough hand clapped over her mouth and she was dragged away.

CHAPTER

12

'**G**et out of here before any of them see us,' the voice said tersely. Cassie could smell the acridity of sweat.

Jordan, she was thinking. The one with the gun. The one in the Pistol Club. The other one was Logan, who was on the MIT debate team, and was younger than Jordan – or was he older? Cassie never had been able to keep Portia's brothers straight, even when Portia was telling her about them, back on Cape Cod.

Her mind was working very calmly and clearly.

They drove her out of New Salem, onto the mainland, keeping her squashed on the floor of the back seat the whole time. Jordan kept his feet on her and kept something cold and hard pressed against the back of her head. As if I were a dangerous criminal or something, Cassie thought. Good *grief*. What do they think I'm going to do, turn them into toads?

The other pair of feet resting on her was feminine. Portia, Cassie guessed. No, Sally. Portia was too aristocratic to tromp on somebody's legs.

Cassie heard the thudding of the tires as they drove over the bridge to the mainland. After that there were a lot of turns, and then a long ride on a bumpy road. When they finally stopped, it was very quiet.

They were in the middle of a forest. Birch and beech and oak, the native trees of Massachusetts, grew thickly all around. They let Cassie out of the car, and then the guys marched her into the woods. Cassie could hear the lighter footsteps of the girls following. It seemed like a long walk, farther and farther away from the road and any semblance of civilisation. As dark fell, they reached a clearing.

Somebody had been here before. Logan's flashlight showed a fire pit, and ropes hanging from a tree. Portia and Sally – Cassie had been right, it *was* Sally – made a fire in the pit, while the guys tied Cassie to the tree. They used a lot more rope than Cassie thought necessary.

And she didn't like the look of that fire.

'Why are you doing this?' she asked Logan as he stepped back from tying her. When she could see their faces she could tell Logan from Jordan – Jordan was the one with shark's eyes.

'Because you're a witch,' Logan said briefly.

'That's a *reason*?'

Portia stepped forward. 'You lied,' she said accusingly. 'About the boy on the beach, about everything. All the time, you were a witch yourself.'

'I wasn't then,' Cassie said, trying to keep her voice steady. 'I am now.'

'Then you admit it. Well, we're going to do now what we should have done then.'

A hard fist of fear clenched in Cassie's stomach, and she looked at the fire again. Jordan was putting something in it, something long and metal.

I'm in trouble, Cassie realised. I am in very, very bad trouble.

She needed help. She knew that, and knew of only one way to call for it. Her only weapon was her power.

All right, she told herself; do what you did to call to Sean. Get ready, stay calm – *now*.

Adam, she tried to call to him with her mind. *Adam, it's Cassie. I'm in trouble.* She wished she had the chalcedony rose to hold while she called; Adam had told her it would help make contact with him. But the chalcedony rose was Diana's.

Don't think about that now. Think about Adam. You need to make Adam hear you.

Adam, she called again, putting all her strength behind it. Strange that the ability to push with her mind, to do whatever she did to send the power lancing out, didn't seem to deteriorate with use. Instead, it was like a muscle, getting stronger as she exercised it. *Adam*, she called again, keeping the message simple and clear. *It's Cassie. I need help*.

He'll come, she told herself. He'll find this place somehow; he'll come if I can just stay calm and wait. It was the thought of what might happen *before* Adam came that chilled the blood in her veins.

So here she was, stuck in the middle of nowhere with four witch hunters. And the silence was getting on her nerves.

'The least you can do,' she said slowly, speaking to Logan and Sally because she didn't think Jordan or Portia would answer, 'is explain yourselves. You've got me out here, and the least you can do is tell me why you hate witches so much. Because I don't understand.'

'Are you crazy?' Logan said, as if it should be perfectly obvious. Then, as she continued to stare at him, he said simply, 'Because they're evil.'

'Logan ... ' Cassie searched his face in the firelight.

'We're just like you. We're more – in touch – with nature, that's all. We study it and we celebrate it, and sometimes we can get it to do things for us. But we're not evil. Look,' she said, as Logan turned away, 'we have our faults like everybody else, but basically we try to be *good*.'

'What about Faye Chamberlain?' Sally snapped, joining the conversation suddenly. 'Is she good?'

'There's good in Faye,' Cassie said, even more slowly. 'Diana said that once to me, and it's true. Faye just has to find it. But anyway, you can't judge all of us by one person.'

'How about what they did to the entire school for years? You're calling that good? They treated everybody like slaves!'

'That was wrong, I admit it,' Cassie said. 'But *Diana* didn't do that – if people treated her like a princess, it wasn't her fault. Faye was the one treating people like slaves. Some of the others went along because they didn't *think* about it. And whatever they did, this isn't the way to solve it!'

'Mr Brunswick is going to solve it,' said Portia briefly.

'Mr Brunswick is a murderer! He is *not* your friend, Portia. He's the one who killed Kori Henderson, Chris and Doug's sister. He killed her because she didn't fit in with his plans. And he killed Mr Fogle, the old principal, because he wanted to take his place. And,' Cassie said, 'he killed Jeffrey, Sally! *Yes.* He did it out of spite as far as I can see – or else to drive the witches and the outsiders farther apart. He wants us to hate each other.'

'That's ridiculous,' Logan said. 'Why would he want that?'

'Because,' Cassie said, shutting her eyes, knowing it was probably useless, 'he is a witch. The bad kind. The only completely bad one I've ever met. And I think he wants us to wipe you out. Or maybe he just wants to take us somewhere else and wipe out the people *there*. I don't *know* what he wants,' she said, opening her eyes, 'but whatever it is, it isn't good. It isn't something that's going to make you happy.'

'Oh, forget this crap. Let's get started,' Jordan said.

'No, wait, I want to get something clear.' Sally stood in front of Cassie, eye to eye. 'You said Brunswick killed Jeffrey – but he couldn't have. He wasn't even in New Salem that night, or when the other murders were committed, either.'

'Oh, he was here, he just wasn't up and around,' muttered Cassie. She looked at Sally. 'He didn't need to be there. He's a witch. He sent out power – dark energy – to do it. Or else maybe he took over somebody's mind and made *them* do it.'

Like Faye, Cassie was thinking grimly. When it came right down to it, Faye could have pushed Kori down the steps to break her neck, and could have dislodged a boulder to start a rock slide on Mr Fogle. She could even have got Jeffrey down to the boiler room on some pretext and then strangled him. All it would take would be sneaking up on him from behind and then somehow getting the rope around his neck. The police doctors had said one person could do it.

'What difference does it make, how?' Cassie asked tiredly. 'He did it, that's all that matters. And he *did* do it, Sally, I promise you. He killed Jeffrey.'

Sally was staring hard into her eyes, her pugnacious face inches from Cassie's. She shook her head and turned away.

'I'm sorry,' Cassie said to the back of her rusty head. 'I liked Jeffrey too. I know what you think, that I was trying to steal him or something. But I wasn't. I was just – I was so excited that night at Homecoming. It was the first dance I'd ever been to when guys wanted to dance with me.'

'Oh, I'm sure!' Sally snapped without turning around.

'It *was*. It's the truth, Sally,' Cassie said passionately. 'Back in California I didn't know any guys at all. I was just too shy. I don't even know why they wanted to dance with me at Homecoming. Sally ...' She gazed at the red-haired girl's tight shoulders helplessly.

Sally turned slowly. 'I guess you don't ever look in a mirror,' she said, but there was less animosity in her voice.

Cassie blinked away the tears that threatened. 'I do, but I don't see anything special,' she said. 'And I didn't want to steal Jeffrey; I was just so flattered that he asked me. It was a beautiful night, and everything seemed enchanted, and then ...' She looked from Sally to Logan, blinking again. 'You don't know how I felt when I realised he was dead. I would have done anything to catch the person who did it.'

Logan took a step towards her, but Portia's voice, sharp as a wasp sting, stopped him. 'She's doing it! She's using her witch powers on you, right now. Don't be stupid, Logan.'

Cassie looked at her. 'Portia, for God's sake...'

'Portia's right,' Jordan said brutally. 'If we listen to her, she'll trick us. She's been a liar from the start.' He pulled the metal thing out of the fire.

'What is that?' Cassie asked.

'A cattle brand.'

Cassie thought about that, and tried to keep her fragile grip on control. Jordan stepped in front of her, holding the long rod which was red-hot at the end. That didn't surprise Cassie. What surprised her was what he said.

'Where are the Master Tools?' he asked.

Cassie was dumbfounded. '*What?*'

'Mr Brunswick told us,' Portia said, her voice thin and hard. 'He told us that they're the source of your power, and that if they're destroyed you lose it all. He wants to destroy them himself and stop you forever.'

Cassie had the wild impulse to laugh, but she knew that would only bring more trouble. So *he'd* put them up to this. And he knew she'd found the Master Tools. Right now, he must be expecting her to tell Jordan to save herself. Or maybe he was around here, hoping Cassie would call on him for help.

I won't, Cassie thought. No matter how bad it gets, I won't do it. I don't want to be saved by him.

She looked around the clearing, especially at the shadows that flickered on the edges of the firelight.

'He wants the Master Tools, all right,' she said distinctly. 'But not to destroy them. He'd use them to destroy *you*, and us, too, if he can't get us to knuckle under.'

Jordan looked unsurprised. 'You'll tell us in a while,' he said. 'I expected you to lie at first.'

Cassie's entire body tightened as he brought the glowing brand closer to her. I am brave, she thought, trying to calm her heartbeat. I am as strong as I need to be. But when she smelled the hot metal, sheer black fright swept through her.

'Wait! Stop right there, Jurgen and Low-down, or whatever your names are.' It was Deborah's voice, angry and filled with elemental savagery. The girl was standing between two trees as if she'd just materialised there this moment. With her tumbled dark hair blending into the black shadows, and her graceful, stalking posture, she might have been some forest goddess come on a mission of vengeance.

Jordan dropped the cattle brand and grabbed his gun, pointing it directly at Deborah.

A new voice spoke quietly from the other side of the grove. 'If you move away from Cassie and put the gun down,' Adam said in low, precise tones, 'we won't have to hurt you.' He had appeared just as soundlessly and he looked just as dangerous as Deborah. Cassie thought of the costume he'd worn at Halloween, the stag antlers and autumn leaves of the horned god. Right now she wouldn't have been surprised to see a stag beside him.

There was another slight movement and Cassie saw Diana.

It was as if moonlight had suddenly stepped into the grove. An unearthly aura hung about the girl who stood with fair hair cascading around her like a shining cloak. Tall and slender, she had such an air of command that she might have been the goddess Diana, with the moon and stars at her fingertips. She looked at the outsiders silently with eyes as green as jewels, and then she spoke.

'Get away from my friend,' she said.

For an instant Cassie thought they were going to do it on the strength of her authority alone. Jordan's gun wavered. Then it snapped up again, pointing towards Adam, and Logan snatched a burning stick from the fire. He held it close to Cassie's face, as Jordan had held the brand.

'Keep back or we'll hurt *her*,' he said.

Adam let out his breath. 'We warned you,' he said softly.

Cassie was looking into Diana's emerald eyes. She glanced at Logan's burning stick, and then back. She could tell that Diana remembered the candle ceremony.

Fire – so close she could feel its heat on her cheek.

The flames changing shape every second, their radiance streaming endlessly upwards. There was power in Fire, as Cassie had discovered when Faye had waved a piece of burning paper at her in the old science building. Power there for the taking...

This time she took it.

The stick flared up as if someone had dumped gasoline on it, and Cassie turned her face away, eyes shut against the brilliance. Logan screamed and threw the stick. Jordan's head jerked sideways, he was distracted for an instant—

—and that was all it took. Jordan went down as the Henderson brothers appeared from nowhere, leaping like twin golden flames. The gun fired a shot skyward, and then they were pinning him, one on each arm. Cassie saw Nick surge up from the shadows and grab Logan from behind. Logan struggled, but Adam joined Nick and the fight was over in seconds.

By the time Cassie looked the other way, the outsider girls were taken care of. Sally was on her face, with Deborah kneeling on her back and Melanie standing over them. Portia was flattened against a tree, very still. Two feet from her, Raj was snarling, lips peeled back, hair bristling. Laurel stood just behind him, looking tall and terrible.

'These trees,' she said to Portia, 'have put up with a lot from your kind. If you try to run you'll end up lost in the middle of them. That's not to mention what the dog might do. If I were you, I wouldn't move a muscle.'

Portia didn't.

Diana walked over and cut Cassie's ropes with a white-handled knife. It took some time.

'Good job,' Suzan said from the sidelines.

'Are you all right?' Diana asked Cassie, still with

that frightening, unearthly aura about her. Cassie nodded.

'We were already on our way when you called to Adam,' Diana said. 'Laurel saw their car speeding down Crowhaven Road and Adam felt there was something wrong. He guided us to their car, but it was Raj who tracked you through the woods.'

Cassie just nodded gratefully. She couldn't speak.

'Since Cassie's all right, we won't hurt you four,' Diana said aloud, then. 'But we're going to take *this*' – she picked up Jordan's gun, holding it as if it were a poisonous snake – 'and we're going to leave you here. Your car has a few flat tyres. You can walk home.'

The four outsiders said nothing. Sally, still on the ground, was panting; Logan, with Nick's arm around his throat, was trembling-still; Portia remained frozen against the tree. But it was Jordan who held Cassie's attention. He was staring at Diana with eyes of pure hatred, like a cornered wild dog.

It will never stop, Cassie thought. They'll hate us even more after this. They'll do something else to us, and we'll do something to them, and it will never stop.

On impulse, she walked over to where Jordan lay sprawled on his back on the forest floor, and she held out a hand to him.

'We don't have to be enemies,' she said. 'Can't we just end it now?'

Jordan spat on her.

Cassie went still, too surprised to be upset. Nobody had ever spat at her before. She looked in shock at her outstretched hand, then wiped it on her jeans.

What happened next she heard later from Laurel, because she was actually looking down at the time. Nick started towards Jordan instantly, but he was hindered by having to get rid of Logan, and anyway Adam was simply *faster*. He moved faster than the eye could follow, grabbing Jordan by the front of the jacket and hauling him up, then knocking him down again with one lightning-quick blow to the face. Behind Cassie, the bonfire shot up in orange flames ten feet high. Jordan landed on his back, both hands clapped over his nose.

'Get up,' Adam said. The flames roared and crackled, sending a shower of sparks floating into the darkness of the woods.

Nick was beside Adam now. His face was emotionless, utterly cool, the old Nick. 'Naw, buddy, I think he's had enough,' he drawled, taking hold of Adam's arm.

Jordan lifted one hand from his nose, and Cassie saw the blood. 'She's a little liar. You'll find out,' he yowled in a thick voice, looking from Cassie to Adam.

For a moment Cassie thought Adam was going to hit him again. Then Adam turned away, as if forgetting Jordan existed. He didn't seem to notice Nick's existence either. He took Cassie's hand, the one Jordan had spat on, turned it over, and kissed it.

Cassie thought that somebody had better do something fast.

'We should tie them up,' Melanie said, her calm, thoughtful voice pervading the clearing. 'Or three of them at least – the fourth can be untying the others while we get away.'

'Not too tightly,' Diana said, conceding. While Jordan, Logan, and Sally were being tied up, she stuck the white-handled knife in the ground by Portia. 'You can cut them free when we leave. Don't try to follow us,' she said. Portia didn't look as if she might follow; her eyes were showing white all around.

Diana followed her gaze to the fire, which was still roaring more like a burning oil well than a bonfire, and spoke softly to Cassie. 'Can you tone that down a little? I think they're scared enough.'

Cassie, who wasn't doing it, mumbled something inarticulate, and hastily went over to check on Sally's bonds.

Sally glanced at her out of the sides of her eyes and spoke without moving her lips. 'I was wrong about you.'

Cassie looked at her in surprise, but said nothing, leaning over as if to examine Sally's tied wrists.

'You may be right about Brunswick,' Sally said, still in almost inaudible tones. 'If you are, I feel sorry for you. He's going to do something on the ninth. There's a full moon or something – and that's when he's going to move. He wanted the tools before then.'

'Thanks,' Cassie whispered and she squeezed Sally's hand behind her back. Then she straightened up as Diana said, 'Let's go.' As they left, Cassie nudged Adam inconspicuously.

'Are you doing the fire?' she whispered.

'What? Oh.' The flames fell, collapsing suddenly into a normal bonfire. 'I guess so,' he said.

They walked through the woods, Laurel and Deborah leading them surely among the dark trees, Raj trotting alongside. Cassie spent the entire walk thinking about Nick.

She got in the Armstrong car with him when they came to the road. He drove silently, one arm along the back of the seat. The other cars were in front of them, headlights shining on the lonely road as they made their way back to New Salem.

Cassie was trying to find the right words to say.

She'd never had to do anything like this before and she was afraid to do it wrong. She was afraid to hurt Nick.

But there was no way around it. From the instant that Adam had kissed her hand she had *known*. Cassie could like it or hate it, but there was no way to do anything about it.

'Nick ...' she said, and choked up.

'You don't have to say anything,' he said, in his old, detached, nothing-hurts-me voice. Cassie could hear the pain underneath it. Then he looked at her, and his tone softened.

'I knew what I was doing when I got into this,' he said. 'And you never pretended anything else. It's not your fault.'

He'd said she didn't have to say anything – but she did. She had to try to explain to him.

'It's not because of Adam,' she said softly. 'I mean, it's not *for* him, because I know there's no hope. I – *accept* that now, and I'm happy for him and Diana. But I just...'

She stopped and shook her head helplessly. 'This is going to sound totally stupid, but I can't be with anybody else. Ever. I'm just going to have to ...' She tried to think of a way to put it, but all she could come up with was a phrase out of one of her grandmother's Victorian etiquette books she'd read one rainy afternoon.

'I'm going to have to live a life of single blessedness,' she mumbled.

Nick threw back his head and laughed. Real laughter. Cassie looked at him, embarrassed, but glad that at least he was smiling. His voice was more normal too, as he glanced at her sideways, taking his arm off the back of the seat.

'Oh, you think so?' he said.

'Well, what else am I supposed to do?'

Nick didn't answer, just shook his head slightly, with

another little snort of laughter.

'Cassie, I'm glad I met you,' he said. 'You're – unique. Sometimes I think you belong back in medieval times instead of now. You and Diana and *him*, all three. But, anyway, I'm glad.'

Cassie felt more embarrassed, and she didn't understand. 'I'm glad I met *you*,' she said. 'You've been so nice to me – you're such a good guy.'

He snorted again. 'Most people would disagree,' he said. 'But I'm not so bad. I'll have to make sure I'm not, or I'll still see you looking at me with those big eyes.' He started to fish a cigarette out of the pack in his pocket, then glanced at her sideways and tapped it back.

Cassie smiled. She wished she could hold his hand, but that wouldn't be right. She was going to have to make it alone now.

She leaned back and looked through the windows at the lighted houses slipping by.

CHAPTER
13

'It's the Moon of Long Nights,' Diana said. 'And it's not just full on the ninth. There's an eclipse.'

'A total lunar eclipse,' said Melanie.

'Is that bad for us?' Cassie asked.

Diana considered. 'Well, all witches' powers are strongest in moonlight. And certain spells are best done at the dark of the moon, or at the full moon, or at some other phase. I'm sure that if Black John is going to move on that particular night, an eclipse must be best for whatever he's going to do. And worst for us fighting him.'

'Except,' Adam said, 'if we know he's going to move – and he doesn't know we know it. He won't realise we're prepared.'

There were thoughtful nods around the Circle. It was the day after Thanksgiving and everyone who had come to rescue Cassie the day before was gathered at Adam's house. Cassie had told them what had happened in the clearing before they came – except about Jordan asking for the Master Tools. This she'd whispered to Adam and Diana in front of Diana's house last night. Now she looked at the two of them with a question in her eyes.

Adam and Diana both regarded the group unhappily. 'Right,' Adam said. 'I guess we'd better tell them. Since *he* knows, it doesn't really matter, does it?'

'Faye must have found out somehow,' Diana said, looking more unhappy than ever. 'She went to Black John—'

'No,' Cassie said.

Diana looked at her, surprised. 'But—'

'Not Faye,' Cassie said, grimly and with absolute certainty. '*Sean*.'

Adam cursed softly. Diana stared at him, then at Cassie. Then she whispered, 'Oh, my God.'

'What about Sean? What did he do?' Deborah demanded. Nick was very alert, his narrow eyes fixed on Cassie.

After a glance at Diana – who nodded and leaned her head on one hand – Cassie said simply to Deborah, 'He told Black John that Adam and Diana and I had found the Master Tools.'

'You found – you mean you guys – you mean you really—?' Deborah was sputtering. The others looked speechless with amazement.

'*Cassie* led us to them,' Adam said. 'They were in the fireplace at Number Twelve. On the way back we ran into Sean, who said he'd seen a light. But you think . . . ?' He looked at Cassie.

Cassie took a deep breath. 'I think Black John has been influencing him all along. I think he was the one who stole the hematite from my room. I figured it out last night, when I was trying to get to sleep. I started thinking about who could have told Black John – and I kept getting this flash of Sean the first time I saw him. He was wearing a belt with his name carved on some shiny stone. I used to see him wear it all the time, but now that it's cold and everybody's wearing sweaters, I haven't noticed it. But I'll bet he's been wearing it underneath, and I'll bet he was wearing it that night he came out in his pyjama top. And I'll bet that shiny stone is—'

'Hematite,' half a dozen bleak voices chorused, and everyone looked at Melanie.

'Hematite or lodestone,' Melanie confirmed. 'Yes, it is; I've seen that belt too. How incredibly stupid of us. It never even occurred to me.'

Nick leaned forward. 'So you think Faye *wasn't* the one who told Black John we were wearing amethysts as protection? You think Sean did that?'

Cassie looked at the hard line of his mouth. 'It wasn't his fault, Nick. If Black John got into his mind – well, I know how I felt when he was trying to get into *my* mind. Sean wouldn't have been able to resist. In fact, *we* saw that he couldn't resist, at the assembly when he volunteered to be a hall monitor. I had to yell at him to break the trance.'

'Sean ... God!' Laurel said, settling back. 'It's just too awful.'

'I'm afraid it's worse,' Cassie said. She stared down at Mrs Franklin's coffee table, pressing one hand flat against it. She didn't know how to say this next. 'You guys, I think ... I think Black John used Sean to commit the murders.'

There was a deafening silence. Even Diana looked too horrified to support Cassie. But Adam looked into her eyes and then slowly, shutting his own eyes, nodded.

'Yes,' he said.

'Oh, *no*,' said Suzan.

'I think' – Cassie swallowed – 'that he could have written a note to Kori the night before, asking her to meet him in front of school. She wouldn't have suspected him; she'd have just thought it was Circle business. He could have come up behind her, and—'

'I'll kill him!' Doug shouted, jumping up. Nick and Deborah grabbed him, but by then Chris was shouting too, lunging for the door. Adam and Melanie wrestled him to the ground.

'It wasn't *him*; it wasn't Sean,' Cassie shouted. 'Listen to me, you guys! It was Black John; *he's* the one who killed Kori. If I'm right, Sean probably doesn't even remember it! He was just a – a *container* for the dark energy to use.'

'God,' Laurel said. 'God – remember the skull ceremony in Diana's garage? The time the second bunch of dark energy was released? Sean and Faye started fighting, the candle went out, and the dark energy escaped. Sean said Faye started it, and we all believed him. But Faye said Sean was trying to break the circle. What if she was right?'

'I'll bet she *was* right,' Cassie said. 'Black John's been with us all the time. Whatever Sean saw, he saw. And when enough dark energy was released from the skull – which Black John *arranged* to happen whenever he could – then it worked with Sean to commit the murders.'

'It would have been easy to get Mr Fogle over to Devil's Cove, too,' Suzan said. 'Sean could have pretended he had something bad to tell about somebody else in the Club. I used to do that all the time; tell the principal things about—' She glanced at Diana. 'Well – that was in the old days. Anyway, Sean could have asked Fogle to meet him under the rocks and then – *foom*.' She made a pushing gesture. 'Good-bye, Mr Fogle.'

'Can we let you up now?' Adam asked Chris, and 'Can we trust you to act sensible?' Deborah asked Doug.

There were incoherent snarls from the Henderson brothers, and when they were released they sat up with flushed faces and blue-green eyes as bright as gas flames.

'We're gonna get that bastard,' Doug said quietly.

'If it's the last thing we do,' said Chris, equally quiet. Cassie hoped they meant Black John.

'But what about Jeffrey?' Diana asked Cassie.

Cassie shrugged. 'I don't know how Sean could have gotten him down to the boiler room—'

'By saying *you* were down there, maybe,' Laurel said.

'—but if he did, he could have just come up behind him and strangled him with the rope – no, Sean's too short. Oh, I don't know how he could have done it—'

'By getting Lovejoy to sit down or lean over,' Nick said, his voice crisp and low. 'That's what I'd have done, anyway, if I were trying to strangle somebody that much taller. And look, if Sean had that dark energy *inside* him somehow, he could have had outrageous strength. He must have had, to be able to put the noose around Lovejoy's neck and haul him up over that pipe afterwards.'

Cassie felt sick. 'It's true – I didn't see either Sean or Jeffrey at the dance for a while before the murder. Then all of a sudden Sean appeared on the dance floor, coming towards me. So I ran to the boiler room ... and found Jeffrey.'

'I think we need to talk to Sean,' said Diana.

'No,' Adam said, with surprising vehemence. 'That's just what we shouldn't do. If we talk to him now, Black John will realise we know. But if we don't say anything, if we play along with Sean and pretend we *don't* know, we can feed him disinformation. Tell him things that aren't true, for him to pass along to Black John.'

'Like tell him we don't know when Black John is going to move,' Deborah said, her dark eyes beginning to snap. 'Tell him we're terrified of Black John – we don't know how to use the Master Tools – we're unprepared...'

'Or that we're all fighting among ourselves,' suggested

Laurel. 'We can't agree on anything. We're deadlocked.'

'Right! And then that night we'll actually be ready for him. When's the eclipse, Melanie?' Adam said.

'Around six forty in the evening. That's what I'd say we have to look out for. The moon in shadow.'

'The moon in shadow,' Cassie repeated softly. 'I think I can understand why he would choose that time.' He's a shadow himself, she thought.

'And until then all we have to do is pretend to be completely disorganised, terrified, and argumentative,' said Melanie.

'Shouldn't be too hard,' Suzan said, raising an eyebrow.

'There's somebody I think we *should* talk to,' Cassie said, 'without giving away any of our secrets. I think one of us should talk to Faye.'

'And I think you're elected,' Nick said. 'I can't think of anybody better for the job.' He winked at Cassie, but it was a grim wink.

'We need you.'

'I'm sure,' Faye said lazily, examining herself in the mirror. She was trying her hair in different ways: twisted back, on top of her head, at the nape of her neck. Cassie hadn't been in Faye's bedroom since the night Faye had set a ring of red stones around the crystal skull and released the dark energy that had eventually killed Jeffrey. The room was as opulent and luxurious as ever: the wallpaper patterned with lush jungle orchids, the bed piled with cushions, the stereo system packed with expensive extras. Faye's vampire kittens once again twined sinuously around Cassie's ankles.

But there was a different atmosphere here than

before. The red candles were gone from the dresser tops; in their place were stacks of paperwork. On the bedspread along with the cordless phone was a beeper. An appointment book was sitting in front of the mirror, and the clothes strewn carelessly about were of the sultry office-girl kind Faye had taken to wearing.

The room felt – pressured. Type-A lifestyle. More like Portia than Faye.

'I suppose you know that Portia Bainbridge and Sally had me kidnapped two days ago,' Cassie said.

Faye shot her an amused glance in the mirror. 'And I'm sure you know you only had to open your pretty little mouth and yell, and Daddy would have been right there to help.'

Cassie tried not to look as sick as that made her feel. 'I don't want his help,' she said, swallowing.

Faye shrugged. 'Maybe later.'

'*No*, Faye. Not later. I don't ever want to see him again. But if you know about me being kidnapped, you must know what they were after. We've found the Master Tools.' Cassie looked at the strange opposite-Faye image in the mirror, and then turned to look the real Faye in the eyes. 'They belong to you,' she said distinctly. 'You're leader of the coven. But the coven is going to fight ... Black John.'

'You can't even say it, can you? It's not so hard. Daddy. Father. Pops. Whatever you want to call him, I'm sure he won't mind—'

'Will you listen to me, Faye!' Cassie almost shouted. 'You're sitting here being fatuous—'

'And she knows big words, too!'

'—while something *serious* is going on! Something deadly serious. He is going to *kill* people. That's all he is, Faye, hatred and the desire to kill. I know it; I can feel it in him. And he's taking *you* for a ride.'

Faye's golden eyes narrowed. She looked less amused.

'I've known you for a while now, Faye, and there've been plenty of times when I've hated you. But I never thought I'd see you become somebody's *stenographer*. You used to make up your own mind about things and you didn't kiss up to anybody. Do you remember how you once asked me if I wanted my epitaph to be "Here lies Cassie. She was ... nice"? Well, do you want yours to be "Here lies Faye. She was a good secretary"?'

One of Faye's hands, with its long fingernails – mauve these days, instead of scarlet – was clenched on the dresser. Her jaw was set, and she was staring hard into her own golden eyes in the mirror.

Cassie's pulse quickened. 'When I looked at you I used to see a lion – a sort of black and gold lion. Now I see' – she glanced down at her feet – 'a kitten. Some rich guy's kitten.'

She waited tensely. Maybe ... just maybe ... Maybe the bond forged during the candle ceremony would be strong enough, maybe Faye had enough pride, enough independence...

Faye's eyes met hers in the mirror. Then Faye shook her head. Her face was closed, her mouth tight.

'I think you know the way out,' she said.

The kittens tangled around Cassie's feet as she turned, and she felt the razor-sharp nick of claws.

No, she told them with her mind, and she felt the kittens freeze, ears back. She picked them up, one in each hand, and tossed them onto Faye's bed.

Then she left.

'We have to give her until the ninth,' Diana said. 'Maybe she'll change her mind.'

' "Maybe later",' Cassie quoted, but there wasn't much hope in her voice.

'We'll wait until the ninth for Sean, too,' Adam said.

They made it through the next seven school days without trouble – except among themselves. At New Salem High, the members of the Club only spoke to each other in public to argue. Laurel's birthday on the first and Sean's birthday on the third of December went uncelebrated, because, according to a distraught Diana, none of them could get along long enough to plan a party. Cassie saw the looks and heard the whispers and knew that the plan was working. She concentrated on being as much like the old Cassie as possible – shy, tongue-tied, easily frightened or embarrassed. The role was uncomfortable, like some old skin she'd outgrown, and she itched to get rid of it. But for the time they were fooling Sean. They were even fooling Faye.

'I hear you and Nick have broken up,' Faye said in the hall one day. The hooded golden eyes were warm and pleased.

Cassie flushed, looking away.

'And the Club isn't much of a club without me, from what I see these days,' Faye went on, practically purring.

Cassie squirmed.

'I may join you sometime – maybe for the next full-moon celebration. If you're having one, that is.'

Cassie shrugged.

Faye looked smug. 'We could have a *wicked* time,' she said. 'Think about it.'

As Faye walked away Cassie saw Sally Waltman at her post as hall monitor. She edged up as inconspicuously as possible.

'We're ready for the ninth, like you told us,' Cassie said softly. 'But can you do one more thing for us?'

Sally looked uneasy. 'He's got everybody watching everybody. Nobody's safe—'

'I know, but when the ninth comes, will you tell us if he does anything unusual? If it looks like he's moving? Please, Sally. Everything I told you about him is true.'

'All right,' Sally said, casting a hunted glance around. 'Now just *go*, will you? I'll try to get a message to you if I hear anything.'

Cassie nodded and hurried away.

The ninth dawned grey and windy, the sort of day that normally made Cassie want to curl up in front of a fire. Instead, she put on extra-warm clothes: a thick sweater, gloves, a parka. She had no idea what they might be facing today, but she wanted to be dressed for action. In her backpack, along with her school notebooks, she put her Book of Shadows.

She was walking out of French class when Sally intercepted her.

'Come with me, please,' the rusty-haired girl said in crisp hall-monitor accents, and Cassie followed her into the empty nurse's office next door. Sally immediately dropped the officious tone.

'If I get caught with you, it's all over,' she said rapidly in a harsh whisper, her eyes on the frosted-glass window in the door. 'But here it is: I just overheard Brunswick talking with your friend Faye. Maybe *you'll* understand what it was about, because I sure don't. They were discussing something about arranging an accident on the bridge – it sounded like they were taking an empty school bus over there, and a car, or maybe it was a couple of cars. He said "They only have to burn for an hour or so; by then the water will have risen far enough." Does that mean anything to you?'

'An accident would block the bridge to the mainland,' Cassie said slowly.

'Sure, but why?' Sally asked impatiently.

'I don't know. I'm going to find out. Sally, if I need to see you again, will you be in the cafeteria at lunch?'

'Yes, but you can't talk to me there. Portia's been looking at me strangely ever since that night in the clearing – I think she's suspicious. Her brothers went away mad, and she didn't believe a word you said about Brunswick. If she catches me with you, I'm dead.'

'You may be dead if I *don't* talk with you,' Cassie said. 'Go on, get out of here, I'll leave in a minute.'

Cassie reached the old science building at a run. Waiting on the second floor was the rest of the Club – minus Faye and Sean, who hadn't been informed of the meeting. The plan had been to nab Sean right after lunch, even if they hadn't learned anything about Black John's plans by then.

'But we do know something,' Cassie said breathlessly, sitting down on a crate. 'Listen.' She told them what Sally had said.

'Well, that explains it,' Deborah put in when Cassie finished. 'I just saw him and Faye walk out of the building, and the secretary said they'd be gone all afternoon. So they're going out to wreck a school bus. Cool.'

'But *why*?' Cassie said. 'I mean, it looks like he wants to block the bridge, but what's the point?'

It was Adam who answered. He'd been sitting by Doug, with one of the earphones from Doug's Walkman pressed to his ear.

'The point,' he said, 'is to keep everybody on the island. There's just been an update on the news – anybody remember that hurricane they were talking about the last couple of days? The one that they were afraid was going to hit Florida, but then it turned north while it was still out in the Atlantic?'

There was head-shaking around the group – most of them hadn't been too interested in the news lately – but Melanie said, 'I thought they downgraded that to a tropical storm.'

'Yeah, they figured it was just going to dissipate out in the ocean. Look, I know a little about hurricanes. This one isn't supposed to be a threat, because they're assuming it's going to turn north-east at Cape Hatteras. That's what hurricanes usually do when they hit the low-pressure trough around there. But we all know what happens when they *don't*.' He looked around the group grimly, and this time there were nods from everyone but Cassie.

'When they don't turn at Cape Hatteras, they come barrelling straight up here,' Adam said to her, then. 'Like the one in 1938, and the one a few years ago ... and the one in 1976.'

The silence was absolute. Cassie glanced from side to side at the faces in the dim room.

'God,' she whispered, feeling dizzy.

'Yes,' said Adam. 'Winds a hundred and fifty miles an hour, and *walls* of water, forty feet high. Now, they're still *saying* this storm is going to turn – they just mentioned on the radio that it's supposed to stay well off the Atlantic seaboard. But' – he looked around again, deliberately – 'anybody want to take bets?'

Laurel jumped up. 'We're got to stop Black John. If that bridge is blocked, everybody on the island is in danger.'

'Too late,' Deborah said briefly. 'He's already gone. Remember? I saw him leave ten minutes ago.'

'And everybody's not just in danger, everybody's *dead*,'

Melanie said. 'That storm a couple of years ago just nicked New Salem, but this one could wipe us out.'

Cassie looked at Adam. 'How fast is it coming?'

'I don't know. Could be fifty miles an hour, could be seventy. If it doesn't turn at Cape Hatteras, they'll issue a hurricane warning – but it'll be too late by then, especially if the bridge is blocked. It could get to us in maybe seven, eight hours. More or less.'

'Around the time of the eclipse?' Cassie asked.

'Maybe. Maybe a little later.'

'But before it hits us, it'll hit Cape Cod and Boston,' Diana whispered. 'It will *kill* people there.' She looked stunned and dazed at the idea.

'Then there's only one thing to do,' Cassie said. 'We've got to stop it before it hits land at all. We've got to make it dissipate, or turn back out to the ocean, or whatever. Or we've got to make *him* do it. And before that we've got to warn people on our own – tell them to do whatever you do in a hurricane—'

'Evacuate,' Adam said dryly, 'which may not be possible, even in boats. Listen to that wind.' He paused and Cassie heard not only the wind but a pattering on the boarded-up windows. Rain.

'If they can't get out, they'll have to dig in,' Chris said. 'Anybody up for a hurricane party?'

'It's not funny,' Nick said sharply, and Cassie said, 'All right, then – tell people to do *that*. Do whatever they can. And we'd better get back to Crowhaven Road—'

'With Sean,' Adam cut in swiftly. 'I'll get him and meet everybody at my house. Let's do it, people.'

They left their uneaten lunches – except Suzan, who bolted hers down and ran after the others – and headed for the school.

CHAPTER
14

'So you have to go now,' Cassie said, trying to get her breath, speaking not only to Sally but to everyone in the cafeteria. 'Forget school, forget everything. Leave. Get out if you can, and if you can't – well, do whatever you can to protect yourselves.' She stopped. 'Look, it's *true*. Sally, tell them.'

The rusty-haired girl had been staring at Cassie, eyes wary, poised on her chair as if to bolt from this social pariah. Now she stared at Cassie another moment, then nodded once, as if to herself. Taking a deep breath, she stood.

'Okay, you heard it,' she said in clear, strident tones that carried through the room. 'We're going to have a hurricane. Everybody tell somebody, and tell them to tell somebody else. Come on, get moving.'

A boy stood up. 'I saw on TV last night that the storm isn't coming anywhere near us. How does she know—'

'She's a witch, isn't she?' Sally yelled back in her raucous voice. 'You telling me witches don't know these things? They know more about nature than you ever will! Now come on!'

'Sally, have you lost your *mind*?' The thin angry voice came from the door of the back room, where Portia was standing in front of a group of students with badges, her face chalky with fury. 'You're a hall monitor—'

'Not any more! I said move, you guys!'

'This is completely against regulations! I'm going to tell Mr Brunswick—'

'You do that, cupcake,' Sally shouted back. '*If* you can find him! Now for the last time, people, get moving! Who are you going to listen to, her or me?'

The hall monitors behind Portia hesitated for an instant, then, as a group, they surged forward to obey Sally. Portia stumbled back as they pushed around her, leaving her the sole inhabitant of the room. Cassie's last glimpse of her showed her standing there, rigid, furious, and utterly alone.

Sally began to shout more instructions to the cafeteria workers, and Cassie turned to go. But as Cassie reached the door, each of the girls paused a moment, and looked back at the other across the room.

'You going to be okay?' Sally said. Cassie knew the 'you' didn't just mean Cassie. It meant the whole Circle.

'Yes.'

'Okay. Good luck.'

'You too. Good-bye, Sally.'

It wasn't much of a brilliant cultural exchange, Cassie thought, running towards the parking lot to meet Diana. But it was a truce, witch with outsider. More than a truce.

And now, she thought, I've got to put them out of my mind – all the outsiders. Sally will take care of her people; we have to take care of ours.

It was raining hard now, and it seemed to get worse as she and Diana drove towards Crowhaven Road.

Gusts of wind swayed Diana's car as they pulled into Adam's driveway.

Right behind them, Adam's jeep was pulling in. 'They've got Sean,' Cassie said, twisting to look. She and Diana hurried to help.

Nick and Doug were holding the smaller boy in the back seat. They marched him to the door the way Portia's brothers had marched Cassie. It seemed a little incongruous; Sean was *so* small – but then Cassie looked into those shiny, darting black eyes.

'You'd better get the hematite off him quick,' she said.

Nick pulled Sean's sweater up – and there it was, the engraved belt Cassie had seen that first week of school. Adam unbuckled it and threw it on the floor, where it lay like a dead snake. 'Where's the other piece?' he asked Sean roughly.

Sean just fought to get free, panting, his eyes wild. It took all three of the guys to hold him, and if Chris, Deborah, and Laurel hadn't arrived at that moment, he might actually have gotten away. Working together, the boys and Deborah managed to strip off his sweater and shirt. Underneath, where the other members of the Circle had been wearing amethysts, Sean was wearing a small leather pouch. Adam shook it gingerly and Cassie's piece of hematite fell out.

'Thief!' Deborah said, shaking a fist in Sean's face. Sean stared at her blankly, still panting, terrified.

'He probably didn't even know he had it,' Melanie intervened. 'He's been under Black John's influence from the beginning. Somebody take that hematite out and bury it. Laurel, is the herbal bath ready?'

'Ready!' came Laurel's shout from the downstairs bathroom, over the sound of running water. 'Get him in here.'

The Circle had been planning this purification ritual ever since they'd found out about Sean, and everyone knew his or her part. The boys dragged Sean into the bathroom while Laurel stood just outside the door. 'I don't care if his clothes are off or on,' Cassie heard her calling. 'Just get him in the tub.'

Deborah scooped up the hematite in a dustpan and went to bury it, and Diana rapidly completed a herbal charm she took from her backpack. She charged the canvas pouch of herbs with Earth, Water, Air, and Fire by sprinkling salt on it, flicking water from a glass on it, breathing on it, and passing it over a lit candle which had been sitting ready on the coffee table.

'Okay, it's done,' she said. 'Melanie, what about you?'

Melanie looked up from laying a ring of white stones on the floot. 'I'm done too. By the time we're finished with Sean, he'll be so pure we won't know him any more.'

Cassie wanted to look something up in her Book of Shadows, but there was another priority first.

'We have to warn the parents around here,' she said, 'the ones who're at home, who don't work. Is somebody doing that?'

'I'll go to my house,' Chris said. 'Both of my parents are home.'

'My mom works,' Deborah said.

'That just leaves Faye's mom,' said Diana.

'I'll go tell her,' Suzan offered, surprising Cassie. 'She knows me, she might take it best from me.'

'And the crones,' Cassie said. 'I mean,' she amended quickly, 'Adam's grandmother and Granny Quincey and Aunt Constance.'

'They're at my house; they came over this morning,' Melanie said. 'Something to do with your mom, I think, Cassie. But I can't leave this circle.'

'I'll go,' Cassie said.

Diana flashed a smile at her. 'I think crones is a good name for them,' she said. 'It's what they are, and I think Granny Quincey, anyway, would be proud to be crone to our coven.'

So would my grandma, I bet, Cassie thought, and she plunged outside again.

There was a strange smell out here, a smell like low tide, like crawling and decaying things. Cassie ran to the edge of the cliff, taking the back route along the bluff to Melanie's house, and she saw that the ocean was dark and wild. The water was neither blue nor green nor grey, but a sludgy, oily colour that seemed to be a mixture of all three. Specks of foam were flying on the wind, and there was white froth everywhere.

Above, the clouds took on fantastic shapes, boiling and changing as if moulded by unseen hands. The rain drove into Cassie's face. It was a savage and awe-inspiring scene.

No one answered her knock at the door of Number Four. Cassie wasn't sure anybody inside could hear it over the wind and rain. 'Aunt Constance?' she shouted, opening the door and peering inside. 'Hello?'

She started towards the room that had been given to her mother, and then stopped, turned back guiltily, and wiped her sandy, muddy Reeboks on the mat. Even so, she dripped water on the spotless, mirror-polished hardwood floor as she hurried to the bedroom. The door was barely ajar, and a strange brightness flickered inside.

'Hello? . . . Oh, my God!' Cassie poked her head around the door and froze. The room was lit entirely by dozens of white candles. Around the bed were three figures, three women whose appearance was so strange and fantastic that for a moment Cassie didn't recognise them.

One was tall and thin, another was short and plump, and the third was tiny and doll-like. They all had long hair: the tall one's was black and thick, longer than Diana's, the plump one's was silvery-grey and untidy, waving down past her shoulders, and the tiny one's was gauzy and white like floating wisps of sea foam. And they were naked.

Cassie's eyes were popping. 'Great Aunt Constance?' she gasped to the one with long black hair.

'Who did you expect?' Melanie's aunt said sharply, her meticulously tweezed eyebrows drawing together. 'Lady Godiva? Now go away, child, we're busy.'

'Don't be unkind to her,' said the plump woman, whom Cassie was now able to identify as Adam's grandmother. She smiled at Cassie, entirely un-selfconscious.

'We're trying something to help your mother, dear,' the tiny figure, Laurel's Granny Quincey, added. 'It's a sky-clad ritual, you see; that's why we're naked. Constance had her doubts, but we convinced her.'

'And we need to get on with it,' Great Aunt Constance said, gesturing with the wooden cup she was holding. Granny Quincey was holding a bunch of herbs, and Adam's grandmother, a silver bell. Cassie looked at the bed, where her mother lay as motionless as ever. Something about the light in the room made that sleeping face look different, just as it made the three women look different.

'But there's hurricane coming,' Cassie said. 'That's why I'm here; I came to warn you.'

The women exchanged glances. 'Well, if there is, there's no help for it,' Adam's grandmother sighed.

'But—'

'Your mother can't be moved, dear,' Granny Quincey said firmly. 'So you go along and do what you have to, and we'll try to protect her here.'

'We're going to fight Black John,' Cassie said. The simple statement seemed to hang in the air after she'd said it, and the three old women looked at each other again.

Great Aunt Constance opened her mouth, frowning, but Granny Quincey interrupted her. 'There's no one else *to* do it, Constance. They have to fight.'

'Then be careful. You tell Melanie – and all of them – to be careful,' Aunt Constance said.

'And you stick together. As long as you stick together you'll have a chance,' said Adam's grandmother.

And that was that. The women turned back to the bed. Cassie stood for one more moment looking at the candles – so white, with their flames even whiter, a golden white like Diana's hair – and at the myriad ghostly shadows on the ceiling and walls. Then she left. As she quietly shut the door, all the candle flames danced wildly, and she had a last glimpse of the three women in the room, arms raised, beginning a kind of dance too. The silver bell chimed softly.

She hadn't noticed the wind inside the room, but now she did. Everything outside that door seemed colder and noisier, and the dim light coming in through the windows looked grey and wintry. Cassie had an impulse to go back into the golden room and hide there, but she knew she couldn't.

She walked back to Adam's house, Number Nine, with the wind pushing her all the way.

She was the last one back. The Circle was in Adam's living room, sitting around Sean, who was sitting within the circle of quartz crystals. Sean's face was very pink and scrubbed-looking, his hair was wet and spiky, and he was wearing clothes too big for him. Adam's, Cassie guessed. Around his neck was the canvas pouch full of herbs Diana had prepared. He looked dazed and terrified, but he didn't seem to be trying to get away.

'Were they there? Did you find them?' Diana asked Cassie.

Cassie nodded. She didn't quite want to tell Diana *how* she had found them. She didn't know how Melanie and Adam and Laurel would feel about their elderly relatives dancing naked around a sickroom. They might think there was something wrong with it; they might not understand about the golden light.

'They said they'd stay where they were,' she said. 'Granny Quincey said my mom couldn't be moved, and that they were trying to help her. They said we should be careful, and Adam's grandmother told us to stick together.

'Good advice,' Adam said, looking at Sean. 'And that's just about the point we've gotten to, here. Are we going to stick together or not?'

'We tried asking him about the murders,' Laurel informed Cassie in a low voice, 'but he doesn't remember anything – doesn't know what we're talking about. We had to convince him that it wasn't a joke. He believes us now, but he's scared to death.'

'So here's the choice, Sean,' Adam was saying. 'You can stand with us, or you can spend the rest of the day locked in the cellar where you can't make trouble.'

'Or,' Diana said softly, 'you can go to *him*, to Black John. It's his right,' she added quickly, as some of the others began to protest. 'He has to make the decision.'

Sean's frightened eyes roved all around the room. Cassie felt sorry for him, sitting surrounded, with everyone looking at him. When he spoke, his voice was squeaky but definitive. 'I'll stand with you guys.'

'Good boy,' Laurel said approvingly, and Deborah

thumped him on the back so hard he nearly fell over. The Hendersons said nothing, simply looked at him out of their strange blue-green eyes, and Cassie had the feeling they might never forgive him for what had happened to Kori, even if it hadn't been his fault. But at least for now, the Circle stood together.

Except...

Cassie looked at Adam, and they both looked at Diana. Diana nodded.

'Now's the time,' she said. 'This is Faye's last chance – let's hope she takes it.'

Cassie didn't have much hope, but she picked up the cordless phone lying on a pile of unfolded laundry on the couch. 'What's her beeper number?'

Diana unfolded a scrap of paper and read it off. 'After it rings, press pound and then dial Adam's number,' she instructed.

Cassie did and turned off the phone. She waited. Nothing happened.

'We should give her a while to get to a phone,' Diana said.

They all waited. Rain beat at the windows, and the wind howled in the chimney.

'Isn't there anything we should do? Like – I don't know, nail boards over the windows or something?' Cassie asked.

'Normally, yeah. We'd put up storm shutters, lash everything down, all that stuff,' Adam said. 'But if this one hits us, I think we're history, so there's not much point.'

They waited.

'Try her again,' Diana said, and Cassie did.

'Her mom hadn't seen her since this morning,' Suzan said. 'I wonder where she and Black John are?'

Cassie wondered too. Wherever they were, Faye wasn't answering her beeper.

'I think,' Cassie said at last, 'that we're missing one coven leader. And – well, I wanted to look this up in my Book of Shadows first, but Melanie, doesn't it say somewhere that in an emergency you can elect a new leader?'

Melanie smiled faintly, then nodded, as if she knew what Cassie had in mind. 'In a crisis,' she said. 'If the remaining coven all agrees, a new leader can be elected.'

There was a shifting around the Circle, people straightening up and looking interested. 'Oh,' said Laurel, 'that's a *good* idea.'

'Especially since we've got the Master Tools,' Adam said.

'Let's do it,' said Deborah.

Cassie was excited. She'd taken an oath while watching Faye draw that circle at the crossroads, and now she was going to see her oath fulfilled. She'd promised that Faye wouldn't be leader for ever, and in a few minutes Faye *wouldn't* be.

She opened her mouth joyfully to say, 'I nominate Diana,' but before she could speak she heard Diana's voice.

'I nominate Cassie,' Diana said clearly.

Cassie simply stared at her, amazed. When she got her breath back she said, 'You're joking.'

'No,' Diana said. Then she turned, speaking to the rest of the Circle, speaking formally. 'Cassie,' she said, 'has shown the most power of any of us, including Faye. She can call on the elements – we've seen her call on Fire. She can communicate over long distances. She's had true dreams, and she was the one who led us to the Master Tools. Her grandmother told her that her family has always had the clearest sight and the most power. And she's strong, stronger than I am for this kind of fight. I nominate Cassie.'

Cassie was stunned, but the others were nodding.

'She's pretty tough,' Deborah said, 'even if she doesn't look like it.'

'She got that dog off me,' said Chris, sticking out his foot and examining it.

'She's smart, too,' said Laurel proudly. Aside from Diana, Laurel had been Cassie's first friend in the Circle. 'She thinks of things most people wouldn't think of.'

'She has ideas,' Suzan agreed, nodding her strawberry-blond head sagely.

'I like her,' Sean ventured hesitantly, from his place in the ring of white stones. 'She's nice to me.'

'She's a natural,' Doug said, grinning his wild grin.

Nick just said, '*Yes*.'

Cassie realised they were serious. 'I'm also Black John's...' She stopped and tried again. 'The fact that Black John is my ...' She still couldn't say the word.

'I think that may actually work *for* us,' Melanie said, looking at Cassie with thoughtful grey eyes. 'If he doesn't really want to hurt you it might handicap him – a little.'

Everyone was still nodding. Cassie swallowed and gazed around the Circle. It didn't seem to have occurred to anyone that she might just be too *scared* to do it, to lead the fight against Black John. In her own heart, she knew she didn't want to face him again – that she wasn't ready. She didn't know if she'd ever be ready.

But they were all looking at her: Diana with earnest faith; Deborah and the Hendersons with innocent confidence. Even Nick and Melanie were nodding, urging her.

Cassie looked at Adam.

His blue-grey eyes were something like the ocean outside – murky and full of turmoil. 'You can do it,' he said tersely, answering her unspoken question. 'And I think it's best for the coven. I don't know if it's best for *you*.'

Cassie let out her breath.

They believed in her. She couldn't let them down.

'If everybody agrees,' she said, scarcely knowing her own voice.

'We'll do it the easy way,' Melanie said. 'All in favour of Cassie as leader, raise your hand.'

Every hand was raised.

Diana jumped up. 'I'll get the things,' she said. She and Adam headed for the cellar and returned a few minutes later with the brass and leather document box. Everyone leaned forward to look as she opened it, and there was a soft hiss of amazement around the Circle.

'They're beautiful,' Suzan said, touching the silver diadem with one perfectly manicured nail.

'Yes,' said Diana, unzipping her backpack. 'Here, Cassie, put this on.' It was the white shift Diana wore at meetings.

Cassie felt heat stealing into her face. She *couldn't* wear that. She would look...

'Don't worry, you won't be cold,' Diana said, and smiled.

'But – you're taller than me. It'll be too long—'

'I hemmed it,' Diana said. And then, in the silence that followed, she said gently, 'Take it, Cassie.'

Slowly, Cassie took it. She went into the bathroom, still slightly steamy now, where the boys had washed Sean, and she put on the raw-silk shift. It fitted perfectly.

Diana had this planned, she realised.

She was embarrassed to walk back out, but she told herself this was no time to be worried about how much skin she was showing. Chris and Doug whistled as she rejoined the group.

'Shut up, this is serious,' Laurel said.

'She might as well stand here, in the circle of white stones,' Melanie said. 'Get out, Sean.'

Sean, looking relieved, stepped out. Cassie stepped in. Silence fell.

'I abjure thee to work for the good of the Circle, to harm none, to be faithful to all. By Water, by Fire, by Earth, and by Air, lead us peacefully and with good will,' Diana said. Cassie realised she was getting the part of the ceremony that Faye had missed when Faye had become leader.

'Look – this is only temporary, isn't it—?' she began.

'Sh,' said Laurel, kneeling. Cassie felt something soft being fastened just above her right knee. She looked down to see Laurel buckling the green leather garter.

Coolness encircled Cassie's upper arm, and she turned to see Melanie clasping the silver bracelet there. It was surprisingly heavy; Cassie knew she'd feel the weight whenever she moved that arm.

'Look at me,' Diana said. Cassie did. Between her two hands Diana was holding the diadem of delicate twisted silver, with the crescent moon on top. Cassie felt it settle into her hair, lightly but firmly. And then, all over her body, from the silver of the garter buckles, to the silver of the bracelet, to the circlet touching her forehead, Cassie felt a rush of tingling warmth. An – aliveness.

These are the real tools; not just symbols, she thought. They have power of their own.

In that moment, she knew she could direct their power. It was part of her, suffusing her with strength. She was a witch, from a line of powerful witches, and she was leader of this Circle.

'All right,' she said, stepping out of the ring of stones

and going over to take her Book of Shadows from her backpack. She was no longer worried about how she looked; she knew she looked good. That didn't matter. They had a little time ahead of them, and she wanted to use it to their advantage.

'All right, look; while we're waiting I think we should go through our Books of Shadows – my grandmother told me to study mine, and it's better than doing nothing,' she said. 'We can take turns reading out loud until it gets dark – he won't move until then.'

'Are you sure?' Melanie said.

'Yes.' Cassie didn't know how she knew, but she knew. Her grandmother had called it the Sight, but to Cassie it was more like a voice – an inner voice, a voice at her core. By now, she knew enough to listen to it.

Nobody argued. Those who had them reached for Books of Shadows. Outside, the wind wailed dismally.

CHAPTER

15

Around four o'clock the power went off. The house got colder. They lit candles and went on reading.

' "For Protection Against Fire and Water",' Cassie read. But Melanie said the spell which came after wasn't powerful enough to protect against a hurricane, and Cassie knew she was right.

'Here, this is 'To Cast Out Fear and Malignant Emotions",' Diana read from her own book. ' "Sun by day/and moon by night/let all dark thoughts/be put to flight." Nice thought.'

They went on reading. A *Charm to Cure a Sickly Child. An Amulet for Power. Three Spells to Bind a Lover. To Raise a Storm* – that, they didn't need, Cassie thought wryly. She read again about crystals: how the larger a crystal was, the more energy it could store and focus. The spell *To Turn Aside Evil*, she read aloud, although she didn't understand it.

' "Invoke the power which is yours alone, calling upon the elements or those features of the natural world which lie closest to your heart. These powers have you over all that is evil: powers of sun and moon and stars, and of everything belonging to the earth."'

She read it again, puzzling. 'I still don't get it.'

'I think it means that as witches we can call on nature, on the things that are *good*, to fight evil,' Melanie said.

'Yes, but how do we call on them?' Cassie said. 'And what do they do when we do it?'

Melanie didn't know.

It got dark. The grey light from the windows got dimmer and dimmer and finally faded altogether. Wind banged the shutters and rattled the glass in the windows. The rain kept coming steadily in the blackness.

'What do you think he'll do?' asked Suzan.

'Something unfriendly,' said Laurel.

Cassie was proud of them. They were scared; she knew them well enough to know that fear was what was behind Deborah's restless pacing and Melanie's stillness, but none of them were running away or backing down. Doug cracked bad jokes, and Chris made paper airplanes. Nick sat tense and silent, and Adam kept Doug's headphones on, listening to the news on the radio.

At six o'clock the storm stopped.

Cassie's ears, used to the drumming of rain and the clattering and banging and howling of wind, felt suddenly empty. She looked and saw the others were all sitting alert.

'It can't be over,' Suzan said. 'Unless it missed us?'

'It's still out in the Atlantic,' Adam said. 'They think it should hit land in about an hour. This is just the calm before the storm.'

'Cassie?' said Diana.

'I think he's making his move,' Cassie said, trying to sound calm. And then every muscle in her body tightened.

Cassandra.

It was his voice in her mind. She looked at the others and saw they'd heard it too.

Bring your coven to the end of Crowhaven Road. To Number Thirteen, Cassandra. I'm waiting for you.

Cassie's fingers clenched on a piece of unfolded laundry lying nearby. She tried to concentrate on the power of the Master Tools, on the warmth where they touched her. Then she pushed with her mind, forming words.

We're coming. Say hello to Faye.

She let out her breath. Doug grinned at her. 'Pretty good,' he said.

It was sheer bravado, and they all knew it, but it made Cassie feel better. She inconspicuously wiped her wet palms on the laundry and stood up. 'Let's go,' she said.

Diana had been right; wearing the symbols of the coven leader and the white shift, she didn't feel cold. Outside, the sky was clear and the earth was silent except for the sound of the waves. Yes, the calm before the storm, Cassie thought. It was a very uneasy calm, ready to erupt into violence again at any moment.

Melanie said, 'Look at the moon.'

Cassie's stomach lurched.

It looked like a crescent moon, a silver disc with a bite out of it. But Cassie sensed the wrongness there. It wasn't a crescent moon; it was a full moon being invaded, overshadowed. She was watching darkness fall on a bright world.

She thought she could actually see the shadow moving, covering more of the white surface.

'Come on,' she said.

They walked up the wet street, making for the headland. They passed Suzan's house with its Grecian pillars, a grey bulk against the moonlight. They passed Sean's house, just as dark. Water gurgled down the sides of the road in little rivers. They passed Cassie's house.

They reached the vacant lot at Number Thirteen.

It looked just the way it had when they had celebrated Halloween here by making a bonfire and calling up Black John's spirit. Empty, deserted. Barren. There was nobody here.

'Is it a trick?' Nick asked sharply. Cassie shook her head uncertainly. The little voice inside wasn't telling her anything. She looked eastward at the moon, and felt another shock.

It was visibly smaller, the crescent very thin now. The shadow was not black or grey, but a dull copper-brown colour.

'Ten minutes until totality,' Melanie said.

'About half an hour until the hurricane reaches land,' said Adam.

A fresh wind blew around them. Cassie's feet, in the thin white shoes Diana had brought for her, were damp.

They stood uncertainly. Cassie listened to the waves crashing at the base of the cliff. Her senses were alert, searching, but nothing seemed to be happening. Minutes dragged by and her nerves stretched more and more taut.

'Look,' Diana whispered.

Cassie looked at the moon again.

The dull brownish shadow was swallowing up the last fingernail-thin edge of brightness. Cassie watched it go, like a candle winking out. Then she gasped.

The sound was involuntary and she was ashamed of it, but everyone else was gasping too. Because the moon hadn't just gone dark, like a new moon, and it wasn't even the coppery-brown colour. As it was covered by shadow it turned red, a deep and ominous red, like old blood. High in the sky, perfectly visible, it glowed like a coal with unnatural light.

Then someone choked and Sean made a squealing noise.

Cassie turned quickly, in time to see it happening. On the empty lot before them, something was appearing. A rectangular bulk was taking shape, and as Cassie watched, it became more and more solid. She could see a steeply pitched roof, flat clapboard walls, small windows irregularly placed. A door made of heavy planks. It looked like the old wing of her grandmother's house, the original dwelling from 1693.

It shone with a dull light, like the blood-red moon.

'Is it real?' Deborah whispered.

Cassie had to wait a moment to get the breath to speak. 'It's real *now*,' she said. 'Right now, for a few minutes, it's real.'

'It's *horrible*,' Laurel whispered.

Cassie knew what she was feeling, what the whole coven was feeling. The house was evil, in the same way that the skull was evil. It looked twisted, askew, like something out of a nightmare. And it gripped all of them with an instinctual terror. Cassie could hear Chris and Doug breathing hard.

'Don't go near it,' Nick said tightly. 'Everybody stay back until he comes out.'

'Don't worry,' Deborah assured him. 'Nobody's going near that.'

Cassie knew better.

The inner voice, silent just a few moments ago, was telling her clearly now what she had to do. What it wasn't telling her was how to get up the courage to do it.

She looked behind her, at the rest of them standing there. The Club. The Circle. Her friends.

Ever since her initiation, Cassie had been so happy to be a part of this group. She'd relied on different members of it at different times, crying on Diana and clinging to Nick and Adam when she needed them. But now there was something she had to do, and not even Nick or Adam could help her with it. Not even Diana could go with her.

'I have to go alone,' she said.

She figured out that she'd said it aloud when she saw them all staring at her. The next instant they were all protesting.

'Don't be crazy, Cassie. That's his territory; you can't go in there,' Deborah said.

'Anything could happen. Let him come out,' Nick told her.

'It's too dangerous. We won't let you go by yourself,' Adam said flatly.

Cassie looked at him reproachfully, because he was the one who'd said that being coven leader might not be good for *her*; and he was right, so he was the one who should understand now. Of course this was dangerous, but she had to do it. Black John – John Blake – Jack Brunswick, whatever you wanted to call him – had summoned her here, and he was waiting for her inside. And Cassie had to go.

'If you didn't want to listen to me you shouldn't have elected me leader,' she said. 'But I'm telling you now, that's what he wants. He isn't coming out. He wants me to go in.'

'But you don't have to,' Chris said, almost pleading.

Of them all, only Diana was silent. She stood, mouth trembling, tears hanging on her lashes. It was to her that Cassie spoke.

'Yes, I do,' she said.

And Diana, who understood about being a leader, nodded.

Cassie turned away before she could see Diana cry. 'You stay here,' she said to all of them, 'until I come out. I'll be all right; I've got the Master Tools, remember?'

Then she started walking towards the house.

The nails in the heavy timber door were set in a pattern of swirls and diamonds. They seemed to glow redder than the wood around them. Cassie touched the iron door handle hesitantly, but it was cool and solid to her fingers. The door swung open before her and she went inside.

Everything here was slightly misty, like a red hologram, but it *felt* real enough. The kitchen was much like her grandmother's kitchen and it was empty. The parlour next door was the same. A flight of narrow, winding stairs rose from the back corner of the parlour.

Cassie climbed the steps, noting with a strange amusement the incongruity of the tin lantern hanging on the wall. It was giving off a cold, eerie red light, barely brighter than the house itself. The stairs were steep and her heart was pounding when she reached the top.

The first small bedroom was empty. So was the second. That left only the large room over the kitchen.

Cassie walked towards it without faltering. On the threshold she saw that the red glow in here was brighter, like the surface of the shadowed moon.

She went in.

He was inside, standing so tall that his head almost touched the uneven ceiling. He was giving off a light of pure evil. His face was triumphant and cruel, and inside, Cassie thought she could see the outlines of the skull.

Cassie stopped and looked at him.

'Father,' she said, 'I've come.'

'With your coven,' Black John said. 'I'm proud of you.'

He extended a hand to her, which she ignored.

'You brought them here very nicely,' he went on. 'I'm glad they had the sense to acclaim you as leader.'

'It's only temporary,' Cassie said.

Black John smiled. His eyes were on the Master Tools. 'You wear them well,' he said.

Cassie felt a slow writhe of panic in her stomach. Everything was going according to his plan, she could see that. She was here, with the tools he'd wanted for so long, on his territory, in his house. And she was afraid of him.

'There's no need to be frightened, Cassandra,' he said. 'I don't want to hurt you. We don't need to quarrel. We have the same purpose: to unify the coven.'

'We don't have the same purpose.'

'You are my daughter.'

'I'm no part of you!' Cassie cried. He was playing on her emotions, looking for her weaknesses. And every minute the hurricane was getting closer to land. Cassie sought desperately for a distraction, and she glimpsed something behind the tall man.

'Faye,' she said. 'I didn't see you there, standing in his shadow.'

Faye stepped forward, indignantly. She was wearing the black silk shift, like a negative image of Cassie's, and her own diadem, bracelet, and garter. She lifted her head proudly and gazed at Cassie with smouldering golden eyes.

'My two queens,' Black John said fondly. 'Dark and bright. Together, you will rule the coven—'

'And you'll rule us?' Cassie asked sharply.

Black John smiled again. 'It's a wise woman who knows when to be ruled by a man.'

Faye wasn't smiling. Cassie looked at her sideways.

Black John didn't appear to notice. 'Do you want me to stop the hurricane?' he asked Cassie.

'Yes. Of course.' This was what she'd come for, to hear his terms. And to try and find his weak point. Cassie waited.

'Then all you have to do is swear an oath. A blood oath, Cassandra; you're familiar with those.' He held a hand out to Faye without looking at her. Faye stared at the hand for an instant, then reached down to pull a dagger out of her garter. The black-handled knife used for casting circles on the ground. Black John held it up, then he cut his own palm. Blood welled out sluggishly, dark red.

Like Adam, Cassie thought wildly, her heart accelerating. Like the oath Adam and I swore.

The tall man held the dagger towards Cassie. When she made no move to step forward and take it, he held it towards Faye. 'Give it to her,' he said.

Faye took the dagger and handed it to Cassie, handle first. Slowly, Cassie's fingers grasped it. Faye moved back to Black John's side.

'It's just a little blood, Cassandra. Swear obedience to me and I'll release the hurricane, let it turn harmlessly back out to sea. Then you and I can begin our reign together.'

The dagger was actually trembling in Cassie's hand. There was no way to steady her pulse now. She knew what she was going to do, but she needed time to get her nerve up.

'How did you kill Jeffrey?' she said. 'And why?'

The tall man looked momentarily taken aback, then he recovered. 'By getting him to sit down for a moment; and to cause dissent between our kind and the outsiders,' he said. He smiled. 'Besides, I didn't like his attention to my daughter. He wasn't one of us, Cassandra.'

Cassie wished Portia could see her 'Mr Brunswick' now. 'Why did you use Sean?' she asked.

'Because he was weak, and he already wore a stone that I could influence,' he said. 'Why all these questions? Don't you realise—'

He broke off then and moved lightning fast. While he was in the middle of speaking, Cassie had thrown the dagger at him. She'd never thrown a knife before, but some ancestor who'd worn the Master Tools must have, because the bracelet seemed to guide her right arm, and the dagger flashed end over end straight towards Black John's heart. But the tall man was simply too quick. He caught the dagger in midair – by the blade – and stood holding it, looking at Cassie.

'That was unworthy of you, Cassandra,' he said. 'And hardly any way to behave to your father. Now I'm angry with you.'

He didn't sound angry; his voice was cold as death and poisonous. Cassie had thought she'd been afraid before, but that had been nothing. Now she was truly afraid. Her knees were weak and the pounding of her heart shook her whole body.

Black John tossed the dagger back and it stuck in the floor in front of Cassie, quivering. 'The hurricane is about to reach land,' he said. 'You don't have a choice; you've never had a choice. Take the oath, Cassandra. *Do it!*'

I'm frightened, Cassie thought. Please, I'm so frightened ... She was wearing the Master Tools, but she had no idea how to use them.

'I am your father. Do as I tell you.'

If only I knew how to use them...

'You have no power to defy me!'

'Yes, I do,' Cassie whispered. In her mind, a door opened, a silver light dawned. Like the moon coming out of a shadow, it illuminated everything. She understood the spell to turn aside evil now. *Invoke the power which is yours alone … these powers have you over all that is evil…*

Suddenly, she felt as if a long line of witches were standing behind her. She was only the last, only one of them, and all their knowledge was hers. Their knowledge and their power. Words rose to her lips.

'Power of moon have I over thee,' she said shakily.

Black John stared at her, seeming to recoil.

'Power of moon have I over thee,' Cassie repeated, more strongly. 'Power of sun have I over thee.'

Black John stepped back.

Cassie stepped forward, searching for the next words in her mind. But she didn't say them. A voice said them for her, a voice behind her.

'Power of stars have I over thee. Power of planets have I over thee.'

It was Diana, her fair hair stirred as if in a light wind. She came to stand behind Cassie, tall and proud and slender, like a silver sword. Cassie's heart swelled; she had never been more glad to have anybody disregard her instructions in her life.

'Power of tides have I over thee. Power of rain have I over thee,' said Adam. He was right beside Diana, his hair shining like firelight, like rubies, in the red glow.

Deborah was behind him, her dark hair tumbling around a small face fierce with concentration. 'Power of wind have I over thee,' she said.

Nick joined her, his eyes cold and angry. 'Power of ice have I over thee.'

And Laurel. 'Power of leaf have I over thee. Power of root have I over thee.'

And Melanie. 'Power of rock have I over thee.'

They were all here, all joining Cassie, adding their voices to hers. And Black John was cowering before them.

'Power of thunder have I over thee,' Doug told him, and, 'Power of lightning have I over thee,' shouted Chris.

'Power of dew have I over thee,' Suzan said, and pushed a small figure in front of her. It was Sean, and he was shaking, seemingly terrified to come face to face with the man who had controlled his mind. But his voice rose in a shriek.

'Power of blood have I over thee!'

Black John was against the red wall of the house now, and he looked shrunken. His features had lost definition, and the red glow had died, leaving him black in reality.

But there were only eleven in Cassie's coven; the Circle wasn't complete. And only a full Circle could stand against this man.

As Sean's yell died, Black John straightened. He took a step towards them, and Cassie's breath caught.

'Power of fire have I over thee!' a husky voice cried, and he fell back. In astonishment, Cassie looked at Faye. The tall girl seemed to have gained height as Black John had lost it, and she looked every inch a barbarian queen as she stood glaring at him. Then she moved to stand beside Cassie. 'Power of darkness have I over thee,' she said, each word a stabbing knife. 'Power of night have I over thee!'

Now, thought Cassie. He was weak, wounded, and they were united. Now, if ever, was the time to defeat him.

But neither Fire nor Water had done it before. Black John had been defeated twice, had died twice, but always he'd come back. If they were going to get rid of him permanently they had to do more than destroy his body. They had to destroy the source of his power – the crystal skull.

If we only had a larger crystal, Cassie thought. But

there was no larger crystal. She thought desperately of the protruding outcrops of granite in New Salem... but they weren't crystal, they wouldn't hold and focus energy. Besides, she didn't just need a big crystal, she needed an *enormous* one. One so huge – so huge...

I like to think of crystals as a beach, she heard Melanie's laughing voice say in her mind. *A crystal is just fossilised water and sand...*

Along with the words came a picture. A glimpse of Cassie's own hand that first day on the beach at Cape Cod. 'Look down,' Portia had hissed, seeing Adam coming, and so Cassie had looked down, ashamed, staring at her own fingers trailing in the sand. In the sand that glittered with tiny flecks of garnet, with green and gold and brown and black crystals. A beach. A beach.

'With me!' Cassie shouted. 'All of you think with me – give me your power! *Now!*'

She pictured it clearly, the long beach stretching parallel to Crowhaven Road. More than a mile of it, of crystal piled on crystal. She sent her thoughts racing towards it, gathering the power of the coven behind her. She focussed on it, through it, looking now at Black John – at the crystal skull with its grinning teeth and its hollow eyes. And then she *pushed* with her mind.

She felt it go out of her, like a rush of heat, like a solar flare with the energy of the entire Circle driving it. It poured through her into the beach, and from the beach into Black John, focussed and intensified, with all the power of Earth and Water combined. And this time when the skull exploded it was in a shattering rain of crystal like the blasted amethyst pendant.

There was a scream that Cassie would never forget. Then the floor of the house at Number Thirteen disappeared from under her feet.

CHAPTER

16

'**A**re you okay?' Cassie asked Suzan, whom she happened to be lying on. 'Is everybody okay?'

The Circle was lying scattered over the vacant lot as if some giant hand had dropped them. But everyone was moving.

'I think my arm's broken,' Deborah said, rather calmly. Laurel crawled over to her to look at it.

Cassie stared around the lot. The house was gone. Number Thirteen was a barren piece of land again. And the light was changing.

'Look,' Melanie said, her face turned up. This time there was joy and reverence in her voice.

The moon was showing silver again, just a thin crescent, but now the crescent was growing. The blood colour was gone.

'We did it,' Doug said, his blond hair dishevelled more wildly than Cassie had ever seen it. He grinned. 'Hey! We did it!'

'*Cassie* did it,' Nick said.

'Is he really gone?' Suzan asked sharply. 'Gone for good this time?'

Cassie looked around again, sensing nothing but brisk air and the endlessly moving sea. The earth was quiet. There was no light but moon and stars.

'I think he is,' she whispered. 'I think we won.' Then she turned quickly to Adam. 'What about the hurricane?'

He was fumbling at his belt with the radio. 'I hope it's not broken,' he said, and put the headphones on, listening.

Limping and crawling, they all gathered around him, and waited.

He kept listening, shaking his head, flicking the channels. His face was tense. Cassie saw Diana beside her, and reached out to take her hand. They sat together, hanging on. Then Adam sat straight suddenly.

'Gale force winds on Cape Cod ... storm moving north-east ... north-east! It's turned! It's heading out to sea!'

The Henderson brothers cheered, but Melanie hushed them. Adam was talking again.

'High tides ... flooding ... but it's okay, nobody's hurt. Property damage, that's all. We did it! We really did it!'

'Cassie did it—' Nick was beginning again, irritably, but Adam had leaped up and grabbed Cassie and was whirling her in the air. Cassie shrieked and kept shrieking as he swooped her around. She hadn't seen Adam this happy since ... well, she couldn't remember *when* she'd seen Adam this happy. Since the beach on Cape Cod, she guessed, when he'd flashed that daredevil smile at her. She'd forgotten, in their months of trouble, that grimness wasn't Adam's natural state.

Like Herne, she thought, when she was deposited, breathless and flushed, back on her feet. The horned god of the forest was a god of joyful celebration. Chris and Doug were trying to dance with her now, both together. Adam was waltzing Diana. Cassie collapsed, laughing, just as something large and furry hit her and rolled her over.

'Raj!' Adam said. 'I told you to stay at home!'

'He's about as obedient as all of you,' Cassie gasped, hugging the German shepherd as his wet tongue lapped her face. 'But I'm glad you came. All you guys, not the dog,' she said, looking around at them.

'We couldn't just *leave* you in there,' Sean said.

Doug snickered, but he slapped the smaller boy on the back. 'Course not, tiger,' he said, and rolled his eyes at Cassie.

Cassie was looking at Faye, who had been sitting a little apart from everyone else, the way Nick used to do. 'I'm glad you came to join us too,' she said.

Faye didn't look anything at all like a stenographer. Her mane of pitch-black hair was loose over her shoulders, and the black shift exposed more pale honey-coloured skin than it covered. She looked a little bit like a panther and a lot like a jungle queen.

Her heavy-lidded golden eyes met Cassie's directly, and a small smile tugged at the corners of her lips.

Then she looked down. 'I can do my nails red again, anyway,' she said lazily.

Cassie turned away, hiding a smile of her own. That was probably as much acknowledgement from Faye as she was ever going to get.

'If you guys are all finished yelling and dancing,' Laurel said, in a carefully patient voice, 'can we go home now? Because Deborah's arm *is* broken.'

Cassie jumped up guiltily. 'Why didn't you *say* so?'

'Aw, it's nothing,' Deborah said. But she let Nick and Laurel help her up.

As they walked back, Cassie was struck by another thought. Her mother. Black John was dead, the hurricane was detoured, but what about her mother?

'Can we take Deborah to the crones?' she asked Diana.

'That's the best place, anyway,' Diana said. 'They know the most about healing.' She looked at Cassie with understanding in her green eyes, then she took Cassie's hand and squeezed it.

I've got to prepare myself, Cassie thought as they approached Number Four. I've got to be ready. She could be dead. She could be just the same as when I left there ... lying on that bed. She could stay that way forever.

Whatever happens, I kept my promise. I stopped Black John. He won't ever hurt her again.

Cassie glanced up at the moon before stepping up to Melanie's house. It was a thick crescent now, a fat, happy moon. She took it as a good omen.

Inside, candles flickered. Cassie wondered for one wild instant if the three old ladies were still dancing around sky-clad, and then she saw the parlour. Great Aunt Constance was sitting as stiff as a ramrod on the rounded seat of a chair, immaculately dressed and looking very proper as she served tea by candlelight to her three guests.

To her *three* guests ...

'*Mom!*' cried Cassie, and she ran forward knocking over one of Great Aunt Constance's fragile chairs as she went. The next minute she was holding her mother, hugging her wildly on Aunt Constance's couch. And her mother was hugging back.

'Good heavens, Cassie,' her mother said a few minutes later, pulling away slightly to look at her. 'The way you're dressed ...'

Cassie felt for the diadem, which had fallen askew. She settled it on her head and looked into her mother's eyes. She was so happy to see those eyes looking back at her, and seeing, that she forgot to answer.

Deborah's voice came from the hallway, tired but proud. 'She's our leader,' she said. Then: 'Anybody got an aspirin?'

'Well, obviously it isn't just temporary,' Laurel said, looking nettled. 'I mean, we *elected* you.'

'And you came through,' Deborah said, taking a large bite out of an apple with the hand that wasn't in a cast.

It was the next day. There was no school, because of minor storm damage and the disappearance of the principal. The Circle was enjoying the unseasonably mild weather by having a picnic in Diana's backyard.

'But we've got *two* leaders now,' said Chris. 'Or is Faye unelected?'

'Hardly,' Faye said, with a withering glance.

Melanie shifted thoughtfully, her grey eyes considering. 'Well, other covens have had more than one leader. The original coven did; remember, Black John was only *one* of the leaders. You could share with Faye, Cassie.'

Cassie shook her head. 'Not without Diana.'

'Huh?' said Doug.

Nick directed an amused glance at her. 'Diana might not want the honour,' he said.

'I don't care,' Cassie said, before Diana could say anything. 'I won't be leader without Diana. I'll quit. I'll go back to California.'

'Look, you can't *all* be leaders,' Deborah began.

'Why not?' Melanie asked, sitting up. 'Actually, it's a good idea. You could be a triumvirate. You know, like in Roman times; they had three rulers.'

'Diana might not want to,' Nick repeated, with rising inflection. But Cassie got up and went over to her anxiously.

'You will, won't you?' she said. 'For me?'

Diana looked at her, then at the rest of the Club.

'Yeah, go on,' Doug said expansively.

'Three's a good number,' Laurel added, smiling impishly.

Faye sighed heavily. 'Oh, why not?' she grumbled, looking in the other direction.

Diana looked at Cassie. 'All right,' she said.

Cassie hugged her.

Diana pushed a strand of fair hair back. 'Now I've got something for you to do,' she said. 'As a leader, you're not a junior member of the coven any more, Cassie, but nobody else can do this. Will you please go and dig up that box I gave you on the night of Hecate?'

'The trust festival box? Is this the time to unbury it?'

'Yes,' Diana said. 'It is.' She was looking at Melanie and Melanie was nodding at her, obviously sharing some secret.

Cassie looked at both of them, puzzled, but then she went down the road to get the box, accompanied only by Raj, who trotted along behind her. It was wonderful to be alone, and to know that nothing was out to get her. She dug in the sand near the big rock where she'd buried it that night, and pulled the damp box out. The sea flashed and sparkled at her.

She brought it back to Diana's house, breathless from the walk, and presented it to Diana.

'What's in there? More Master Tools?' Doug said.

'It's probably some girl thing,' said Chris.

Diana bent over the box, an odd expression on her face. 'You didn't open it,' she said to Cassie.

Cassie shook her head.

'Well, I know you didn't,' Diana said. 'I knew you wouldn't. But I wanted *you* to know. Anyway, it's yours; and what's inside it, too. It's a present.' She blew drying sand off the box and handed it back to Cassie.

Cassie looked at her doubtfully, then shook the box. It rattled lightly, as if there were something small inside. She glanced at Diana again. Then, hesitantly, with an almost scared feeling, she opened it.

Inside, there was only one object. A little oval of rock, pale blue swirled with grey, embedded all over with tiny crystals which sparkled in the sunlight.

The chalcedony rose.

Every muscle frozen but her eyes, Cassie looked at Diana. She didn't know what to do or say. She didn't understand. But her heart was beating violently.

'It's yours,' Diana said again, and then, as Cassie just crouched there, immobile, she looked at Melanie. 'Maybe you'd better explain.'

Melanie cleared her throat. 'Well,' she said, and looked over at Adam, who was sitting as still as Cassie. He hadn't said much all morning, and now he was staring at Diana wordlessly, riveted.

'Well,' Melanie said again. Adam still wouldn't look at her, so she went on anyway. 'It was when Adam was telling us about how he met you,' she said to Cassie. 'He described a connection – what you called a silver cord. You remember that?'

'Yes,' said Cassie, not moving otherwise. She was looking at Diana now too, searching Diana's face. Diana looked back serenely.

'Well, the silver cord is something real, something in the old legends. The people it connects are soul mates – you know, meant to be together. So when Diana and I heard about it, we knew that's what you and Adam are,' Melanie finished, sounding glad to be done explaining to people who wouldn't look at her.

'That was why I was surprised about Nick, you see,' Diana said to Cassie, gently. 'Because I knew you could only love Adam. And I was going to tell you at the very beginning, but then you were asking me to give you another chance, to let you prove you could be faithful... and I thought that was a good idea. Not for me, but for you. So you'd know, Cassie, how strong you are. Do you see?'

Cassie nodded mutely. 'But – Diana—' she whispered.

Diana blinked, her emerald eyes misting over. 'Now you're going to make me cry,' she said. 'Cassie, with all the unselfishness that's been going on around here, do you think I'm not going to do my part? You two have been waiting for months because of me. Now you don't have to wait any more.'

'There's nothing anybody can do about it,' Melanie put in, sympathetically but pragmatically. 'You and Adam are linked, and that's it. There isn't anyone else for either of you, so you're stuck together for this lifetime. Maybe for a lot of lifetimes.'

Cassie, still frozen, shifted her eyes to Adam.

He was looking at Diana. 'Diana, I can't just ... I mean, I'll always—'

'I'll always love you, too,' Diana said steadily. 'You'll always be special to me, Adam. But it's Cassie you're in love with.'

'Yes,' Adam whispered.

Cassie looked down at the rough little stone in her palm. It was sparkling crazily and she felt very dizzy.

'Go on, go over to him,' Diana said, pushing her gently.

But Cassie couldn't, so he came to her. He looked a bit dazed, but his eyes were as blue as the ocean in sunlight, and the way he smiled at her made her blush.

'Go on, kiss her,' Chris said. Laurel smacked him. The rest of the Circle looked on with great interest.

Adam glared at them and kissed Cassie formally on the cheek. Then, under cover of the groans, he whispered 'Later,' to her in a way that made her pleasantly nervous.

Can I handle Herne? she wondered, looking up at his hair that was so many colours: dark like garnet and bright like holly berries, threaded with gold in the sunshine. I guess I'm going to have to, she thought. For a lifetime, Melanie had said; maybe a lot of lifetimes.

For some reason that made her look at Faye and Diana.

She didn't know why, and then she had a flash of memory. Sunlight. Golden sunlight, the smell of jasmine and lavender, a laughing voice singing. Kate. Kate's hair had been the impossible fair colour of Diana's. But, Cassie realised now, Kate's laughing, teasing eyes had been *Faye's*.

An ancestress of both of them, Cassie thought. After all, they're cousins; they've got most of their ancestors in common.

But something deep inside her seemed to smile, and she wondered. Was Melanie right; was it possible to have more than one life? Could a soul keep coming back to Earth? And if so, could a soul ever – split?

'I think,' she said suddenly to Diana, 'that you and Faye are going to have to learn to get along. I think you two ... need each other.'

'Of course,' Diana said, as if it were something everybody knew. 'But why?'

It was probably a crazy theory. Cassie wouldn't tell her about it, or at least not right now. Maybe tomorrow.

'I'm going to do a picture, I believe,' Diana was saying

thoughtfully, 'to add to my collection. What do you think of the Muse, with the moon and stars around her, looking inspired?'

'I think it's a good idea,' Cassie said unsteadily.

'What we really have to talk about,' said Melanie, 'is what we're going to do with the Master Tools now. We have power; the coven has power, and we need to decide what to do with it.'

'Naw, what we need to do is *party*,' Doug said. 'To make up for all the birthdays that we missed. Chris and me didn't get a real party, and neither did Sean or Laurel...'

'Environmentalism,' Laurel was saying firmly to Melanie. 'That should be our first cause.'

'I didn't get a party either,' Suzan pointed out, delicately peeling the wrapper off a Twinkie.

Faye examined her nails, jewel-red, in the sunlight. 'I know some people I want to hex,' she said.

Cassie looked at them all, her coven, laughing and arguing and debating with each other. She looked at Nick, who was leaning back, looking amused, and he caught her eye and winked.

Then she looked at Diana, whose clear green eyes shone at her for a moment. Then, 'Yes, environmentalism is good,' Diana said, turning to Laurel. 'But we have to think about how to improve relations with the outsiders, too...'

Cassie looked at Adam and found him looking at her. He took her hand, closing it in his own, both of them holding the chalcedony rose.

Cassie looked down at their intertwined fingers, and it seemed that she could see the silver cord again, wrapping around their two hands, connecting them. But not just them. Filaments of the cord seemed to web out and touch the others of the group, linking them together with silver light. They were all connected, all part of one another, and the light shone around them to touch the earth and sky and sea.

Sky and sea, keep harm from me. Earth and fire, bring my desire.

They had. And they would in the future. With her inner vision, Cassie saw that the Circle was part of something bigger, like a spiral that went on and on forever, encompassing everything, touching the stars.

'I love you,' Adam whispered.

From the centre of the Circle, Cassie smiled.

Two compelling novels in one . . .

THE VAMPIRE DIARIES: Part I
The Awakening
The Struggle

The Awakening
Elena Gilbert is used to getting what she wants, and she wants mysterious new boy, Stefan. But Stefan is hiding a deadly secret, one that will change Elena's life, for ever . . .

The Struggle
Elena is torn between her boyfriend Stefan and his brother Damon. The boys hide a dark and tragic past that threatens them all. Damon wants to lead Elena astray . . . and he'd rather kill Stefan than let him possess her . . .

Also by L. J. Smith

Two compelling novels in one . . .

THE VAMPIRE DIARIES: Part II
The Fury
The Reunion

The Fury
Faced with the ultimate evil, Stefan and Damon must put their feud behind them and join forces with Elena to confront it – little knowing that in doing so, they are finally sealing her fate . . .

The Reunion
Elena, rising from the dead, summons Stefan and forces him to keep his promise to her, even though it means fighting the most terrifying evil he has ever had to face. Together at last, the vampire trio must once more challenge their fate . . .